Angel Baby

ALSO BY RICHARD LANGE

Dead Boys

This Wicked World

RICHARD LANGE

MULHOLLAND
BOOKS

HODDER

First published in Great Britain in 2013 by Mulholland Books
An imprint of Hodder & Stoughton
An Hachette UK company

1

A CIP catalogue record for this title is available from the British Library

Trade Paperback ISBN 978 1 444 75514 5
eBook ISBN 978 1 444 75515 2

Printed and bound by CPI Group (UK) Ltd, Croydon, CR0 4YY

Hodder & Stoughton policy is to use papers that are natural, renewable and recyclable products
and made from wood grown in sustainable forests. The logging and manufacturing processes are
expected to conform to the environmental regulations of the country of origin.

Hodder & Stoughton Ltd
338 Euston Road
London NW1 3BH

www.hodder.co.uk

For Kim Turner,
who loves the lonely places.

Now there was a day when the sons of God came to present themselves before the Lord, and Satan came also among them.

The Lord said to Satan, "From where have you come?"

And Satan answered the Lord and said, "From going to and fro on the earth, and from walking up and down on it."

—Job 1:6–7

We are constantly on trial.
It's a way to be free.

— Smog, "River Guard"

ANGEL BABY

1

Luz didn't think things through the first time she tried to get away. It was a spur-of-the-moment decision. One night Rolando beat her so badly that she peed blood, and the next morning, as soon as he and his bodyguards left the house, she limped downstairs and out the front door, across the yard, and through the gate in the high concrete fence that surrounded the property.

Barefoot and wearing only panties and a black silk robe, she stumbled down the street, trying to hail a taxi. The drivers slowed and stared, but none would stop. Tears of frustration blurred her vision. She tripped and fell but got quickly back to her feet. Scraped knees and skinned palms wouldn't keep her from Isabel's third birthday party. She was determined to be there, no matter what. She'd appear at the front door with a giant pink cake and an armful of gifts and, oh, wouldn't Isabel be surprised to see her?

Maria, the housekeeper, stuck her head out of the gate and shouted for her to stop. Luz tried to run, but the pills that got her through the day back then made her feel like she was slogging through mud. Maria caught up to her before she reached the corner and grabbed her by the hair. Luz fought back, kicking and clawing, but then El Toro, the house guard, was there too.

"Help me," Luz called to a man on a bicycle. "Please," to a woman pushing a stroller, but they, like the taxi drivers, ignored her. This was Tijuana, see, and if you valued your life and the lives of your family, you minded your own business. El Toro and Maria dragged her back to the house. They locked her in her room and laughed at her vows to get even.

Rolando killed her dog when they told him that she'd run away. He stormed into the bedroom and yanked Pepito from her arms, placed the heel of his boot on the toy poodle's head, and crushed its skull. Then he forced Luz to the floor, twisted her arms up behind her back, and raped her there on the white shag carpet.

"Why do you make me do these things?" he screamed at her when he finished. "Why do you make me hate myself?"

It will be different this time. In the year since she last made a run for it, Luz has been putting together a plan, and now, finally, she's ready. Isabel turns four next Tuesday, and Mommy will be there to watch her blow out the candles on her birthday cake, or Mommy will die trying.

She pretends to be asleep when Rolando comes out of the bathroom. He squeezes her foot through the sheet.

"Hey, Sleepy, time for breakfast."

"Mmmmm," Luz says. "Give me a minute."

He's dressed for business in a dark suit, white shirt, and shiny black cowboy boots. Luz has consulted the calendar on his desk and committed today's schedule to memory: An 11 a.m. meeting at Las Rocas Resort with Mr. Volkers from San Diego to talk about opening another KFC franchise. Lunch at the same place with Alvarez, his attorney, then on to Ensenada to see Flaco. Though it says on the calendar that they'll be discussing horses, the real topic will be a shipment of heroin from Apatzingán. Luz has been listening closely to her husband over the last year and has learned all of his nicknames and code words. So Flaco and the dope, and afterward dinner with the whore he keeps down there. This means he won't be home until at least nine.

When he goes downstairs, Luz crawls out of bed and walks into the bathroom to wash her face. The room still reeks of his shit. She brushes her long black hair until it shines, lifting it off the back of her neck to glance at the words tattooed there, *Angel Baby*. She convinced Rolando to let her get the tattoo by telling him it was her pet name for him. In reality, it's the title of a song she used to sing to Isabel during the year they had together. She's been careful never to let Rolando find out about the little girl because she knows he'd use anything she loved as a weapon against her or a chain to bind her more tightly to him.

Wrapping herself in a white robe, she leaves the bedroom. Her footsteps echo in the two-story foyer as she walks down the marble staircase. On the street Rolando is known as El Príncipe, the Prince, and this is his palace. A four-thousand-square-foot house with five bedrooms, six bathrooms, faux granite and gold leaf everywhere, leather and stainless steel. Everything is expensive but nothing goes with anything else. Rolando decorated by pointing at pictures in magazines. A fake Picasso hangs above a scorpion made of rusted iron. A $10,000 couch from Milan sits between two La-Z-Boy recliners with massage motors and heated cushions. And the house itself is so poorly constructed, new cracks appear in the walls every day.

It's a stucco-and-laminate fantasy that won't last much longer than Rolando does.

He stands and pulls out a chair for her when she enters the dining room. Such a gentleman this morning. It's because she let him fuck her last night and even went to the trouble of thrashing and moaning as if she were enjoying it. She wants him to think everything is perfect between the two of them when he leaves today. She fumbles with her napkin, yawns, and looks somewhat confused about exactly where she is, playing the stoned princess to the hilt. It's an act she's perfected in the six months since she managed to wean herself off the pills, the Xanax and Valium, Vicodin and Oxycontin, that used to keep her from adding up her sins and hanging herself in the shower.

She threw away the dope because she needed a clear head to plan her escape and because she didn't want to be strung out when she finally got free, but she's kept Rolando thinking that she's using. He'd become suspicious if he discovered she'd stopped, and besides, he likes her high. It makes him feel superior.

He returns to his chair across the table from her, and she smiles and asks in a sleepy baby voice when he's going to take her shopping for the shoes she showed him on TV the other night.

"Shoes?" he says. "You think I have time to think about shoes?"

She plays the game, scrunching her face into a pout and whining, "But you said, Papi. You said I could have them."

"I did?"

"You know you did. But when?"

"How about when we fly to Acapulco this weekend?"

"Acapulco!" Luz exclaims and claps her hands.

It wasn't easy quitting the drugs. In fact, to this day there are moments like this when her mind and body beg for the distance they provided. When this happens, she conjures the face of her daughter and prays to it as fervently as a primitive supplicating the only star in a pitch-black sky.

Maria bustles in from the kitchen carrying a platter of *pan dulce* and a bowl of fruit salad.

"Good morning, *señora*," she says to Luz, sweet as can be. They've made peace since Luz tried to walk away, or at least Maria thinks they have. Luz has done her best to convince the housekeeper that she barely remembers that day, but she still can't tell if she's bought it. The woman is hard to read.

Maria lifts the carafe from the table and fills Luz's cup with coffee. The sleeve of her blouse slides up to reveal a scar on her arm. It's from an injury she got in prison, where she did time for fencing stolen goods. She was the mother of one of Rolando's boyhood friends, a kid named Gato who was killed early in Rolando's rise. Gato made Rolando swear he'd take care of his mother if anything happened to him, and Rolando kept the promise by hiring the woman to oversee his household.

"Do you need anything else, *señora?*" Maria asks Luz.

"No, *gracias*," Luz replies.

"*Señor?*"

"No, Maria. *Gracias*," Rolando says.

The woman returns to the kitchen, and Rolando spoons fruit salad onto a plate and hands the plate to Luz. One of the parrots he keeps caged in the living room squawks, "My name is Gladiator! My name is Gladiator!"

"Where are you going, all dressed up?" Luz says.

"To fight a bull, what do you think," Rolando says, then bites into a pastry.

Luz pokes at her fruit. Her stomach is tight with anticipation and worry, but she manages to swallow a piece of pineapple, makes sure Rolando sees her eating.

"And you?" he says with food in his mouth, the fucking pig. "Let me guess: a massage? A manicure?"

"Both," Luz says with a laugh. "Why not?"

"It's a good life, no?"

"A good life," Luz says, the words burning her tongue. She reaches across the table and takes one of Rolando's hands in both of hers.

Rolando lifts a red rose from the vase on the table and slips it into her hair above her ear. He smiles and starts to say something tender, but then his phone rings, and his eyes go ice-cold. The human thing is all an act. He can turn it on and off like that. What he is inside is a monster, a shark, something soulless and ravenous. He stands and walks out of the room, barks *"Qué?"* into the phone.

El Toro, the guard who helped drag Luz back last year, lumbers in and grabs a sugary *concha* off the plate of pastries. Luz can feel the man's contempt for her, the boss's dope-fiend whore of a wife, has always felt it.

"Tell El Príncipe the car is ready," he says before walking back to the kitchen.

Luz passes the message on to Rolando when he finishes the call. He kisses her on the forehead and leaves without another word. She watches from the window as he climbs into the Escalade with Ozzy and Esteban. El Toro opens the heavy iron gate and gives a quick wave as the truck drives out.

And, so, it's time.

Her first stop is the bedroom, where she turns on the television and crawls between the sheets again like she does every morning. Today, though, her fists are clenched and sweaty, her legs tensed to run.

At 10:15 there's a knock at the door.

"Yes," she croaks, making her voice froggy.

Maria pokes her head in. "Any laundry, *señora?*"

Luz motions to the bathroom without looking away from the TV and ignores Maria as she walks in and empties the hamper into a plastic bag and walks out again. She begins counting to thirty after the housekeeper closes the door but only gets to ten before she can't stand it anymore and pops out of bed.

She has fifteen minutes to make her escape. She knows Maria's and El Toro's schedules as well as she knows Rolando's: Maria will be in the laundry room at the back of the house, and El Toro sneaks off to the garage every day from 10 to 10:30 to watch a soap opera on a little TV he keeps out there.

She dresses quickly in jeans, a T-shirt, and tennis shoes. No makeup, no jewelry. A fleece jacket and a pink baseball cap, nothing more, go into a zebra-striped backpack, something a child would carry to school. She's traveling fast and light. Anything else she needs she can pick up when she reaches the U.S. Heart pounding, she opens the door and checks the hall, then quietly descends the stairs. A radio plays in the room where Maria is sorting clothes, the DJ telling a dirty joke.

When she reaches the ground floor, she hurries to Rolando's office and slips inside. On the walls are shelves of books the man has never read, the heads of animals somebody else shot, and paintings of sailing ships and knights in armor bought in bulk by a decorator. The only personal addition is a large framed photograph of a dark-haired woman lying nude on a bed, legs spread wide. Rolando likes to tell people that it reminds him of Luz.

As soon as the door closes behind her, Luz relaxes a bit. She's been in here on numerous dry runs during the past few months, and now it's only a matter of following her plan. She goes to the big wooden desk and picks up the letter opener, a German

World War II dagger with a swastika engraved on the handle, and uses it to pry open the lock on the top drawer. Inside is a fluorescent green Post-it with the name *Angelina* and a phone number scrawled on it. Angelina is the name Rolando's mother gave to a daughter who died more than twenty years ago, the one the whole family now reveres as a stillborn saint, and the number, entered backward, is the combination to the wall safe, which is hidden behind a painting of a wolf hunt: men with fur hats riding in sleds, rifles, bloody snow.

Luz sets the painting on the floor and punches the numbers into the safe's keypad. The lock clicks, and the safe swings open. Inside are stacks and stacks of rubber-banded U.S. currency, hundreds and twenties, and a shiny silver gun, Rolando's custom-engraved, silver-plated Colt .45. Snakes twine around skulls on the barrel, and an image of Santa Muerte is carved in ivory on the grip. Luz transfers the money, all of it, to the backpack and lays the gun on top. Bowing her head, she murmurs a childhood prayer, and God's name is still on her lips as she grabs the pack, stands, and opens the office door.

"You dropped this, *señora,*" Maria says, holding out the rose that Rolando stuck in Luz's hair at breakfast. "Out here, in the hallway."

El Toro stands behind the woman, a mean grin on his ugly face. He's looking forward to hurting her. Both of them are. And then Rolando will finish the job.

Luz backs up and reaches into the pack for the .45. Rolando taught her how to use it on the house's basement firing range. At first he had to force her, because she couldn't stand the sound and the thump in her chest when the gun went off, but over the past year, thinking it was a skill that might come in handy during her escape, she's practiced whenever she could and become a pretty decent shot.

She racks the slide and points the .45 with both hands, doesn't flinch at the *BOOM BOOM BOOM* when she squeezes the trigger. Maria flies backward into El Toro, a jagged black hole under her left eye, a bloody volcano erupting out of the back of her head. The other two rounds hit El Toro in the chest and throat. He and the housekeeper go down together, tangled in death.

The horror of what she's just done paralyzes Luz for an instant, like an icy hand suddenly gripping her neck. When she can move again, she drops the gun into the backpack and steps over the bodies, being careful not to look down at them. There's only one thought in her head: Isabel. When the big front door doesn't open on the first try, she panics and jerks the knob a few times before realizing that the deadbolt is engaged. A second later she's on the porch. Four seconds later she's out the gate and on the street. Ten seconds later she's gone, another scrap swept up in the noisy, stinking whirl of the city.

2

MALONE STEPS OUT OF HIS MOTEL ROOM, AND THE SUN SURPRISES him like an unexpected slap in the face. He wobbles a bit, then sets off for the OXXO store down the road to buy something to take the edge off.

On the hill above the motel is the dog track, Agua Caliente. Malone has Freddy put him up out here so he can walk to the races while killing time before a run. Better than being downtown, where some whore always manages to slip her hand into his pocket. At least this way he might get lucky and make a little money instead of spending every last dollar on pussy, coke, and shitty tequila that comes out of a Patrón bottle but damn sure isn't Patrón.

Traffic is heavy on Paseo de los Héroes. Trucks coughing up clouds of exhaust, cars with blaring radios, scooters buzzing like angry insects. If Malone stuck out his hand, he could touch the river of rattling steel. One step and he'd be swallowed up by it and torn to shreds before he knew what hit him.

It's that kind of morning. He arrived in Tijuana last night, took the trolley down, and started drinking without dinner at a soccer bar across the street from the motel. When the joint closed and they threw him out, he somehow made it back to his room, saw his true face in the mirror, began to weep, passed out, and woke up in hell.

A buzzer sounds when he enters the convenience store. Neatly shelved cans of tuna and beans and menudo show off their labels beneath fluorescent lights that are reflected in the freshly waxed floor. There's a whole rack of instant noodles, a whole aisle of potato chips. Microwave burritos and cheeseburgers, a soft drink dispenser. It's almost exactly like a 7-Eleven or AMPM in the States. Too much like one.

Malone walks to the cooler for a six-pack of Tecate and a quart of Gatorade. The girl at the register smiles briefly before ringing up his purchases. She's wearing a red and yellow uniform, and her hair is pulled back into a tight bun. Very professional. She tells him how much he owes in Spanish, then English.

Malone is dressed like a typical *gabacho,* in knee-length Bermuda shorts, a tourist T-shirt from Cabo San Lucas, and flip-flops. It's his way of blending in. Every third American down here looks exactly like him. The scraggly blond hair, the sunglasses. A surfer who's somewhat off course. He glances at a digital clock on the wall: 10:31 a.m.

"Is that the real time?" he asks the girl.

"*Sí,* yes," she replies.

The little restaurant next door is painted a soothing shade of pale blue. It specializes in seafood—cocktails, soups, ceviche. Malone sits at a plastic table under a tin awning and orders three fish tacos and a shrimp cocktail. He opens the Gatorade and drinks half of it in a gulp, then pops a beer and sucks that down too.

By the time the old woman in the frilly apron brings his food, he's doing okay. He opens another beer and digs in. The cocktail is served in a tall Styrofoam cup. Malone pours ketchup and Tapatío into it and mixes everything with the shrimp and chunks of tomato and avocado.

A skinny brown stray with sad eyes and enormous teats watches him eat. He tosses the dog a saltine. The traffic still bucks and roars, and the cell phone store next door is blasting *banda* at tooth-rattling volume, but it doesn't feel like the end of the world anymore, just another day, no harder, no easier.

Malone walks back to the motel when he finishes. It's a two-story cinderblock bunker with bars on the windows. Looks like a hot pink prison. He always gets a room on the second floor in case there's an earthquake, envisions himself riding the building down if it collapses. The mattress sags, the TV only gets three channels, all in Spanish, and the air conditioner gives off a smell like mildewed towels. Stay drunk, though, and you don't even notice.

He sets the beers on the dresser and goes into the bathroom to take a shower. The water temperature veers back and forth between lukewarm and scalding hot every thirty seconds, keeping him on his toes. He cuts his chin shaving, presses toilet paper to the wound. Another beer and he'll be ready for the walk up the hill to the track. He stares out the window while sipping, watches a VW bug try to make a U-turn, everyone ignoring the driver's frantic hand signals.

The boys bring the dogs for the third race onto the track and parade them past the grandstand. Malone moves to the rail to check them out. There's no reason to, really. He doesn't know squat about greyhounds, what signs to look for that one will run any faster than another. He normally makes his bets based on

14

some combination of name and odds. This race he has his eye on Prometheus, going off at 8 to 1. Who the fuck would name a dog Prometheus? That alone is enough to pique his interest.

He walks back into the Hippodrome to place his wager. Most of the seats in the grandstand are empty. A few old Mexican men chattering in the shade, a couple of day-trippers down from San Diego. The clerk at the betting window takes his money and slides him his ticket without interrupting her cell phone conversation. Ten bucks on Prometheus to win.

His morning buzz is wearing off, so he stops at the bar for a rum and Coke, drinks it standing there, listening to the electronic chortles of the casino's slot machines bounce around in the rafters of the grandstand. Walking this tightrope gets mighty old. Sober, he can't stand himself, and drunk it's even worse. That's when he thinks about jumping off a bridge or getting hold of a gun.

The bartender, an old man with dyed black hair and mustache, is shuffling a deck of cards. He smiles at Malone and fans the deck, facedown.

"Pick one," he says.

Malone finishes his drink and sets the plastic glass on the bar. "The race is about to start," he says over his shoulder as he walks away.

He's at the rail again when the dogs come out of their boxes. They run past, chasing the lure, a scrap of fur attached to the end of a pole. Prometheus is out of it before the pack reaches the first turn. Malone crumples his ticket and drops it to the ground. His phone rings.

"You winning?" Freddy says.

"What do you think?" Malone replies.

"Some people here need a ride," Freddy says. "Come on over."

★   ★   ★

Malone's anxiety kicks in during the cab ride to Freddy's house. The only thing that gets his blood pumping anymore is making these runs, but he also swears he's going to have a heart attack every time.

He met Freddy one rotten night in a bar in National City, a bar he shouldn't have been in. Freddy pegged him right off the bat as a bad machine and said he had a job that would be perfect for him. Malone's bank account was about to bottom out, so he couldn't afford to be choosy. Ever since then he's come to TJ once or twice a month to drive a load of illegals across the border into the U.S. *Pollos,* Freddy calls them. Chickens.

It's nothing fancy: You stack them in the trunk of a car, head to the crossing at San Ysidro or Otay Mesa, answer the inspector's questions without stuttering, and say thank you when he passes you through. And the odds are excellent that he will pass you through. With sixty thousand to seventy thousand vehicles crossing every day, the inspectors can only be so thorough. Put a halfway respectable-looking white man behind the wheel, and it's practically a sure thing.

If you do get sent to secondary and asked to open the trunk? Again, the odds are in your favor. All those cars and trucks coming across, and only about three hundred people a year are actually prosecuted for bringing in illegals. Malone has never been caught, but he knows someone who has. The border cops sent the load back over the border and cut the driver loose in a couple of hours. They aren't going to waste their time trying to hold back the ocean.

Once on the U.S. side, Malone off-loads the *pollos* at a drop house, gets rid of the car, and goes home to his place in Imperial Beach. At $500 a head, it's the easiest money he's ever made.

The cabbie shifts into low and grinds up a steep, rutted dirt road leading to a hilltop neighborhood of rambling cinderblock and stucco houses all crowned with bare rebar, the first hopeful step toward second floors. Freddy's house is the nicest on the street, with a two-car garage, lime green paint job, and tile roof.

Freddy is standing on the porch, yelling into his phone, when the cab pulls up. Whoever he's talking to is a *pinche pendejo* and can kiss his fucking *culo.*

"Are you hungry?" he calls out as Malone is paying the driver. "My mom is making chicken."

Malone tells him nah, he's fine, had a big breakfast. Last time he took Freddy up on the offer of a meal prepared by his mother, some kind of goat stew, he was chained to the toilet for a week. Even now the thought of it makes his stomach flip.

He walks up the driveway past a couple of flunkies with buckets and rags who are washing an old Crown Victoria. Freddy bops around, pointing out spots they missed. He's short and wiry and weighs the same as he did when he used to box in club matches all over town. His hair and goatee are going gray, but there's still a fighter's bounce in his step, a disquieting quickness to his movements.

"Check out your ride," he says to Malone.

"A narcker."

"I got it at auction, real cheap."

A pack of children are playing in the yard, some kicking a soccer ball, others reciting sing-songy chants and rhythmically clapping their hands. There are always children around: Freddy's sons and daughters, nieces and nephews, even a few grandkids. Malone can't keep them straight, and they only add to his nervousness. Whenever one of them takes a tumble or starts to cry, he has to stop himself from running over and scooping her up, and every wail stiffens his spine and tightens his throat.

17

He and Freddy walk into the house and back to the kitchen. Along the way Freddy points out some new furniture he bought recently at Ikea in San Diego.

"This one's called Gustav," he says. "Can you believe it? A fucking chair named Gustav?" He reaches out and pats the chair. "Hello, Gustav. How are you?"

His wife and mother are chopping vegetables. Malone says *hola,* and they smile and nod. Freddy opens the refrigerator and pulls out a Budweiser. "You want beer or a Coke or something?" he asks Malone.

"Coke's good," Malone replies.

They step through a sliding glass door onto a patio, and Freddy motions Malone to a deck chair. Malone sits and sips his soda. The view is to the west here. Tijuana lies gray and smoking beneath a milky sky, an ugly city spread haphazardly across a series of ugly hills. A small patch of ocean sparkles in the distance, something Freddy is extremely proud of, something he's worked his whole life for.

The little man picks up a watering can and chatters away about the bugs eating his gardenias as he sprinkles the flowers growing in various pots. He's always moving, can't sit still, and Malone bets this means he wasn't much of a fighter. Probably couldn't stick to any kind of plan, just got in the ring and punched and punched until he ran out of gas, at which point his opponent turned him into hamburger. That would explain the scars on his face and his ruined nose. The crowd must have dug him, though. Nothing gets them going like a bleeder.

After a few minutes, Freddy checks through the slider to see where his wife is, then says to Malone, "Hey, when you were married, did you have women on the side?"

"No," Malone says. "No, I didn't." This is the last thing he wants to talk about. He watches a buzzard circle in the sky above a trash heap in the distance.

"But you were only married how long? A year?" Freddy says.

"Five years," Malone says.

Freddy hisses between his teeth and gestures dismissively. "See, I been with Sonia twenty years," he says. "Twenty. Think about that. I love her, okay, but she's not the same woman I married. After six kids." He mimes a pair of sagging tits, a giant ass. "She's not the same."

Malone shifts in his chair, uncomfortable. He'd rather not be privy to the details of other people's lives. They're too often sad and too often lead him to places he's trying to avoid.

"So I have girlfriends," Freddy continues, lowering his voice to a whisper. "One or two, only for fucking, to remember what it's like with someone who wants it. My friend says, 'Man, you spend too much money on those *putas*.' He says, 'You should go to the Internet'"—he pumps his fist in front of his crotch, as if masturbating. "But I tell him, 'Hey, I'm not a schoolboy, I'm a man, and I need a real woman.' This"—he pumps his fist again—"makes me feel stupid. I'd rather fuck my wife."

Freddy's phone rings. He detaches it from the clip on his belt and is yelling into it before he even puts it to his ear. Malone stares out at the man's prized glimpse of the Pacific. The sun hits it and turns it so bright, his eyes have trouble adjusting. He finishes his Coke and taps his fingers on the can.

"You ready to make some money?" Freddy says, holstering his phone.

"That's why I'm here," Malone says.

A loud bang makes them both jump. One of the kids, a toddler, has run smack into the sliding glass door and is now screaming his head off on the kitchen floor.

"No, no, no, *mijo*," Freddy coos as he opens the door and bends to gather the little boy in his arms. "Don't cry. Don't cry."

Malone drives the Crown Vic through the gate in the chain-link and razor-wire fence surrounding Goyo's, a body shop in a gritty neighborhood not far from the San Ysidro crossing. Freddy is right behind him in his dented Nissan pickup. Goyo is a fat man in a dirty blue work shirt with a patch that reads *Sam* sewn to the breast pocket. He slides the gate shut, and he and Freddy begin to argue in Spanish, speaking too fast for Malone to follow.

Malone climbs out of the Vic and stands in the dirt lot. It's about time for another drink, but he'll wait until he gets over the border. His nervousness about the crossing is building. He can feel it in his back and neck.

Goyo and Freddy agree to disagree, and Goyo walks into the shop while Freddy yells at Malone to open the Vic's trunk. A few seconds later Goyo herds five frightened men into the sunlight, where they stand staring at the ground and shuffling their feet. Malone doesn't look into their faces, doesn't want to know them.

Goyo moves to the gate to check the street and signals Freddy that it's all clear.

"*Ándale, ándale,*" Freddy says to the *pollos*. He practically has to kick them in the ass to get them moving toward the car. One by one they climb into the trunk, lying on their sides so they all fit. Freddy gives them last-minute instructions: Don't panic, there's plenty of air. Stay quiet, and in an hour you'll be in the land of the free and the home of the brave.

"*Tiene agua?*" he asks them as he prepares to close the trunk.

"*Sí,*" they reply in unison, one man holding up a bottle of water.

"*Buena suerte,*" Freddy says, and slams shut the lid.

Freddy's mechanic did a good job modifying the Vic's suspension. The rear end doesn't sag a bit, even with all that weight in the trunk. Malone slides into the driver's seat and starts the engine, and Freddy bends down to talk to him through the open window.

"You cool?" he says.

"Coolissimo," Malone says.

"Then get the fuck out of here."

Goyo opens the gate and Malone backs out. He takes it nice and slow, trying not to jostle the load too much, but it's difficult with all the potholes.

A few minutes later he's in line to cross the border with a thousand other cars, twenty-four lanes in all. This far back he figures it'll be at least half an hour. He waves over one of the vendors working the creeping traffic and buys some water. Other entrepreneurs hawk churros and ice cream, sombreros, and plaster statues of Bart Simpson. A juggler tosses oranges, and a kid blows fire for tips. Last chance to score that good American green before it disappears back into the U.S.

Malone clenches and unclenches his jaw in time to the music playing in the truck beside him. He used to dive in high school and got the jitters like this before every meet, felt like he wanted to rip his skin off. But the anxiety went away as soon as he launched himself off the platform and was replaced by the peacefulness that came with the inevitability of falling.

The Vic wobbles a little, someone moving around in back. Malone turns the air conditioner on high and hopes the cool air reaches the trunk. He had a kid freak on him once, start screaming and trying to kick his way out when the car was less than fifty yards from the crossing. The guy's panic spread to the other pollos, and pretty soon they all lost it.

Hemmed in by other vehicles, Malone did the only thing he could think of: He got out, opened the trunk, and took off run-

21

ning back to TJ, abandoning the car. The other drivers sat there open-mouthed as, one by one, six Mexicans scrambled out of the trunk and fled the same way.

This time they settle quickly. Someone's arm must have fallen asleep or something. The Vic continues to crawl toward the border, and Malone removes his sunglasses and cleans them on his shirt. His pulse is racing when he's three cars away from the inspector. Two cars away, it's even worse. But then, as always, perfect calm as he pulls up to the booth.

The inspector is a heavyset Latina, almost busting out of her uniform. Her hair is dyed blond, and she's wearing too much makeup. Malone hands her his passport, and she gives the car a quick once-over.

"How long were you in Mexico?" she asks as she punches his info into her terminal.

"Two days," Malone replies.

"Where'd you go?"

"Rosarito. My folks have a condo there."

"How much dope you bringing in today?"

A funny one. You got them sometimes. "Come on," Malone says.

The woman shoots him a quick smile and waves him through, already focused on the next car in line. Malone keeps checking the freeway behind him until he's a couple of miles down the road. Even after twenty-two runs, he still can't believe it's so easy. Rolling down the window, he pushes all the old scared air out of his lungs and fills them with fresh stuff.

Per the plan, he exits the 5 in National City and pulls into a gas station. Freddy is all business when Malone calls for directions to the drop-off. No girlfriend talk now, just left here, right there, left here.

The house is a rundown stucco ranch in a neighborhood of rundown stucco ranches. Someone's dream home thirty years ago. Now you've got *cholos* on the corner, pit bulls in the yards, and a ten-foot-tall gang *placa* painted in the middle of the street. Everything goes to shit.

Malone turns into the driveway of 1520 and honks once. A big bald gangster jogs out of the house and opens the garage door. Malone pulls inside, and the door goes down behind him. Two more thugs come into the garage from the house.

"Whassup?" one of them, the one with *13* inked on his throat, says to Malone. It sounds more like a challenge than a greeting. Malone gets out of the car and unlocks the trunk. The first *pollo* climbs out on his own, then helps the others. They're red-faced and sweaty in the harsh light from the bare bulb overhead, and their eyes widen in fear when they get a look at their hosts. Malone doesn't blame them. These goons scare him too.

"Get in the house," 13 barks at them in Spanish, and they shuffle off, heads down, looking more like prisoners than men about to start new lives. The one who helped the others out of the trunk shakes Malone's hand.

"*Gracias, señor,*" he says.

"*De nada,*" Malone says. "*Buena suerte.*"

13 hands Malone an envelope with $2,500 inside. Malone climbs into the car, and someone lifts the garage door so that he can back out. Five minutes later he's on the freeway again, headed to the trolley station where he parked his own car. He'll drop the Vic there, stash the keys under the bumper for whoever Freddy sends to get it, then drive home. Everything went fine today except for that fucker thanking him. Now Malone is going to remember him, wonder about him, hope for him, and, man, that's not cool at all.

3

It's been a long time since Luz has walked in Tijuana. She grew up roaming the city's hectic streets but went north at thirteen and stayed away for six years. When she returned, it was as the mistress of Cesar Reyes, El Samurai, who put her in a beachfront condo in Playas. She didn't walk then because Cesar was a jealous man and worried about her straying. He assigned a driver to take her where she wanted to go and to keep an eye on her. After that she was with Rolando, and he did the same. Pampered in this way, she began to think that only the poor and crazy relied on their feet to get around.

She heads downhill now toward a busy thoroughfare and scuffs along beside it, following two uniformed schoolgirls. The noise is overwhelming, the stench of burning rubber, the heat rising from the concrete. A gritty blast of wind spun off by a passing truck almost knocks her over. She knew her first few hours back in the world would be difficult—she's been away for a long time—but this, it's as if her hometown has suddenly turned against her. She looks around for a taxi, but there are none in sight.

She veers onto the next quiet street she comes to and follows it past brightly painted little houses lined up one beside the other with barely any breathing room between them. A woman sweeping the sidewalk nods and smiles, and a curious dog falls in behind her for a couple of blocks before flopping onto the porch of a blood-red storefront church. She stumbles upon a park—a sad patch of dirt with a few benches and a knot of rusty playground equipment—and stops there to pull herself together.

Sitting on a bench, she places the backpack containing the money and the gun between her feet and fans herself with her hand. Five minutes and she'll be ready to go. The hardest part is over, getting away from the house. Now all she has to do is keep moving north, toward Isabel, her lodestar. Every time she closes her eyes she sees the look of disbelief on Maria's face when she shot her, so she keeps them open, watches a balloon vendor push his cart, watches two children, a boy and a girl, climb the ladder of the slide and slide down, then run screaming to the swings.

A little girl appears beside her and stares up at her, fingers twisting the neck of her Minnie Mouse T-shirt.

"What are you doing?" the girl asks.

"Resting," Luz replies. "What are you doing?"

The girl frowns like this is a trick question, doesn't answer.

"Conchita!"

A woman runs up, out of breath, and kneels in front of the girl. She grabs her by the shoulders and shakes her. "One more time, and that's it," she says. "When I say stop, you stop. Understand?"

The girl nods but is now watching the children on the swings.

"I'm serious," the woman continues. "Look at me."

"I understand," the girl says.

"Good. Now go. You have ten minutes."

The girl dashes off to the playground.

"She's pretty," Luz says to the woman, who sits beside her on the bench.

"My granddaughter," the woman says. "Her mother works at the Sony factory, so I take care of her during the day. And here I thought I was done raising kids when my own moved out."

The woman sighs and straightens her dress over her legs. "What about you?" she says. "Any children?"

"A girl," Luz says. "About the same age as your granddaughter."

"How nice!" the woman says. "They're cutest right now, aren't they? Learning so fast, but not too smart yet, where they think they know everything."

The chaos of the city and the weight of all the years she's missed with Isabel combine to knock the wind out of Luz. A tear gets away from her and races down her cheek. Now isn't the time for regret, she tells herself, now is the time to be strong, but it's no good, the tears keep coming.

"Is everything all right?" the woman says. She digs through her purse and comes up with a packet of tissues.

"Problems with my husband," Luz says.

"I kicked my bastard out years ago," the woman says. "Never been happier."

Luz takes a tissue and blows her nose, tries to smile.

A man standing near a shoeshine kiosk draws her attention. He's staring at her and talking into a cell phone. How stupid she was to stop so soon, with Rolando always bragging about having eyes everywhere. She stands suddenly and picks up the backpack.

"What's the matter?" the woman asks.

Luz hurries away without answering. Rolando could be

watching her right now, toying with her before finishing her off, like a cat with a mouse. At the edge of the park she comes upon a taxi parked in the shade of a dead tree and hops into the backseat. The driver awakens, startled from a nap, and begins to protest.

"I'm off duty."

Luz opens the backpack and slides a hundred-dollar bill off one of the stacks of money inside. She shows it to the driver and says, "This is yours if we leave right now."

The driver hesitates, ducking his head to see if Luz is being followed. After weighing the risks, he starts the car and pulls away from the curb with a loud screech. They're soon lost in traffic, one taxi among hundreds.

"And so?" the driver says, sizing up Luz in the rearview mirror.

Luz drops the bill onto the passenger seat.

"Take me to Lomas Taurinas," she says.

The *colonia* looks the same as it did when Luz left it. A maze of tin-roofed shacks clogging a dry, dusty canyon next to the airport. A slum cobbled together out of plywood, old garage doors scavenged from the U.S., cinderblocks, and blue plastic tarps. A *barrio* where fear rules, and anger flares quickly into violence.

When Luz was three, Luis Colosio was shot in the plaza down the street from the hovel she shared with her mother and two brothers. The presidential candidate had come to campaign in the neighborhood, and it was like a party, with music and cheering and vendors selling tacos and *raspados*. Luz thought he was a movie star, the way everyone called out his name and pushed in to listen when he climbed onto a truck to give a speech. She whined and whined until her Uncle Serafin lifted her onto his shoulders so she could see.

Colosio waded into the crowd after he spoke, shaking hands and hugging supporters. That's when a man sidled up to him, put a pistol to his head, and pulled the trigger. Luz didn't understand what was happening but was frightened by the screams of those who did. The gunman was apprehended on the spot, a deranged factory worker. There were rumors, however, that others were involved, policemen and rival politicians.

Luz directs the driver through the maze of narrow streets, past the little store where she used to buy chips and sodas with quarters begged from tourists down on Revolución, past the school with its broken windows and cracked basketball court, past the corner where the neighborhood girls taunted her because of her ratty clothes and bare feet. She shivers to see it all again, everything she ran away from. Stupid, ugly, filthy Taurinas. Her hatred for the place hasn't cooled.

They finally reach her mother's house, a two-room concrete bunker with tattered lace curtains hanging in the barred windows and gang graffiti sprayed across the front door. Luz tells the driver that if he waits for her, there's another hundred in it for him.

"Only if you hurry," he says. "This place is a den of thieves."

The welter of electrical lines overhead casts a spider-web shadow onto the house. Two men up to their elbows in the engine of a pickup watch suspiciously from across the street as Luz climbs the crumbling steps to the porch. She smells sewage and burning trash, and her whole childhood returns to her at once. She wants to vomit, to leave immediately, but it's finally come to this: Her mother is the only person who can help her.

She knocks once, and the door, unlatched, swings open with a creak. It looks as if someone has emptied a Dumpster in the front room. Beer cans and wine bottles everywhere, dirty clothes, boxes of greasy car parts, a giant stuffed pink elephant, four or

28

five TVs. The only furniture is a worn-out couch. Luz recognizes it as the same one her brothers took turns sleeping on when they were kids. Flies buzz around plastic bags filled with empty cans of beans and fast food wrappers, and someone is snoring in the bedroom.

"Mamá," Luz calls from the doorway.

The snoring turns to coughs.

"Wake up," a man grunts. "Someone's here."

"Who?" Luz's mother asks.

"How the fuck should I know?"

"Who is it?" Luz's mother yells into the front room.

"It's me, Mamá, Luz," Luz says.

"Luz?"

"I need to talk to you."

Silence, then urgent whispers. A few seconds later her mother, Theresa, staggers in from the bedroom. She's wearing an oversized Iron Maiden concert T-shirt as a nightgown. The bright red dye job on her hair is growing out, her roots showing black and gray, and yesterday's mascara is smeared around her eyes. She squints at Luz and says, "Yeah, it's you," then walks to the couch and digs out a pack of cigarettes from between the cushions, lights one.

"I've forgotten how many years it's been," she says.

"Nine," Luz says, clutching the backpack to her chest.

"Seriously?"

"Add it up."

Theresa sits on the couch, legs curled beneath her. She's gotten fat. Her face is swollen, her belly. She used to be so beautiful, the most beautiful whore in the *colonia,* people said. It gives Luz satisfaction to see her looking this bad but also breaks her heart.

"Carmen wrote to tell me you were living with her in L.A., but I never heard from you," Theresa says.

"I didn't think you cared," Luz says.

"I knew how you felt about me. It was stupid to keep pretending."

She's right, Luz thinks. At least the bitch gave her that, the gift of truth. She made sure that Luz and her brothers knew the score from the start: Assume that everyone you meet is a liar, a cheat, a rapist, a murderer. A wolf waiting to rip your guts out. And if anyone claims not to be, trust him even less than those who have their crimes tattooed across their foreheads.

"Carmen was good to me," Luz says. "I stayed with her and her family and went to school. I did okay, you know, even got A's in math and in science, but I had to drop out when I got pregnant. The baby was a girl. Isabel. Her daddy died right after she was born."

Theresa focuses on a patch of sunlight on the couch, moves her fingers through it. "I don't need to hear this," she says.

But Luz thinks she does, so she continues. "I went to work at Taco Bell after that," she says. "It was fine. Not fun or anything, but fine. One day I was at the register and this guy, this sweet-talking *pendejo,* came in and told me I could be doing a lot better, that I was too pretty to be making burritos. He got me a job at a club, a place where gangsters went, *narcos.* I started out waitressing, then did some dancing."

Then did the other thing. Luz doesn't say this, though, won't give Theresa the satisfaction.

Theresa blows out a cloud of smoke, her foot jiggling impatiently. "And? And? And?" she says. "Just tell me why you're here."

"I'm here for her, for my baby," Luz says. "I met a man at the club. He asked me to move back here to be with him, offered me an allowance. I was only thinking of Isabel when I said yes, that she should have a future. I left her with Carmen and said I'd send money. Things were good for a while, until another man decided he wanted me, that I should be his woman instead. He and my old man fought, and the other man won. El Príncipe."

Theresa's eyes widen in recognition of the name. "My God," she gasps, and springs to her feet as if Rolando were about to storm in and shoot her dead.

"Calm down," Luz says. "I've left him, and I'm going back to Isabel. But I need your help."

"I can't help you," Theresa says. "I don't have anything."

"I need someone to take me across the border. Give me a name."

"No, get out now."

"You owe me, Mamá."

"I don't owe you shit."

Luz thrusts out a hundred-dollar bill pulled from the backpack. Theresa looks at the money, looks at Luz, then drops her cigarette into a beer can sitting on the arm of the couch.

"Your little brother, Beto, was killed last year," she says. "They cut off his head and left his body in a ditch. And Raúl's in prison in Texas. He'll never get out. They were idiots who took after their fathers." She snatches the bill from Luz's fingers. "I thought you were smarter."

A voice comes from the bedroom: "Who the fuck are you talking to?"

"Shut up, you fucking dog," Theresa yells back.

Luz feels like she'll never get away if she doesn't go this instant. The old witch will put a spell on her, steal her breath, and feed her to the monster in the other room.

"A *pollero*," she says.

"Go to Goyo's Body Shop in Libertad," Theresa says. "But don't you dare tell him who sent you."

Luz turns to leave without a good-bye, riding the runaway

horse of her fear and revulsion down the stairs and out to the waiting cab. Theresa appears in the doorway, a mocking sneer twisting her face.

"Tell Isabel Grandma loves her," she calls after Luz. "Give her kisses for me."

A jet roars low over the house on its way to a landing at the nearby airport. The noise drowns out Theresa's cackle and rousts a flock of ravens that had been commiserating on the sagging electrical lines, sends them flapping into the dirty brown sky.

Luz tells the driver where they're headed. He holds out his hand and watches in the rearview as she takes another hundred from the backpack and passes it to him. Sensing his hunger, Luz reaches into the pack and grabs the .45. It flashes like a mirror when she pulls it and points it.

"Don't be stupid," she says.

The driver lowers his eyes and shoves the money into his shirt pocket. It takes two twists of the key to get the car started, and then he heads down the hill. Luz slides low in back and returns the gun to the pack but keeps her finger on the trigger. She breathes easier with every turn that takes her farther from her mother's house. Now if only it were possible to set fire to the past and everyone in it.

Colonia Libertad lies right on the border. It's a crowded, noisy slum with clear views of the new Mediterranean-style subdivisions spreading across the hillsides in California. Residents heave their household trash over the border fence into the U.S., and the Border Patrol launches tear gas canisters into the neighborhood to drive off the rock-throwing kids the smugglers hire to create diversions for their crossings. The Border Patrol agents and the residents know one another by name. They exchange taunts at night and waves and hellos in the morning.

Luz's driver pulls into a gas station and asks the other drivers gathered there about the body shop. One of them has heard of the place, gives him directions. Goyo himself turns out to be a sweaty *gordo* who plays stupid until Luz throws some money around. A hundred dollars gets him on the phone to his boss.

"Freddy's on his way," he says when he finishes the call. "You want to wait in the office?"

The office contains a cot, a hot plate, and a pile of porno magazines. It smells like the monkey cage at the zoo.

"I'm fine here," Luz says.

She sits on a stack of tires and keeps a tight hold on the backpack. Goyo goes to work with a rubber mallet on a dented fender. Every blow makes Luz jump.

Freddy shows up half an hour later, a wiry little crook with a busted nose who talks too fast and constantly shifts his weight from one foot to the other, making him look like a snake about to strike.

"Who sent you?" is the first thing he asks.

"Who cares?" Luz replies.

"Obviously I do," Freddy says.

Luz hands him a bundle of hundreds from the backpack. She realizes it's dangerous to reveal that she's carrying so much money, but she needs to let him know she's serious about doing business with him. Freddy thumbs the bills and purses his lips.

"Whose is this?" he says.

"Mine," Luz says.

"Whose before?"

Luz reaches out to take the bundle back, but Freddy, he's quick, pulls it away.

"You seem like trouble," he says. "Are you trouble?"

"If you can't help me, say so," Luz says.

"What else is in there?" Freddy asks, gesturing at the back-pack.

Luz hauls out the pistol and gives him a good look at the business end. His eyes widen, but he recovers quickly and shows his teeth. *The smiles these men have,* Luz thinks. *Never a bit of truth in them.*

The gun goes back into the bag, and Freddy flips through the money again. The racket of a passing truck drowns out most of what he says next. All Luz hears is "...lady, right?"

She shrugs.

"So I think you want to go first class," he continues.

What she wants right now is to get so high that the world falls away and leaves her floating in that place where nothing hurts and nobody can touch her. What she wants is to be done with all this walking and talking and trying, to lie still in a dark room, her only sensation the crisp coolness of clean sheets against her skin.

"Don't fuck around," she snaps. "Say what you mean."

"I mean I can stick you in the trunk of a car and send you out like some Indian from Oaxaca, but that's always a gamble," Freddy says. "You might make it, you might not. Or, for more money, I can pull some strings and guarantee you get across."

Luz pictures Rolando drawing nearer every minute, creeping up on her.

"Look, I know you're fucking me over," she says, "but I'll pay whatever it takes to be sure I get to the U.S. The only condition is, I need to go today."

Freddy frowns and fingers his mustache. "That I don't know about," he says. "A guaranteed crossing takes time to arrange."

"Today or nothing," Luz says.

Freddy taps his palm with the stack of cash she gave him, considering this demand. After a few seconds, he shrugs and says, "I'll do my best. Maybe this evening."

"So get to work," Luz says.

Freddy motions her to a filthy couch sitting in the shade, tells her she'll be more comfortable there. She says she's fine where she is. He offers her cookies, a soda, and she refuses both. She tries to listen in when he gets on his phone, but he ducks inside the shop and keeps his voice low.

A fly buzzes round, sent by the devil to drive her crazy. She swats at it once, twice, then gives up and watches it land and skitter over her sweaty forearm. It pauses and taps at a freckle of dried blood on her wrist, Maria's or El Toro's. She scrapes the spot off with her fingernail, and a bigger one on the back of her hand.

4

THE WAVES ROLL IN PALE GREEN, VEINED WITH WHITE FOAM LIKE liquid marble, bellies full of sunlight. They rise only waist-high before flopping with barely enough energy left to make their runs up the sand. Malone sits cross-legged above the high-tide line south of the Imperial Beach pier and watches a flock of plovers work the swash zone. The skittish little birds chase the retreating waves, pausing now and then to peck the wet sand in search of mole crabs.

No alcohol is allowed on the beach, but the cops and life-guards recognize Malone as a local, another sunstruck idler who's dead-ended in this last-stop surf town, so they ignore the Tecate in his hand. He hides the can anyway, leaving it wrapped in the paper bag the clerk at the liquor store slid it into when he bought it. He has a thing about keeping up appearances, a conceit his parents beat into him, and one that he likes to think sets him apart from other drunks. Deep down he knows it's a ridiculous distinction, but so what, a man needs his signifiers.

Not many people are out on this warm Thursday afternoon. A family of what might be Germans, pale going quickly to pink; a couple of Mexican kids giggling under a blanket; two jarheads tossing a football. Malone finishes his beer and could use another. It's been an exciting day, with the crossing and the drop-off, Mr. Toad's Wild Ride, and his nerves have taken a pounding. He stands and brushes the sand off his ass, wonders if Pablo Honey is drinking.

The pier is a rickety mess of planks and pilings. Malone can see the ocean below, through the gaps between the boards, and feel the entire structure rise and settle with the swell as he walks out on it. To the north, the view is all the way up the coast to downtown San Diego, to the south, Tijuana, the bullring rising like Rome's Colosseum out of the clutter.

A few surfers are riding the breaks at Boca Rio and the Sloughs, where the Tijuana River empties into the sea. It's one of the most polluted stretches of beach in California, but this doesn't scare the hard-cores. Raw sewage, floating garbage, and the occasional dismembered *narco* do nothing to discourage them from paddling out to catch the world-class waves. The county has given up trying to stop them, offering free hepatitis vaccines instead.

Pablo Honey is fishing in his usual spot halfway down the pier, his line just back of where the waves are breaking twenty feet below. Elbows on the rail, he reels in some slack: *CLICK, CLICK, CLICK*. He's using a live anchovy on a number four hook, hopes for halibut. Nothing in his bucket yet. Malone doesn't mean to startle him, but his "What's up?" sends the kid tripping over his shoelaces.

"Easy, dude," Malone says. "It's just me."

Pablo laughs and nods and fiddles with his Padres cap for a while, pulling himself together. "Got a new girlfriend," he barks when he finally calms down. Words tend to explode out of him, everything an exclamation.

"Another one?" Malone replies.

"White chick, big ol' titties."

"Come on."

"No shit. We're getting married."

"So let's celebrate. You got a bottle on you?"

It's a crapshoot. Some days Pablo likes a nip while he fishes, other days he feels the Lord all around him and packs a New Testament instead. Malone gets lucky: The kid reaches into the pocket of his camo cargo shorts, pulls out a pint of Popov, and hands it over.

Pablo Honey is half Chinese, half Mexican, and his real last name is Estrada. He and Malone lived in the same building in L.A. a few years back, a hundred-buck-a-week flophouse in Hollywood, Little Armenia. Pablo washed dishes to pay his rent while Malone pissed away a nice chunk of change his grandfather had left him.

Malone was generous with his money, treating his down-and-out pals to drinks and steak dinners at Sizzler, and Pablo was the only guy who tried to pay him back. He was also the only guy who never asked what the hell someone like him was doing in a dump like that. Malone appreciated the kid's uncomplicated acceptance of his and others' circumstances, found wisdom in it even, and the two of them helped each other along as best they could, like friends Malone had only read about in books.

He was heartbroken when Pablo announced one day that he'd inherited a little house in Imperial Beach from an aunt and would soon be moving down there.

38

"Good for you," he said. "But I'll be awful lonely."

"Huh?" Pablo said.

"I'm going to miss you, man. You're my bud."

Pablo frowned, deep in thought for a few seconds, then smiled and said, "So come with me, then."

Malone had moved up to L.A. and settled into the flop when his life in Orange County ended, and he figured he'd be there until he drank himself into an early grave. But Pablo's offer got him thinking. After five years of slipping in vomit on the way to the liquor store and passing out at night to the sound of men in other rooms wrestling with their nightmares, he hated the constant madness of Hollywood. Whatever misery he'd been seeking, he'd experienced; whatever point he'd been trying to make to himself, he'd made it. So, after throwing one last party for all of his Tinseltown cronies, he packed his stuff in the Louis Vuitton bag he'd ended up with after the divorce and followed Pablo to the beach, crashing on the kid's couch until he found his own place. It's been two years now, and he's still here and still alive—quite an achievement, he's decided, for someone who so often wants to die.

He guzzles some vodka and passes the bottle back to Pablo, who reams the neck with a T-shirted finger and has a drink himself. A gull touches down on the railing, looking for something to steal. Finding nothing, it takes off again and glides toward the beach on stiffly arched wings.

"What's your girl's name?" Malone asks Pablo.

"What?" he replies.

"Your new girlfriend."

"I met her on the Internet," Pablo says. "She lives in Dallas. Come over tonight, and I'll show you naked pictures."

They stand silently then, the sun warming their backs, the breeze ruffling their hair. They often go an hour or more without speaking, and Malone is always grateful for the quiet. He's had talk enough to last him a lifetime.

He heads for home a while later, to kill the rest of the afternoon there. His place is a couple of blocks inland, a guesthouse in the backyard of a slightly larger house. The guesthouse was a tool-shed until someone drywalled and added a bathroom, and there's barely enough space in it for a futon and a television, but Malone is okay with that. The beach is there when he wants to stretch out.

The yard of the house is an overgrown jungle prowled by feral cats as wild as tigers. On his way back to the shed, Malone rousts the big gray one he calls Smoke, interrupting the cat's snooze in a patch of sunlight. The cat crouches and hisses at him before diving into the bushes.

Inside his room, Malone kicks off his flip-flops and snags a beer from the mini-fridge. That and a microwave are the extent of the kitchen facilities. After opening the windows to get the air moving, he stretches out on the futon and turns on the TV. He runs through the channels until he happens upon *Jaws,* a film he knows by heart but still watches whenever he comes across it.

Quint is in the middle of his story about the USS *Indianapolis* when Gail calls Malone's name. She presses her face to the screen of his side window in order to peer inside.

"You decent?" she says.

"No," he says. "But come on in."

Gail rents the front house with her teenage son Seth. She's forty, a skinny blonde who's starting to wrinkle from too much sun but still has a nice smile and kind blue eyes. She's been di-vorced for years but isn't bitter, doesn't blame all men for her troubles with one of them. She opens the door and pokes her head inside.

"You gonna be around later?" she says.

"Could be," Malone says.

"Seth's going to his dad's."

"Yeah?"

"So . . . ?"

"I'll be around."

Once or twice a month she sneaks back to Malone's place with a joint and a bottle of wine, and they make each other feel good for a night. It's straight-up sex, and both of them know that's all it'll ever be. She wants someone more stable than him, and he doesn't want anyone at all. He gave everything he had the first time around, emptied himself out.

"Care for a beer?" he says.

"Come on," she says. "How are we ever gonna get to Maui if you keep spending all your money on booze?"

It's their running joke—sad in a way—sneaking off together to Hawaii, starting over.

"I'm gonna hit the Mega Millions this week," he says. "Jackpot's up to what?"

"One hundred seven million."

"The numbers came to me in a dream. You watch."

"You're fucking nuts," Gail says. "You hear about Jordan and Nikki?"

"No."

"They finally split for Alaska last night."

"No shit."

"Yeah, and then Nikki called me this morning and said the apartment was unlocked and whatever they'd left behind was up for grabs. I went over a couple hours ago, and it looked like everything they owned was still there. Furniture, clothes, everything. I scored a blender and a set of knives. You should go see what's left."

Probably nothing but junk, but you never know. When the next commercial comes on, Malone hauls himself up off the futon, grabs another beer, and strolls over to the gray stucco apartment building across the street. Jordan and Nikki's place is on the second floor. Two guys he's never seen before are struggling to carry a sofa out of the apartment, and after a few rounds of "You lift your end," "No, you lift *yours*," they finally manage to slide it through the front door.

Malone steps inside. The place has been pretty well picked over by now. A couple of surf rats are looking through the kitchen cupboards, and a homeless woman Malone knows as Daisy has piled a bunch of blankets and sheets on the bedroom floor. The only furniture left is a homemade bookcase and an ugly nightstand.

Mike the Hippie comes out of the bathroom carrying five rolls of toilet paper.

"Dude," he says. "What a trip, huh?"

Malone kneels next to a stack of magazines and flips through them to see if there's anything worth taking. It's mostly old *Peoples* and *Enquirers*. They were a nice couple, Jordan and Nikki. She was a waitress somewhere, and he was always talking about applying at the post office, had it in his head that delivering mail would be the perfect job for him. "You get to wear shorts" was his reason.

"Check it out," one of the surfers says. He draws back his fist and punches a hole in the living room wall.

"Aww shit, it's on!" his buddy yells, then jumps into the air and puts both feet through the wall before falling to the floor.

A bewildered Jordan walks into the apartment.

"What the hell's going on?" he says.

Everyone is silent until Mike the Hippie says, "We thought you moved out."

42

"What?"

"Nikki called Gail and said—"

"That fucking bitch!"

Mike drops the toilet paper and slips out the front door. Malone follows him. He hears Jordan screaming at everyone else to get the fuck out as he and Mike hurry down the stairs.

"What a trip," Mike says again.

Malone is walking back across the street when his phone rings. It's Freddy.

"I got something for you tonight," he says.

"Tonight?" Malone says. "I just got back."

"Yeah, yeah, I know," Freddy says. "But this is something special."

"So special that I'm gonna want to come all the way down there again?"

"And you'll have to use your own car, too. I can't get another one so soon."

"No way, man, no way."

"Hold on now," Freddy says. "I'm talking big money."

"Big money," Malone says. "What's that in dollars?"

"How's ten grand sound?" Freddy says.

It sounds pretty damn good to Malone. It sounds like he'd be able to hang up on Freddy the next couple of times he calls, take a little break.

"What are you trying to pull?" he says as he watches the evening fog creep in, the sun a dead red dot behind it. "If you're giving me ten, that means there's a lot more in it for you."

"See, that's what I like about you," Freddy says. "You don't let me get away with nothing."

5

A CRUISE SHIP IS DOCKED IN ENSENADA THIS MORNING, SO THE streets of the grimy port city are filled with tourists. The shopping district has sprung to sudden, noisy life, with mariachis playing, taxis honking, and smiling touts standing in front of every restaurant and souvenir store, running through their pitches in an effort to pull customers from the crowd.

"Real Cuban cigars, my friend."

"Lunch special, two-for-one margaritas."

"Mr. Whisker, Mr. Whisker, come look at my junk. Buy your girlfriend something."

Rolando watches the hustles from the second floor of Fuego, the disco he owns here. He's cleared enough space in a storeroom for a desk, a couch, and some chairs, hung a few posters of bikini-clad Tecate girls on the walls, and calls it his office. Music is playing downstairs, and the bass tickles the soles of his feet. Carlos opens the club during the day when a boat is in and has

44

a couple of girls dance on the poles. Guys wander in looking for cheap tequila shots and end up springing for a quick blow job, and Carlos moves a bit of coke and weed, too, letting the purchasers get high in the bathroom.

Rolando tried grinding tourists in Tijuana when he was a kid, got paid a few pesos for steering shoppers to a cousin's leather store on Revolución. He never learned enough English to make people trust him, though, and couldn't bear looking stupid in the eyes of the foreigners. The first man he ever stabbed was a marine who made fun of his accent. "Jew guys wan' belt? Jew guys wan' boots?" the jarhead said, mocking him, and Rolando flipped open his knife and stuck it in the boy's thigh. The police caught up to him later and beat him black and blue but didn't arrest him. The *pendejo* was only a tourist, after all, and who hadn't wanted to let the air out of a tourist at one time or another?

Rolando turns away from the window to face the two cops sitting in his office now. Look how far he's come. The men are here to pick up their monthly payoffs and want to know if there's anything they can do to earn extra money. One is young and thin, the other fat and older. The fat one does the talking.

"Maybe you need some bodyguards?" he says. "Maybe you need our guns?"

Rolando gestures at Ozzy stationed by the door and Esteban lounging on the couch.

"I've got all the guards and guns I need for today," he says. "But tomorrow, who knows? I'll remember your offer when the devil comes to call."

The cops chuckle and shake their heads.

"Seriously," Rolando continues. He lowers himself into the chair behind his desk. "I've committed sins even he can't abide."

The men's smiles disappear, and the young one dabs sweat off his forehead with the sleeve of his uniform. The police are always scared when they come to see El Príncipe. They know he's connected to the cartel. They know about the beheadings, the dismemberments, the barrels of acid. They've mopped up the blood and hauled the mutilated corpses to the morgue. But still they sit across from him, desperation outweighing fear, and offer to violate their oaths and piss on their honor in exchange for an envelope stuffed with cash. Rolando understands that a man who'd do this can never be trusted, but he may be useful.

He reaches into his briefcase for their pay, tosses it onto the desk, and smiles inwardly as they reach for the packets.

"Keep your eyes open," he says, "except when I tell you to close them."

The men chuckle again, already standing, eager to be on their way. Ozzy opens the door for them and locks it when they go out, then makes a face and spits on the floor. He can't stand a crooked cop either.

Rolando gets up and walks to the window again, looks down on the milling cruise ship passengers. Indian kids circulate among them with trays of string bracelets and chewing gum, dirty hands upraised, begging for pennies. The passengers ignore the children and wonder why the city doesn't keep them out of the tourist areas.

Fucking Americans.

Esteban's phone beeps. "Flaco's here," he says.

A few seconds later there's a knock at the door. Ozzy steps out into the hall to pat Flaco down, then escorts him in.

"Hola, Tío," Flaco says to Rolando. They shake hands. Flaco is tall and skinny with bulging eyes and big ears that stick straight out from his head, a country boy from top to bottom, with his boots and hat, his jeans and silk western shirt, a cockfight embroidered on the back. He's up from Michoacán, Apatzingán, where his family grows poppies and processes the resin from the

46

plants into black tar heroin. With the permission of the Tijuana cartel, Rolando buys heroin from Flaco, smuggles it into the U.S., and distributes it all over California and Arizona. It's a good business. Even after paying taxes to the cartel, Rolando makes much more money than he can spend.

"How's your father?" he asks Flaco.

"Still busting everyone's balls," Flaco says.

"That's good, huh?"

"The Lord has really blessed him."

These farmers are religious, won't drink or fuck a whore. All they care about is money. They're Rolando's mother's people. She grew up down there, and Flaco is Rolando's cousin or something, someone he can rely on.

They discuss the next shipment, one hundred pounds arriving on Saturday. The deal could easily have been set up by phone, so Rolando suspects there's something else behind this visit. Sure enough, after a bit of hemming and hawing, Flaco finally gets around to the real reason he made the trip north.

"I want to buy some new trucks," he says. "Three F-450s, one red, one black, one gold." He blushes, embarrassed by the extravagance of his request. Rolando wishes everyone he dealt with was as humble as this boy.

"Three?" he says, playing with the kid.

"Do you know somebody who can get them?" Flaco says.

Rolando assures him that the purchase can be arranged, give him a couple of days. All it'll take is a call to San Diego. He might even have them bring up an extra one for himself. He asks the boy about his mother. She had an operation recently, some kind of cancer. His phone rings as Flaco begins to respond, and Rolando raises his hand for silence when he sees that it's Jorge, one of his street guys.

"Boss," Jorge says. "Something fucked's happened."

He stopped by the house to collect some money El Toro owed him but got worried when the big man didn't come out to open the gate. Climbing the wall surrounding the property, he saw that the front door of the house was wide open and decided to investigate. Inside, he found El Toro and Maria shot dead and Luz missing.

"I'm in the yard now," he says. "What should I do?"

"Do you have a gun?" Rolando asks him.

"*Simón.*" Of course.

"Stand guard until I return. Don't let anybody in."

Rolando punches out and hits the button for Luz. Her phone rings and rings until voice mail picks up. "What the fuck is going on?" he says. "Get in touch with me as soon as you can."

Everyone's staring at him, wondering what's happened, but all he can think about is Luz. The men responsible for this will hurt her, he knows. Women, children—nobody's off-limits anymore. He covers his mouth with his hand, keeps himself under control, but a scream still echoes in his head: *Where are you, baby? Where are you?*

He spends the drive back to Tijuana trying to figure out who killed his people and kidnapped his wife. Carlos Avila was squeezed out when the cartel gave Rolando his territory, and word is that he's still holding a grudge five years later. There's also a rumor that the cartel intends to do away with independents like Rolando and take over the heroin business in addition to cocaine. This might be their first move.

Then again, it could have been someone he brushed against on his way up, someone whose brother he killed, whose sister he fucked, whose son OD'd on his dope. A powerful man has enemies, a successful man breaks hearts, and the losers will always try to destroy the winners and drag them back down into the mud.

Whoever it was, he's dead. He's dead, his family's dead, his friends. Even the memory of him will be erased.

The road hugs the coast, passing luxury condo developments filled with American retirees and tumbledown fishing villages where dogs fight over garbage in the streets. Behind it all is the Pacific, the first flash of sunset imparting a pink tinge to the surf that batters the rocky shore.

Rolando learned to swim there, learned to catch and ride a wave. He remembers being out in the water at this exact time of day some long-ago summer, how the sea cooled his sun-burned skin, how the spray solidified the light, how humbling it was when the sea took control, lifting him, cradling him, then hurtling him toward shore. He had friends who never needed anything more than this, and he used to tell them it was because the salt water had softened their brains. But they were the smart ones, he sees that now, Paulito and Juan and El Gato; Chino, Zap, and Sid Vicious.

Dusk is settling over Tijuana by the time they get back. The dusty air gilds every tire shop and shack cantina with a golden aura, and evening's shadows soften the daytime glare. The city's roar has quieted, and worried wives let out sighs of relief when their husbands return home safe from work.

The twilight calm does nothing to ease Rolando's mind, however. The house is dark when they pull up in front, and as the gate slides open, he wonders whether he might be walking into an ambush. He climbs out of the Escalade with his Beretta in hand, ready for anything.

"Here I am, boss," Jorge says, stepping out of the dark, hands over his head.

"You're alone?"

"Only me."

"You didn't see Luz?"

"I didn't see nobody."

Rolando turns to Esteban and Ozzy. "Keep watch out here," he says, and motions for Jorge to accompany him into the house.

The two men walk up the steps leading to the front door. Rolando starts to push the door open.

"Get ready," Jorge says. "They're right here in the hall."

Rolando turns on the light in the foyer. A huge crystal chandelier throws a lacy pattern over the walls and floor. The bodies lie in a heap in front of the office. Rolando moves toward them and switches on another light. Blood everywhere, and the smell of it too. Flies buzz around the corpses, skittering across their dull, dead eyes and darting in and out of their noses and mouths and the new holes the bullets made.

"Luz!" Rolando shouts. His thought is that she might be hiding somewhere, too frightened to show herself. "Luz!"

One of the parrots in the living room screeches. Rolando calls Luz's phone again, hears it ringing upstairs. Taking the steps two at a time, he races to their bedroom, bursts in, and finds the phone on the nightstand.

Room by room he searches the rest of the house, checking inside every closet and under every bed. Don't be frantic, he tells himself, be thorough. There's no sign of her, but also no signs of more violence.

"Send in Esteban," he tells Jorge.

He kneels next to the corpses. The shock has passed, and now his anger is building. Two people he trusted, who trusted him, gunned down like dogs.

Esteban comes through the front door and walks over to stand beside him.

"Jesus Christ," he mutters when he sees Maria and El Toro.

"Get rid of the bodies and clean up the mess," Rolando says.

He enters his office. It'll be an easy matter to find out what went on here today. There are cameras all over the house, inside and out. They record everything that happens and feed it into his computer. A better setup than the president's, the salesman said.

He sits at his desk and turns on his laptop. He left the house at 9:45, so he starts there, cycling through various cameras. The footage jumps forward one minute with each tap of his finger. At 10:06 Luz goes to the bedroom and lies down. The rest of the house is quiet, just Maria puttering about. At 10:15 Maria walks upstairs to fetch the laundry, then, with the next tap of his finger, she's gone. Luz gets out of bed. She dresses quickly, puts a few things into a backpack, and Rolando tracks her as she walks downstairs.

The muscles in his back tighten when she approaches his office. He switches cameras and watches her open the safe. She removes the money and the gun he kept in it and puts them in the pack. Then she turns and looks right into the lens, right at him. She knows about the cameras, knows he'll be watching her, but doesn't care. In fact, something like triumph shines in her eyes.

Two cameras, one in the office and one in the hall, capture what happens when she turns to go. He watches the footage again and again, hoping each time to see someone else do the killing, but it's always and from every angle Luz who pulls the .45 from the backpack and, in a series of blinding flashes, guns down Maria and El Toro, then runs out the front door and through the gate.

He didn't have to marry her after he took her from El Samurai. The old man treated her like a whore, and he could have, too, could have used her up and thrown her out with the trash. But little things about her got to him. The sadness that made her every smile a gift, the tender heart revealed when she dropped her guard, how she'd reach for him sometimes, so desperately, as if she really needed him. He fell for all of it, even though in the next instant the bitch would slice him open with a hooded glance or hateful word. That was her real power, that she could hurt him. She knew all his fears, all his weaknesses, and how to use them against him. And that's why he married her, he sees it now, the real reason: to keep his greatest enemy close.

He makes his decision quickly, has been formulating it ever since her betrayal began to play itself out on the computer screen. The money and the gun mean nothing to him, but he does want her. When she ran last year, he put it down to the drugs. This, however, is something different, something she planned. She killed Maria and El Toro, stole his money, and made him look like a fool. As much as he loved her yesterday, he hates her now, and this won't end until she begs him to die. He'll catch her and bring her back, start on her with his fists and move on to the knife.

Esteban is preparing to roll Maria's body onto a tarp he brought in from outside. He crouches beside the corpse and takes hold of her dress.

"Before you do that, call our friend at La Mesa," Rolando says. "I want to see El Apache."

"Now?" Esteban replies, exasperated.

"Yes, now," Rolando snaps, then goes back to his desk to once again watch Luz look up at him, point the pistol, pull the trigger, and run out the door like a woman on fire.

6

Jerónimo Cruz, El Apache on the street, reaches up to adjust the reading lamp mounted on the wall above his bunk, shifting the beam to better illuminate the pages of the worn paperback romance novel that he's a few pages from finishing. He'll forget the story as soon as he's done, but books are scarce in La Mesa, so he reads everything that comes along, in Spanish or in English. One week it's Stephen King, the next something about white women shopping in New York. Doesn't matter to him. He can only pump so much iron and watch so much TV. Reading forces his mind to work, helps pass the time, and keeps him off the yard, which is where most trouble starts.

Ronald McDonald pokes his head into the cell, his bright red hair standing up like he just saw something that scared the shit out of him. He has freckles, too, and the joke is his mom fucked a clown.

"Spare a Fanta?" he asks.

"Go ahead," Jerónimo replies.

Ronald slips inside and bends to pull a cold can of soda out of the small refrigerator under Jerónimo's bunk. "They locked the block up early," he says. "I can't get over to the commissary."

"The Jew isn't open?"

Ronald backs out and looks down the tier to where the old man called the Jew peddles soft drinks and snacks out of his cell. You can buy whatever you want in this place, from tacos to dope to TVs to birthday cards for your kids. Jerónimo has never seen anything like it in any of the prisons he's done time in on both sides of the border.

"He might be in the infirmary," Ronald says, stepping back into the cell. "I heard his liver is fucked."

"Have a seat."

A square of plywood covers the open toilet, and there's a cushion on top of it for visitors. That's where Ronald sits now and sips from his Fanta.

"I heard something else too," he says.

"Yeah?"

"That *pendejo* Salazar over in B Block says he's going to kill you for disrespecting him."

"I didn't disrespect him," Jerónimo says.

Ronald shrugs.

"He asked me to play cards, and I didn't want to," Jerónimo continues.

He's made an effort to keep to himself this time around, and a year into his three-year bit has only had to fight twice. That's an accomplishment, considering what a sensitive bunch convicts are, always looking for reasons to get their feelings hurt and stomp a mudhole in someone's ass.

That he's under the protection of El Príncipe helps, because nobody wants to piss off the Prince. But the association also leads to resentment. Less well-connected prisoners see his one-man cell, his TV and microwave and electric fan, then look around the filthy, sweltering dormitory they share with five hundred other snoring, farting, stinking prisoners and say, "Fuck that ass-licker."

Salazar is one of the jealous ones.

"You're too good to play with us, huh?" he said when Jerónimo declined his offer to join the poker game. "So go to hell then."

The kind of threat Ronald just reported usually goes in one of Jerónimo's ears and out the other, another dumbshit talking tough. But Salazar is something else. He's serving max time for murder and has killed two other men while inside, left them holding their guts in their hands. A loco like that, you take seriously.

Somewhere on the block someone starts singing a hymn at the top of his lungs. Another prisoner yells at him to shut up.

"Jesus is coming," the singing con roars, slurring drunk. "Better get ready."

"Jesus can suck my cock," is the reply.

Ronald hands Jerónimo a cigarette, and he sits up on his bunk and leans forward to reach the match.

"They say Salazar cut someone's head off during the riot," Ronald says. "Then ate the guy's eyes."

In 2008, before Jerónimo began his stint, the inmates here rioted to protest the overcrowded, unsanitary condition of the prison and the brutality of the guards. At that time eight thousand men and women were packed into the facility, which had originally been designed to hold three thousand. The authorities regained control after three days by storming the cellblocks and opening fire on the rioters. The official death toll was twenty-one inmates killed and scores injured, but darker rumors swirled that hundreds of additional bodies were bulldozed into a common grave in the prison cemetery.

Everyone who was here then has a riot story: nightmare atrocities committed by prisoners or guards, harrowing close calls, selfless rescues performed under fire. A whole new pantheon of heroes and villains was born out of the blood and flames. Jerónimo listens politely to the tales but doesn't put any stock in them. He's spent enough time behind bars to understand that myth quickly eclipses truth in places where the truth is always suspect.

So, "Ate his eyes?" he says to Ronald. "Fuck."

"Just so you know," Ronald says.

"What I'm up against, huh?"

Ronald finishes his Fanta and checks his watch. "*Malcolm in the Middle*'s on," he says. He has a cell to himself, too, and a TV, paid for by his parents. He's halfway through two years for beating his wife and says he'd do it again tomorrow if the bitch spoke to him like she did the night he lost control.

Jerónimo shuts out the light when Ronald goes, lies back on his bunk and closes his eyes. He thinks about his own wife, Irma, and their kids, Jerónimo Jr. and Ariel. They're living with Irma's sister now, and Irma says everything is fine, there's enough money, enough room, and the children are happy. She offers to bring them to visit, but Jerónimo won't let them see him here. He won't let Irma come for conjugals, either, because he isn't even sure he'd be able to get it up in one of the dirty little rooms they stick you in. Junior will be five when he gets out, Ariel, seven. Three years for kids that age is half their lives. They'll barely remember him.

Before Irma, before the kids, he didn't give a shit about anything, not even himself. He was born in El Paso, the fourth of eight children. His mom and dad were illegals but got amnesty in 1986 and moved the family to L.A., to Inglewood. Dad repaired sewing machines in a clothing factory downtown, and they lived in a converted garage off Prairie, near Hollywood Park, the four boys sharing one bedroom, the four girls the other. They had decent food, clean clothes, cable TV, but Jerónimo always felt like he was just crashing there. One of his sisters was retarded, so she got most of Mom's attention, and all his dad did was work and sleep.

His oldest brother, Arturo, joined Inglewood 13 at age twelve and was wounded in a drive-by a few years later. He's been sitting in a wheelchair and shitting in a bag ever since. Tony, two years older than Jerónimo, joined the gang next, and at sixteen was tried as an adult for the murder of a liquor store clerk and sentenced to fifty years. Jerónimo was jumped in shortly afterward. He started as a lookout for one of the set's drug corners, soon wound up slinging crack himself, and then became a tax collector, shaking down local merchants and forcing them to pay for protection.

He committed his first murder at eighteen, killed some punk who was messing with his crippled brother, trying to muscle in on the little slice of the dope business the gang had given him. Jerónimo warned the dude a bunch of times to back off, but he wouldn't listen, so Jerónimo stepped up to him one day, put a gun to his head, and pulled the trigger. He didn't feel any guilt afterward, had no nightmares or regrets. It was something that had to be done, and he did it. Like a soldier.

The cops never even came close to solving that one, but his luck ran out soon afterward, when he put together a crew of his own and began robbing other drug dealers, relieving them of their stash and cash. The money was rolling in until they hit a rock house that turned out to be an LAPD sting operation. Jerónimo ended up doing five years in Corcoran behind that.

He got out when he was twenty-four, went back in at twenty-six for robbery, got out at twenty-eight, and was back in by the end of that year for some bullshit assault charge. Looking at serious time if he was popped in the U.S. again, he moved down to Mexico, to Juárez, after his release. A cousin there set him up with a job at a *maquiladora,* a place that made TVs. It was supposed to be a new start, but six months later he was busted for selling flat screens he'd smuggled out of the factory.

An inmate laughs maniacally, another gives a *grito.* Steel doors clang, toilets flush, and someone bounces a basketball off a wall. Jerónimo is usually able to block out the ceaseless cacophony of prison life, but not this evening. Tonight every sound makes him squirm.

He rolls off his bunk and washes up at the sink, shaves his face and head, then changes out of his shorts into a prison-issue gray T-shirt and sweatpants. Leaving his cell, he walks down the tier to see Armando. Armando is a little guy with one eye who also did work for El Príncipe on the outside. He has a phone hidden in his cell.

"You know anybody in B Block you can call?" Jerónimo asks. He doesn't have to say "anybody you can trust."

Armando looks up from a magazine. "Sure."

"Can you find out which bunk Salazar's in? You know, the killer?"

Armando has Jerónimo keep a lookout while he retrieves the phone from behind the air shaft grate and makes the call. Two minutes later Jerónimo has the information he needs: last row, last bunks, bottom.

Jerónimo has a small shank hidden inside his mattress, but

this calls for something more certain. He walks down the stairs to the second tier. El Punisher is sitting on the edge of his bunk, doing bicep curls with a dumbbell and watching a beauty pageant on TV.

"*Órale, hombre,*" Jerónimo says.

The big man motions him into the cell with a nod.

"I need something nice for like half an hour," Jerónimo says.

El Punisher drops the barbell and reaches for a Bible. The pages of the book have been glued together and a space carved out to hold contraband. There's an ice pick inside, a steak knife, and two good-sized blades with duct-tape grips.

"I can get bigger," El Punisher says. A tattoo of two dogs fucking covers his bare chest.

"I bet you can," Jerónimo says, reaching for the pick. He tests the point with his thumb.

"Seriously. You need a gun, give me an hour," El Punisher says.

"This'll do," Jerónimo says. He drops a twenty-dollar bill onto El Punisher's bunk, stashes the pick in his sweats, and leaves the cell. Glancing up at the skylight in the ceiling of the corridor, he sees that night has come down.

He did a year in the federal pen at Juárez for the TVs. With no money coming in from outside, he had to find a way to rent a bunk and buy decent food, because everything costs in a Mexican prison, right down to the guards charging fifty centavos a day to mark you present at head count.

A stroke of luck saved him from having to shine shoes or wash clothes or fetch meals for the more well-off inmates. His second day in, a *vato* from L.A. who didn't like his Inglewood tattoos jumped him. Jerónimo managed to twist the shank out of his hand and turn it on him. Dude was dead and Jerónimo was back playing dominos before the guards knew what was happening.

Vincente, El Príncipe's brother, saw it all go down and was impressed by how Jerónimo handled himself. He was doing time for shooting a judge and had a thriving drug business in the prison. He summoned Jerónimo to his cell and offered him a job delivering heroin to his customers. You didn't say no to someone like Vincente, so Jerónimo spent the rest of his time in Juárez running tar and coming down hard on junkies who fell behind on their payments.

When he was released, Vincente gave him a thousand-dollar bonus and told him to see his brother in Tijuana if he needed work. A month later Jerónimo joined El Príncipe's crew. By day he acted as muscle for the Prince, collecting on loans he had on the street, and at night he lay in his tiny, noisy room—a room no bigger than his cell had been—and tried to figure out what next. Because death was closing in on him, he was sure of it. There were no old gangsters. You were considered ancient if you made it to forty, and Jerónimo wanted to live longer than that, didn't want to be shot down doing someone else's dirty work. Staring up at the ceiling, his mind aflame, he prayed and made promises. "Help me change the end of my story," he begged.

The central corridor of A Block is called Revolución, after Tijuana's main drag. The inmates congregate there, playing cards on the picnic tables and sitting stoned against the concrete walls, seeing nothing and everything. Music blares out of a hundred radios, and cons stand in the middle of the corridor and carry on shouted conversations with other prisoners in the three tiers of cells towering above them. Jerónimo nods to a couple of acquaintances as he moves through the chaos. He keeps his circle small. The fewer motherfuckers who know your business, the better, especially if you're trying to avoid trouble.

When he reaches the guard station at the end of Revolución, he motions to the pig inside to get his ass up from his desk and come to the window.

"Hey, boss," he says. "I need to take a walk."

"So?" the pig replies. *Tío Pelón,* the inmates call him, Uncle Baldy. He has a thing for young cons, trades them cigarettes and Cup O' Noodles for blow jobs. Jerónimo unfolds a twenty and presses it to the scratched and smeared Plexiglas that separates them. Baldy waves him to the door. When the buzzer sounds, Jerónimo steps into the sally port. Baldy is waiting for him there. He takes the money and signals another guard in the office through a barred window. Another buzzer goes off, and Baldy pushes the door that opens onto the yard.

"How long?" he says to Jerónimo.

"Fifteen minutes," Jerónimo says, stepping outside.

Baldy stands in the doorway and whistles. The guard in the east tower waves his rifle. Baldy points at Jerónimo and gives the thumbs up. The tower guard waves his rifle again. Baldy moves back inside the cellblock and closes the door.

Jerónimo pauses for a few breaths of fresh air. The sounds of a Tijuana night rise over the wall and drift across the deserted yard. A car honks, music plays, a mother shouts for her children to come inside for dinner. The prison festers right in the middle of the city, surrounded by houses, restaurants, and shops. During the riot, people with loved ones inside climbed onto the roofs of neighboring buildings and tried to catch glimpses of their fathers, sons, and lovers when the assault team finally herded the surviving inmates onto the yard.

Jerónimo sets out for B Block, walking across the basketball court and the weight pit. It's a hot night but still a relief from the swelter of the cellblock. And he can see the stars out here, faint in the purple sky, at least until the tower guard decides to fuck with him by shining a spotlight in his face. Jerónimo raises a hand to block the beam and keeps his eyes on the ground, not missing a step.

When he reaches B Block, he pushes a button next to the door that sounds a buzzer. A guard appears at the window in the door, and another twenty gets Jerónimo inside.

He met Irma at the pharmacy where she worked. He liked how classy she looked in her white coat and pants, but she cut him off with a cold stare when he tried to flirt with her as she rang up his chewing gum and deodorant. Catching a glimpse of his shaved head and tattoos in a mirror on his way out, he couldn't blame her. A woman like that could do a lot better than a thug like him.

Still, he couldn't stop thinking about her. He found himself remembering her eyes while he ate lunch and mooning over her dainty hands as he drove to a barbershop to squeeze a payment for El Príncipe out of the owner. He returned to the pharmacy the next day for more gum and asked Irma if she could recommend some vitamins, said he'd been feeling a little run-down. She came out from behind the counter and spent ten minutes with him, explaining the different pills and what they were supposed to do for you. When he asked if she knew of anything that'd make him better looking, she smiled the faintest of smiles and said, "You're a funny one, aren't you."

"I'm trying," he replied.

He replayed this exchange over and over for the rest of the day, searching for deeper meaning in Irma's every word, every gesture. And then, that night, as he once again tossed and turned in his narrow bed, feverish with visions of his bleak future, it came to him as suddenly as a bullet to the head: He loved her, and loving her was the only thing that would save his life.

He began to court Irma with all the desperation this realization inspired, showing up at the pharmacy every day with a small gift and a compliment. After two weeks she agreed to have coffee with him, two weeks later, lunch. Every time he was with her, he found something new to admire. There had been other women in his life, but none like her. Her sincerity and kindness seemed to alter the composition of the air he breathed and transform the chemistry of his blood.

He told her the truth from the very beginning, that he was a murderer, a thief, a weapon in the hands of evil men.

"But there's something good in me," he said. "It's growing every day, taking over."

Irma told him later that his honesty had taken her by surprise. She'd been expecting gangster posturing and crude boasts, but instead was moved by the tears she saw in his eyes when he expressed his desire for a new kind of life. After a month of listening to him lay himself bare, she finally reached across the table and took his hand.

"That's enough looking back," she said. "From now on, we only think about the future."

This was all the encouragement Jerónimo needed. He met with El Príncipe the very next day to tell him that he'd soon be starting a family and wanted to switch to a safer line of work. It was a dangerous announcement to make—you didn't just up and walk away from El Príncipe's crew—but Jerónimo was now determined to be a free man, dead or alive.

At first the Prince scoffed at him. "What the fuck else do you think you're going to do?" he said. "All you're good at is scaring people." Then he got angry, deciding that Jerónimo's wanting to go straight was some kind of insult. He drew a gun and pointed it across his desk, called Jerónimo a traitor and threatened to kill him then and there.

Jerónimo didn't flinch. He stared down the barrel of the gun and again asked for the Prince's understanding. "You know I've been loyal to you," he said. "And I'm here now as one honorable man speaking the truth to another honorable man."

El Príncipe pressed the gun to his forehead.

"On your knees," he said.

"Respectfully," Jerónimo replied. "I'll take it standing."

A clock in the room ticked five times, and then the Prince sat down, the gun lying on the desk in front of him. The agreement was this: Jerónimo wouldn't be allowed to leave the gang. Instead, he'd be moved down into the reserves. He'd no longer work directly for El Príncipe but would still be called upon to do favors for the crew from time to time. And God help him if he ever refused such a request. It wasn't the clean break Jerónimo had been hoping for, but he knew better than to push his luck.

The main corridor of B Block has been converted into a dormitory. Rows of steel bunks stacked two high, narrow walkways between them, fill the cavernous space. The din is even more intense here than it is in Jerónimo's block, a good thing in this case. Nobody even notices when he steps inside.

As he makes his way across the room, he hardens into something less human than he was moments before and pulls the ice pick from his sweatpants. Arriving at the last row of bunks, he starts down it, a wrecking ball in mid-swing, prepared to smash anyone who gets in his way. The cons he encounters in the cramped aisle feel the heat coming off him and fall onto their racks or step aside to let him pass.

All he hears now is his own breathing, a rasping in his

head. Salazar is lying on his bunk, thumbing a PlayStation. He looks up an instant before Jerónimo reaches him. His eyes widen. Jerónimo thought he might try to reason with him, warn him, frighten him, but an image of the last man the fucker killed—splayed in the dirt, opened up from throat to groin—comes to him, and in one swift motion he clamps his hand over Salazar's mouth and plunges the pick into his bare chest.

One-two-three-four-five. He stabs him as quickly as he can yank the pick out and slam it back in. Six-seven-eight-nine. He leaves the pick in on the last thrust and jerks the handle back and forth in order to do as much damage as possible. Salazar dies without a struggle, without a sound, his eyes rolling back in his head, a trickle of black blood spilling from the corner of his mouth.

Jerónimo withdraws the pick and wipes it clean on the sheet. He's sweating like crazy, panting, as he makes his way back up the alley between the bunks. Nobody tries to stop him as he hurries to the guard station. Someone will toss a blanket over the corpse, someone else will steal the dead man's shoes. It'll be tomorrow morning before a guard finally discovers the body.

The pig controlling the doors barely looks up at Jerónimo when buzzing him out. A dog barks somewhere in the night as he walks across the yard, a car alarm goes off, a plane flies low overhead. He blocks his nostrils one at a time and blows them clear. When he spits, he tastes blood. An empty plastic bag rolls toward him on the wind. Before he can get out of its way, it wraps around his feet and nearly trips him.

After meeting with El Príncipe, Jerónimo used all the money he had saved to pay the various bribes that would allow him to drive a taxi. He rented a cab and began working sixteen-hour days ferrying passengers around Tijuana. He and Irma married and settled into a little house in a quiet neighborhood. He worshiped her, she rooted for him, and they were happy. Ariel came along, then Junior, and the plan was to save $10,000 and move to San Diego or L.A.

The errands Jerónimo was required to do for El Príncipe were usually simple tasks. Every couple of months a call would come: Pick this up here and drop it off there. One night, however, he was ordered to torch a car, and on another occasion he beat an old man who owed money. That kind of thuggery weighed on him now like it never had before, and he looked forward to the day he and his family would cross the border and he'd leave the gangster life behind for good.

They were three months from making the move when he drove his cab to an address El Príncipe's man gave him, honked twice as instructed, and waited for someone to come out of the house and get the package he was carrying in the trunk. The car was suddenly surrounded by masked soldiers dressed in black. They laid him facedown in the street and kicked him in the head after showing him the five pounds of heroin he'd been hauling. Whose is it? they wanted to know.

"Whose do you think?" he said. "It's mine," and he's been in La Mesa ever since.

El Príncipe rewarded him for taking the fall. He gets enough money to live like a man in here, and every month Irma picks up an envelope full of cash for her and the kids. Now all he has to do is survive the two years remaining on his sentence. He's been keeping his hands clean and taking it day by day. Until now.

Back in his cell he strips and washes up, then puts on aftershave and a clean T-shirt and shorts. Lying on his bunk, he aims the fan at his face and sets it to high. The Dodgers are playing. He plugs

66

his headphones into the TV and turns it up so that the crowd is the loudest thing in his head. When Baldy comes for him, the pig has to step into his cell and jab him in the shoulder with his club to get his attention. Jerónimo takes off the headphones, and the clamor of the block returns.

"Let's go," Baldy says.

"Where to?" Jerónimo says.

"Your friend wants to see you."

7

N IGHT HAS FALLEN, AND LUZ IS STILL WAITING AT THE BODY SHOP
for the driver to arrive. She asks again when he'll be there, and
again Freddy says, "Soon." She needs to leave town *now*. It's
agony being stranded here in the dark and imagining Rolando
moving from shadow to shadow, closing in, murder on his mind.

She paces the parking lot, walks from the stack of tires she's
been sitting on to the fence and back. She keeps one hand in
the pack, finger curled around the trigger of the pistol. Once or
twice today she's caught Freddy staring at her and going over in
his mind various ways to take the money. She stared right back
at him, thinking, *Try it, you* hijo de puta, and if he comes after her, she will, she'll shoot him, no problem. The money is
Isabel's, the down payment on their future, the foundation for
their new life.

She reaches the fence, turns, and starts back toward the tires.
When she's halfway there the lot is flooded with light. A car

has pulled into the driveway. Freddy and Goyo freeze, but Luz draws the .45 and crouches beside the fence. Dust swirls in the beams of the car's headlights, and Freddy and Goyo, hands raised weakly against the glare, are bleached into ghostliness.

The car's horn bleats twice, and a voice calls out in English, "Open up, already."

Goyo waddles over and takes hold of the gate, drags it sideways. A beat-up silver BMW pulls into the lot. The engine sputters and dies, and darkness and quiet return. Luz lowers the gun into the pack but stays where she is, back pressed against the chain-link fence.

A white man steps out of the car, some beach bum, tall and thin, older, maybe thirty, thirty-five. He's wearing a T-shirt advertising a surf shop, plaid shorts, and black Converse tennis shoes. Surely this isn't the guy Freddy's been talking up all day, his best driver. This *pendejo* can't even keep his hair out of his eyes, has to brush it back every time he turns his head.

"Just so you know, this isn't going to be a regular thing," he says to Freddy. "Nighttime is the wrong time to be fucking around down here."

"If you have trouble with anyone, tell them you know me," Freddy says.

"Yeah, right," the bum says. "I do that, I'll end up in the river."

"Hey, we're all going to end up in the river someday," Freddy says.

He leans in close to speak quietly to the bum. The bum listens for a while, nodding agreeably, but then suddenly stops Freddy and says, "In the morning? You didn't say anything about in the morning." Apparently there's a disagreement over the details of the trip. Not being able to hear what's being said, all Luz can do is watch the men argue in urgent whispers. The bum puts up a fight, but Freddy is relentless and eventually gets his way. He slaps the bum on the back and steers him to where Luz is waiting.

"Now come and meet our friend," he says. "She needs our help."

"There any beer around?" the bum asks.

"Goyo," Freddy calls and tips an imaginary can into his mouth. Goyo grunts and walks into the office.

Freddy brings the bum over, and Luz moves away from the fence, standing up straight to squint down her nose at him. His blue eyes are bloodshot, and he looks as if he could use a shower.

"*Señorita* Luz, this is Kevin Malone, who's going to take you across," Freddy says.

Malone lifts his chin by way of greeting, doesn't even meet her gaze. It's like he could take or leave this job. This infuriates Luz. She can't believe she'll be putting her life in the hands of this *cabrón*.

"This is what I have arranged for you," Freddy continues. "Tomorrow morning you two will drive to Tecate, where a friend of mine will be working at the crossing. At ten a.m., you and Kevin will pass through his station into the U.S. It will be very quick and very simple with no possibility of being stopped. You won't even have to hide; you can sit right up front in the car. Then, once you are across, Kevin will drop you wherever you would like, and you can be on your way."

"I told you I need to leave today," Luz says. She struggles to keep her voice under control.

Freddy raises his hands in a gesture of helplessness. "I know, I know, but it's late, *señorita,* and my man isn't on duty until tomorrow."

"I want to cross tonight. I want to cross right now."

"I'm sorry, but that's impossible. Everything will be fine

70

though. I promise you'll be safe and comfortable. Kevin will take you to a nice hotel, and —"

"No," Luz interrupts. "I want to leave tonight, and I'm not getting into a car with him."

"What do you mean?" Freddy says.

"I want another driver."

"Another driver? But Kevin is the best. He's already taken five people across today."

Goyo returns with a can of Modelo. Malone opens it and has a sip.

"Look at him," Luz says. "Drinking like this is nothing. And he doesn't even speak Spanish."

"Sure, I do," Malone says in Spanish. "A little. Do you speak English?"

"Fuck you," Luz replies in English. "How's that?"

Freddy steps between them. "Listen," he says.

"You listen," Luz says. "I'm paying you a lot of money—more than I should be—for this special deal or whatever it is, and I want someone sober, I want someone smart, and I want to cross tonight."

Malone turns to Freddy with a shrug. "Customer's always right," he says. He takes another swig of beer and walks to his car, leans against the trunk, and tilts his head back to look up at the sky.

"Chingada madre!" Freddy shouts. He advances on Luz with clenched fists and bulging veins. Luz's breath catches in her throat. She draws the Colt and stops him in his tracks. He mutters to himself, tugs his goatee, then points at the gate.

"Get the fuck out of here," he says.

"Fine," Luz says. "Give me my money back."

Freddy reaches into his pocket for the stack of bills he took from her earlier. He pulls off five hundreds—"For my trouble," he says—and throws the rest at her feet.

"And you better make your peace with God," he continues. "Because whoever you took that money from is gonna get you real quick."

Luz picks up the cash and shoves it into the backpack. She heads for the gate but slows as she reaches it. The dark, empty street outside frightens her. Freddy's right: She's dead if she leaves here. Rolando is waiting in every doorway, all the alleys, and she has nowhere else to go, nobody else to turn to. Though it wrenches her pride all the way to its roots, she wheels to face Freddy again.

"Okay," she says.

"Okay what?" Freddy replies. He's going to make her say it.

She nods at Malone. "He can drive."

"Why, thank you, *señorita*," Freddy says with a sneer. "Thank you very much."

"But we leave for Tecate now," she says. "I'm not spending another night in this city."

Malone smiles and lifts his beer in a mock toast, and Luz tightens her grip on the gun inside the backpack. So he thinks this is funny, does he? Well, that's okay. She's got more than enough bullets left to make a joker like him cry.

As he pulls away from the body shop, Malone sticks his arm out the window of the Beamer and flips Freddy off. It's thirty miles to Tecate on the toll road. He and the girl will be there in less than an hour. He'll check her into a hotel, go out for a few beers, drive her across the border in the morning and dump her where she wants, and then he's done. His money will be waiting for him at one of the drop houses in San Ysidro.

He sneaks a look at his passenger. She's staring out the windshield, her backpack clutched to her chest. There's money in it, Freddy told him, and he saw the gun himself. Definitely not your typical *pollo*. She speaks English for one, and you can tell someone has put her on a pedestal, spoiled her a little. Most of the people he hauls are so meek they won't even look him in the eye. This girl has an attitude. That's what happens when you're as nice-looking as she is. Even dressed down, she's a natural beauty. Long black hair, dark eyes, smooth brown skin. The kind of woman men make all kinds of mistakes for.

"The air-conditioning's busted," he says, "but you can roll down the window."

No response, not a twitch.

"Roll down your window if you want," he says again, louder, thinking she didn't hear him.

"I'm fine," she snaps.

Good deal. If he doesn't even have to talk to her, this job'll be cake. He turns on the radio and fiddles with the knob until he picks up a classic rock station out of San Diego that's playing a Neil Young song he's never heard before. He passes a little pickup chugging along with a load of old refrigerators, and then a big black SUV with tinted windows and chrome wheels blows by both of them. A *narco*, most likely. They're the only ones who can afford vehicles like that around here.

He's almost at the entrance to the toll road when flashing lights appear in the rearview mirror. It's where he'd wait, too, if he was a cop looking to shake down tourists with a bit of money in their pockets. He searches for a place to pull over as the fuckers give their siren a workout.

Luz glances over her shoulder at the police car, and all the haughtiness drains out of her. She turns to Malone with panic in her eyes and says, "Don't stop."

"Are you kidding?" he says.

"They're going to kill us."

"What are you talking about? You know how it goes. They'll

73

tell me I ran a stop sign, I'll give them twenty bucks, and we'll be on our way."

"Please," Luz says.

Malone switches off the radio. The girl is scared, and that scares him.

"Look," he says. "I have to stop, but it'll be okay. Stay cool and, whatever you do, don't let them see that *pistola* you're carrying."

Luz starts to say something else, but then sits back and chews her lower lip.

Malone eases to the shoulder in front of a Home Depot. The cruiser rolls up behind them, and the Beamer is suddenly filled with white light. Luz sets the backpack on the floor at her feet.

"Tranquila," Malone says. He watches in the side mirror as a shadow slides out of the cruiser and comes toward the BMW. It's impossible in the glare to make out any details, so he sits and sweats, waiting to see who appears at the window.

"Buenas noches."

It's a cop, a regular old cop.

"Buenas noches," Malone says.

The officer asks in English for his license, and Malone removes the card from his wallet and hands it to him.

"Where you going so fast?" the cop says. His partner has moved up to stand on the passenger side of the car.

"We're meeting friends for dinner in Tecate," Malone says.

The cop nods at Luz.

"Who's she?"

"My girlfriend," Malone says.

"Buenas noches, señorita," the cop says to Luz.

"Buenas noches," she replies.

"You like Mexican girls?" the cop says to Malone.

"I like this one," Malone says.

74

The cop smiles. He's missing a tooth. He adjusts his hat and puts his hand on his gun.

"You were speeding," he says. "Follow us to the station to pay your fine."

"Oh, man," Malone says. "Is there some way to take care of this here? We don't want to be late for dinner."

An eighteen-wheeler rockets past, stirring up dirt and trash and shaking the BMW. The cop stands up straight and presses himself against the door. Two more trucks pass in quick succession.

When the road clears, the cop bends to look in the window again. "Forty dollars," he says.

Malone can tell the man is eager to move on. He slips two twenties from his wallet and hands them over. The cop folds them carefully and tucks them into his ticket book. He glances once more at Malone's license before returning it.

"Slow down, Mr. Malone," he says.

"I will," Malone says. "Sorry to trouble you."

The cop then nods at Luz and says something to her in Spanish that Malone doesn't catch, something that tightens her jaw. This makes the cop smile. He motions for his partner to return to the cruiser, and Malone waits until they get in and turn off the spotlight before starting the Beamer.

"Do you know how many times I've been through that?" he says to Luz. "I'm surprised I didn't recognize the guy."

Luz doesn't respond, is back to staring blankly out the windshield.

Malone doesn't feel completely in the clear until they hit the toll road and are beyond the jurisdiction of the city cops. He sits back in his seat then and releases his death grip on the steering wheel. A sliver of moon is rising over the scrub-covered hills, and the warm air smells of sage. He reaches for the radio but decides against it, enjoying the silence. The sky is full of stars.

Luz finally stirs, rolls down her window. Malone notices a tattoo on the back of her neck, up under her ponytail. *Angel Baby.*

"What'd that fucker say to you back there?" he asks her.

"He wanted to know how much for me to suck his cock," Luz replies.

"Awww, man, that's terrible," Malone says.

Luz shrugs and sticks her hand out the window to feel the air rushing past. Malone is sad looking at her, sad thinking about her life. He should have brought a bottle along. You've got to be ready for moments like these, ready to drown your ruined heart as soon as it starts beating again.

8

BALDY AND THE OTHER GUARD WALK JERÓNIMO TO THE MAIN GATE of the prison. Neither will answer any questions. They allowed him to put on jeans and a shirt, but then hurried him out of his cell before he could grab anything else. As he was being escorted off the tier, he hollered to Ronald McDonald to watch his stuff, said he'd be back soon, hoped it was true.

Waiting at the gate are two big dudes, one with a shaved head, the other with short dark hair. He's seen them before: Ozzy and Esteban, El Príncipe's bodyguards. Baldy opens the gate and says "Go," and Jerónimo steps into the street. He's dreamed of the day he'd leave La Mesa, but the relief he should feel is tainted by the strangeness of the situation. He knows trouble when he sees it.

Ozzy orders him into a black Escalade parked at the curb. Jerónimo climbs in and settles uneasily in the passenger seat. Ozzy gets behind the wheel, and Esteban sits in back.

A banana-shaped air freshener dangles from the rearview mirror, and the Escalade is filled with its sickening chemical scent. When Ozzy turns the key, a *corrido* erupts out of the truck's speakers at full volume. He reaches for the CD player and shuts it off.

"What's up?" Jerónimo asks.

"El Príncipe wants to talk to you," Ozzy replies.

Jerónimo nods. Trouble, like he thought. He puts a hand on the dash when Ozzy shifts into gear and pulls out into the street. He's always been a nervous passenger, can't relax with someone else driving. Ozzy sighs and rubs his temples with his thumb and middle finger, and this makes Jerónimo even more uneasy, muscle like him showing strain.

They cut through the center of town, and every corner holds an ugly memory for Jerónimo. There's where he sliced off a man's ear, and there's where another man fell to his knees and offered his twelve-year-old daughter as payment for a debt. Jerónimo was damaged before he got here, but this place made him worse. There's a ruthlessness here he's encountered nowhere else, as if all that glitter right across the border has driven everyone crazy.

An old man riding a bicycle wobbles into the street in front of the Escalade. Ozzy swerves but still clips him with the mirror, knocking him to the pavement.

"Fuck," Ozzy grunts.

He stops at the corner and stares into the rearview.

"He's dead," Esteban says, twisting to look out the back window.

"The fuck he is," Ozzy says.

"I'm telling you, he's dead," Esteban says. "Drive on."

Jerónimo watches in the side mirror as the old man raises his head, then slowly sits up. Blood is running down his face from a cut on his forehead.

"Okay, maybe he's not dead," Esteban says.

"That's one tough old bastard," Ozzy says.

"Probably got nothing but rocks in his head," Esteban says. "Let's go."

They drive up a hill toward El Príncipe's house. It's a fancy neighborhood with paved roads and gutters, private security, and plenty of streetlights. The houses are all big, all new. Stucco mansions surrounded by high walls. Jerónimo has been here twice before: once when he started working for El Príncipe, and once when he quit. Both times he wondered on whose backs all this was built.

The Escalade turns into the driveway of the house. A man steps out of the shadows and opens the gate, and the truck pulls forward into a parking area. Two other men are standing on the porch, guns in hand, and every light in the house is on. It blazes like a palace awaiting the arrival of guests. Ozzy gets out, then Esteban, and Jerónimo follows their lead. He's one of them after all, one of El Príncipe's men.

They walk up the steps to the front door of the house, past the guard stationed there, and go inside. A man is on his hands and knees in the hall, scrubbing the floor with a brush that he rinses in a bucket of soapy pink water. There are dark stains on the wall behind him. He sits back as they approach and wipes his mouth with his hand. Ozzy reaches over him to tap on a door.

"Come in," El Príncipe calls from the other side.

Ozzy opens the door and motions for Jerónimo to enter.

El Príncipe is sitting at his desk in his office, the same office where he welcomed Jerónimo to the crew, and the same office where he pulled a gun on Jerónimo when Jerónimo told him he wanted out.

"Apache," he says. "Good to see you."

When Jerónimo was born, he looked so much like a little Indian, with his dark skin, slanted eyes, and high cheekbones, that his dad insisted on naming him after the legendary Apache leader. He said he was honoring his great-great-grandfather, an Apache warrior who fled from Arizona to Mexico in the late 1800s, when the Apaches in the U.S. were being shipped off to reservations or hunted down like dogs. Mexico was paying a bounty for Indian scalps too, but great-great-grandfather managed to find refuge in the Sierra Madre and married a woman there.

That was the story Papá told when he had a few beers in him, anyway. Jerónimo liked the yarn because it gave him a history and explained the restlessness that sometimes gripped his soul. The kids called him the Apache growing up, and he kept the nickname as he got older. The fierceness it hinted at was useful in the world he lived in, one more thing to make someone think twice before crossing him.

Ozzy shuts the door and stands in front of it. Rolando tells El Apache to sit in the chair on the other side of the desk. The Indian has his prison face on, a mask that shows nothing, but Rolando knows he must be confused. One minute he's behind bars, the next he's being offered a drink by the Prince himself.

"Beer? Tequila?" Rolando says. "I got brandy too."

"No, *jefe*," El Apache says. "Thanks anyway."

He's always been respectful, always known his place. Got none of that *cholo* cockiness that assholes from L.A. usually have. Rolando liked him from the beginning, when he showed up fresh out of Juárez, looking for a job. He was older than most of the locos who came to him wanting work, but he proved to be a good man, one who could follow orders, one who got things done. In fact, he might even have been somebody if he hadn't decided he'd rather drive a cab, though that took balls, too, to come in and ask to be cut loose. Which is why Rolando thought of him first thing for this job.

They sit in silence, listening to the clock tick, and Rolando guesses the Indian would wait all day for him to speak. They're stubborn that way. He finally stretches in his chair and laces his fingers behind his head.

"How are things in La Mesa?" he asks.

El Apache shrugs. "It's La Mesa," he says. "But thanks for the money you send, and the money you give my family."

"You earned it," Rolando says. "You didn't disappoint me like so many others have."

El Apache shrugs again, unreadable.

"How much time is left on your sentence?" Rolando says.

"Two years, if everything goes like it should," El Apache says.

"But, wait, here you are now," Rolando says with a smile.

El Apache smiles too, but doesn't respond.

Rolando taps his fingers on the arm of his chair.

"You were born in the U.S.?" he says.

"El Paso," El Apache says.

"But then you lived in L.A."

"Yeah, I grew up there."

"And you speak English?"

"Read and write it, too."

There's a commotion out in the hall, shouting. Rolando reaches into the desk drawer for his Beretta. Ozzy's gun is already in his hand. The big man opens the door a crack. The painter who's supposed to cover the bloodstains on the wall has arrived, and he's arguing with the guy scrubbing the floor.

"Shut up and get back to work," Ozzy says. He closes the door and tucks his pistol into his waistband. Rolando leaves the Beretta out, on top of the desk.

"I have a mission for you," he says to El Apache.

El Apache's eyes narrow. "A mission?"

"It's the last thing I'll ever ask you to do for me," Rolando says. "How does that sound?"

"Depends on what it is," El Apache says.

Rolando slides three photos of Luz across the desk. "This morning my wife killed two of my people and ran off with some money," he says. "I want you to find her and bring her back."

El Apache looks down at the photos but doesn't touch them.

"She may be somewhere in Mexico or she may have crossed into the U.S.," Rolando continues. "She has relatives there, I think, in Los Angeles."

"Mexico's a big country," El Apache says. "And L.A.'s a big city."

"So I'm lucky you know your way around both," Rolando says.

"*Jefe*— " El Apache begins.

Rolando cuts him off. "I'll set you up with a car, cash, everything you'll need."

"You're asking too much of me," El Apache says. "I'm a taxi driver."

"Simply for looking for her, I'll pay you $50,000," Rolando says. "Return her to me, and you can keep all of the money she took. And you won't have to go back to La Mesa either. I'll see to that."

El Apache swallows the next excuse he was about to make, lets the offer dance in his head. Rolando smiles to see it.

"How's that sound, taxi driver?" he says.

"Respectfully, *jefe,* I'm not the man for this," El Apache says. "I only want to finish serving my time and get back to my wife and kids. I'm done with the crazy life."

"I know your family is important to you," Rolando says.

"The most important," El Apache says.

Rolando nods thoughtfully, but inside he's gloating. Today's lesson, you fucking idiot, is *Never love anything too much.*

The air-conditioning is on high in the office, but sweat still skitters down Jerónimo's chest. Once again, here he is, sitting across from El Príncipe and a gun, telling him he doesn't want to work for him. The proposal is definitely tempting. The money would be great, but more important is the free pass out of La Mesa. If the officials investigate the killing of Salazar, he could be looking at twenty years tacked on to his sentence.

El Príncipe motions for Ozzy to leave the room. He runs his fingers lightly over the pistol on his desk.

"Do you know where the name Jerónimo comes from?" he says.

"He was an Indian, an Apache," Jerónimo says. "My dad's hero."

"Yes, yes, but why was he called Jerónimo?"

Jerónimo shrugs, wonders if the man is going to shoot him, wonders if he can get to the gun first.

"He had another name in the beginning," El Príncipe continues. "Big Bad Wolf Dick or something, Man Who Smells Like Horse Shit. But one night his god came to him in a dream and told him he had special powers, that he'd be a great leader, and that no bullet could ever kill him.

"The next morning he and his warriors ambushed a squad of Mexican soldiers. Believing the words he'd heard in his dream, Old Owl Tits led the charge, riding into battle carrying only a knife. All the soldiers shot at him, and all of them missed. People said the bullets swerved around him like bees returning to a hive.

"This scared the shit out of the soldiers, of course, and they began to cry out to Saint Jerome for help, 'Jerónimo, Jerónimo,' as this crazy Indian tore into them with his knife, cutting throats and gutting fuckers left and right. 'What better way to frighten my enemies than to take the name they shout when they're about to die,' the Indian thought, and from then on he called himself Jerónimo."

"That's a good story," Jerónimo says.

"That's history," El Príncipe says like he's giving him a magic word. He then picks up one of the photos of the beautiful woman, his wife, the one in which she's wearing a red dress and a flower in her hair, and stares down at it.

There's a knock at the door. The Prince drops the photo and picks up his gun.

"Come in," he says.

Jerónimo falls off a cliff when his daughter, Ariel, walks in, followed by Irma carrying Junior. Rising to his feet, he doesn't know whether to go to them or to rip El Príncipe's head off. The gun pointed at his belly decides for him. He hurries across the room to gather Ariel into his arms and hug his wife and son.

"A gift from me to you," El Príncipe says. "The best gift a man can receive, right?"

Jerónimo ignores him. His son is confused. He was only two when Daddy went to La Mesa, has only seen him in photos since, and doesn't recognize him now.

"It's me, *mijo*," Jerónimo says. "Your Papá."

"I didn't want you to worry about them while you were away, so I brought them here, where they'll be safe until you return," El Príncipe says.

Jerónimo kisses Irma, Ariel, Irma again. He should have known that El Príncipe didn't spring him from prison to *ask* him to find his wife; he's ordering him, and neither he nor his family will leave this house alive if he refuses. Newly elected officials down here often receive a package in the mail containing a bullet and a bundle of cash. It's a message from the local cartel: *Plata o plomo?*— Silver or lead? Cooperate or die. That's what El Príncipe is asking him now: *Plata o plomo?* Your choice.

"Did they hurt you?" Jerónimo whispers to Irma.

She's close to crying but keeps it under control. "No," she says.

"And the kids, they're all right?"

"What do you think? Two men come to the house in the middle of the night, carry them out, drive them all over town."

"I'm sorry," Jerónimo says.

"So this is your fault?" Irma says.

It's a difficult question. She always asks the difficult questions. That's one reason he loves her.

"I can't explain right now," he says, glancing at El Príncipe's gun, directing Irma's eyes toward it. "Do what they tell you, and I'll be back in a day or two."

"Do you promise?" she says.

He straightens the collar of her blouse and pats Junior's head. "What good would that be, coming from a *cabrón* like me?" he says with a grim smile.

"Promise me, Jerónimo," Irma says. "Promise your wife."

"On my life," Jerónimo says.

"So, listen," El Príncipe says. "Why don't you spend this evening with your family, and you can get started in the morning."

Jerónimo kisses Ariel once more, then sets her down and turns to face the Prince. His rage has contracted into something small and hard that beats like a second heart in his chest. He can go for days like this, without sleep, without food.

"I'm ready now," he says.

El Príncipe smirks, his gun still trained on him. "See, I knew you were the right man for the job," he says.

You don't know how right, Jerónimo thinks. *And you better hope you never find out.*

9

Luz is relieved when she and Malone arrive safely in Tecate, happy to be farther away from Rolando and closer to Isabel. They drive into the grim border city on a badly paved road lined with tire repair shops and taco stands, ending up at a tree-filled park a few blocks from the crossing. Malone circles the park and pulls over in front of the Hotel Tecate.

"How's this?" he says.

"Why are you asking me?" she says. "It's your job to handle this stuff."

"Right," Malone says.

Not wanting to wait in the car alone, she accompanies him when he goes inside to see if there are any rooms available, taking the backpack with her.

The hotel is on the second floor of the two-story stucco building, above a Subway sandwich shop. Luz follows Malone up a flight of stairs to the reception desk, which is staffed by an old woman in a wheelchair. Malone's Spanish is terrible, so Luz steps in and handles the negotiations. She asks for two rooms, but the woman says there's only one, with a double bed.

"Take it," Malone says when Luz relays this to him. "I'll sleep on the floor."

"There's got to be someplace else," Luz says.

"Maybe, but it's late, and I don't want to go looking."

Luz starts to push it, then decides not to. She tells the woman fine, and Malone pays in cash.

The woman grabs a key from a hook on the wall and hoists herself onto a set of crutches. Her left leg is shorter than her right, and a child's bare foot dangles uselessly from the ankle. She leads them down a dimly lit hallway lined with numbered doors. A baby cries in one room, the TV is on in another. The hall smells of cigarette smoke and disinfectant.

When they reach their room, number 10, the woman unlocks the door and motions them inside. It's tiny. A bed, a wooden chair, and a TV. The woman turns on the light, and a ceiling fan begins to spin, stirring up shadows. The window looks down on the park. There's music playing somewhere.

"Don't put paper in the toilet," the woman says. "Use the can next to it."

She hands Malone the key and heads back to the desk, the rubber tips of her crutches squeaking on the linoleum. The door to room 9, across the hall, opens a crack, and whoever's inside peeks out. Malone closes the door to their room and twists a flimsy deadbolt that wouldn't stop anybody. Luz is glad she has the gun.

Malone doesn't say anything, and neither does she. The room is too warm, and the air tastes like all the oxygen's been breathed out of it. Luz sits on the tropical print bedspread and closes her eyes, the full weight of the day pressing down upon her. She'd kill for something from her old stash right now, a pill to round off the edges and mute the clanging in her head.

Malone walks to the window and slides it open. The noise from the park is too loud, so he closes it again. He sits in the chair and looks down at his hands as if he's never seen them before.

"I'm going for a sandwich," he finally says. "You want something?"

"No," Luz says.

"I'll be back in a few minutes."

Don't leave me, Luz wants to say, but that's ridiculous. She can take care of herself. As soon as the door closes behind him, she bolts it and drags the chair over and wedges it under the knob. She then pulls the gun from the backpack and sits on the bed with it. Everything's going to be fine. Rolando has no idea where she's run to. Still, a cough in the next room makes her bones itch. Maybe a shower will help.

She steps into the bathroom and turns on the water. A dead beetle lies on its back in a corner of the stall. She picks it up with a handful of toilet paper and drops it into the trash can. She wants to be finished before Malone returns. He might get the wrong idea if he catches her, might think she meant for it to happen. She places the gun on the counter, within easy reach, then strips down.

The water is lukewarm, the stream not much more than a trickle. She unwraps the tiny cake of soap and passes it quickly over her body and between her legs, scrubs herself with the thin washcloth.

A loud bang stops her cold. She reaches for the gun and points it at the bathroom door. After a few seconds she steps dripping from the stall and eases the door open to look into the other room. Nobody there. Back in the shower she rinses quickly, cupping her hands to collect enough water.

By the time Malone shows up again, she's dressed and sitting on the bed, the gun lying beside her, hidden under a pillow. The door is stopped by the chair after opening only a few inches.

"What's going on?" Malone says.

Luz gets up and moves the chair out of the way. Malone smiles when he comes in and sees her standing with it.

"So that works, huh?" he says. "I thought it was a movie thing."

Luz doesn't respond.

He sits in the chair and pulls a sandwich out of the Subway bag, then tosses the bag onto the bed.

"I got you one too," he says. "They were two for one."

Luz ignores him, but her mouth waters as she watches him tear into his turkey and Swiss out of the corner of her eye. She hasn't eaten since morning and is feeling lightheaded. She decides that it's dumb to be stubborn at a time like this. She needs to keep her strength up.

When she reaches for the bag, Malone digs into another one at his feet and brings out a bottle of Coke.

"There's one of these for you too," he says. "Can I turn on the TV?"

They eat watching an old movie about high school kids in the U.S. Luz remembers seeing it on television with her mother, who knew all the songs and sang along in English. Mamá's favorite was one that went "Don't you forget about me." Hearing it now makes Luz think of Isabel. It makes her sad to realize that the little girl probably has no memory of her after all these years.

"Something weird's going on, isn't it?" Malone says.

"Weird how?" Luz says.

"You with that money and that gun, always looking over your shoulder."

"I'm going to L.A. to be with my daughter. What's the problem?"

"Should I be scared too?"

"Don't be stupid," Luz says. "I'm not scared."

"Okay," Malone says.

"Just do your job. Drive."

"All right."

"And don't say shit to me. Mind your own business."

Malone stands and brushes crumbs off his shirt. He drops his sandwich wrapper into the wastebasket and walks to the door.

"Where are you going?" Luz blurts before she can stop herself.

"Wherever I want," Malone says.

"When will you be back?"

Malone gives her a look like *You've got to be kidding* and slams the door on his way out.

Luz props the chair under the knob again, then tries to finish her sandwich but can't get any more down. She opens the window and stands for a moment looking down at the park. Couples stroll hand in hand along lighted paths and circle the bandstand. Laughing children chase one another from tree to tree. An ice cream vendor, a sidewalk preacher, a fusillade of accordion bleats from the radio of a passing pickup. It's all so familiar, yet all so strange, like the last image of an otherwise forgotten dream, an orphaned instant that haunts the dreamer forever.

She goes back to the bed and sits against the headboard with the money on one side of her, the pistol on the other. She glances at the clock: 9:30. Morning is a long way off.

Malone gets a sidewalk table at a restaurant facing the park. He orders two beers at once, downs the first in a gulp, takes his time with the second. It's cooler here than up in the room, a nice breeze blowing. He wipes his sweaty forehead with a napkin, and the paper comes away black. Dampening another napkin with the condensation beaded on his beer can, he rubs his cheeks and the bridge of his nose.

The locals are out in force in the park. The old people take the benches while the teenagers congregate on the edges, where they can keep an eye on who's driving by, sometimes stepping out into the street for quick conversations. A family—mom, dad, a pack of kids—approaches a clown twisting balloon animals. The kids are shy at first, but warm up when presented with colorful giraffes and poodles. The youngest throws a fit when it's time to go, and his cries carry all the way to Malone's table.

A trio of mariachis stroll up, one of them strumming a guitar. "A song, *señor?*"

"No, *gracias,*" Malone says. He doesn't want to pay five bucks to hear "La Bamba" or "Guantanamera" and doesn't know any other songs to ask for.

The musicians move on. If they're hoping for tourists, they're out of luck. The retirees who come over during the day to have lunch and tour the Tecate brewery are long gone, and the rich women staying at the luxury spas scattered across the surrounding hills have been locked in for the night. That leaves trouble like the two shitbirds at the next table: a rangy, hawk-faced dude with a collection of random tattoos and his fatboy buddy, who's dressed preppy in khaki shorts and a pink polo but looks like he's about to hit bottom after a long, slow slide.

The border closes at eleven, but these two are in no hurry. They're making an evening of it. They'll stock up on Valium and Viagra at one of the pharmacies, score some blow at whatever strip club they stumble into, then end up in a brothel, drunkenly trying to put it to a couple of bargain-basement whores. A bowl of menudo and a couple of beers for breakfast, and if they stagger back across the border right when it opens at five, they'll be home in Santee or wherever by six.

Malone has another beer and, why not, a shot of tequila too. He planned on keeping it together tonight to show Luz she was wrong about him, but, really, what does he have to prove to the bitch? Pretty funny how she acted all badass until he got up to go, then all of a sudden didn't want to be alone.

"I'm going to be with my daughter," she said, like that excused everything.

Yeah, well, hey, I had a daughter too, he could have said.

Annie, my Annie.

The only thing that upset him about Val getting pregnant was her being sneaky about it, not telling him when she went off the pill. She knew he hated working for his dad's construction company, and they'd agreed to hold off on having a baby until he got his own thing going. It'd be a couple of spec houses to start—green-certified, solar-heated, gray-water-reuse system, all the trendy bells and whistles—and then he'd find investors and bump up to apartment buildings and office complexes. Val couldn't wait, though, wanted what she wanted, and suddenly faced with having to provide for a child, Malone lost his nerve and decided to stay under his dad's thumb for a few more years.

The old man had always ridden Malone hard. Every opinion he ever had was wrong, every decision he made a bad one. By the time Malone was twelve he'd given up trying to figure out why his dad hated him and had set about plotting his revenge instead. He knew other boys who were at odds with their fathers, and many of them threw themselves into booze or drugs, attempting to punish the bastards who'd brought them into the world and then made their lives miserable. But Malone went another way with it.

He took every insult and every bit of abuse the old man dished out, stood tall under the constant barrage of criticism and unexpected verbal jabs, and never let the son of a bitch see that he'd hurt him. His plan was to outlast him, to let him punch himself out, and then lean over him as he lay gasping for air and spit in his face. He'd leave the ring having proven himself the stronger man without ever laying a hand on him.

With this in mind, Malone did well in school—honor roll, student council, all that crap; he got to work earlier than everyone else and left later; he married the right girl, moved into the right neighborhood, and drove the right car. And when Annie came along, he loved her like his father had never loved him.

She was a beautiful baby and grew into a beautiful child, with wispy blond hair and round blue eyes. Malone was awestruck by her innocence and the sweet simplicity of her affection. "Up, Daddy, up," she'd say. He'd sweep her into his arms and hold her close, and the gentle tap of her heart against his chest became the secret cadence that kept him going.

But where is that heart now, those little hands, and those blue, blue eyes?

Malone orders more beer and more tequila from the waiter with the tired smile, then raises his empty can to the thrill-seekers at the next table, Fatboy and Tattoo Slim.

"How you doin'?" Slim says.

"Great," Malone says. "You guys?"

"Ah, you know, getting there."

Fatboy chuckles and repeats his friend's assessment. "Yup, yup, getting there."

"Let me help you out," Malone says as the waiter returns. "Another round for these gentlemen too, boss. *Por favor.*"

"Thanks," Slim says.

"Yeah, thanks," Fatboy says.

Malone waves it away. He and his new buddies watch two soldiers stroll by with assault rifles hanging across their chests. They look like kids, mean little kids. One of them whistles and gestures to a man on the other side of the street, and he and his partner walk over to talk to him.

"See that TV," Slim says. He points to an older model Sony showing *Law & Order* inside the restaurant. "It used to be mine. I got a new flat screen and put that one out on the curb, and somehow it ended up down here."

"Come on," Malone says.

"I know my own TV, bro," Slim says. He turns to Fatboy. "It's mine, right?"

"It's his," Fatboy says.

"I mean, I don't mind," Slim says. "The thing's twenty years old. But, still, how crazy is that?"

"What's that they call it, the trickle-down theory?" Malone says.

Both guys laugh like they know what he's talking about. Slim has a tattoo of a Harley logo, an American flag, and what looks like a '65 Mustang on one arm, and Bart Simpson, a top-hatted skull, and the words *9/11, Never Forget* on the other. Bunch of junk.

"So, you guys up to no good?" Malone asks.

"We're gonna check out this titty bar up the road," Slim says.

"Oh yeah?"

"There's usually a couple hot bitches there. You're welcome to come along."

"I just might do that."

A bat swoops in to feed on the moths swarming the streetlight above their tables. The three of them tilt their heads back to watch.

"A guy I know got a bat tangled in his hair," Slim says. "The bad thing was, he had a gun in his hand at the time. Fucker was so freaked out, he started shooting at it and blew his own head off instead."

"My brother," Fatboy says.

"What?" Slim says.

"It was my brother who did that."

"Really?"

It's not funny, but Fatboy laughs. Malone does too.

The three of them move on after another round. Their first stop is a small, dark bar with a jungle painted on the wall. A black light makes the lion's fangs shine like the moon on a winter night. Malone drops onto a stool and orders a beer and a shot. The tequila is finally working. His sorrow is nothing but a cold hard pearl now. He and Slim and Fatboy are the only gringos in the place. There are no women either. The music is Mexican, and loud.

Slim and Fatboy huddle with a little guy sporting a perm and lots of gold around his neck. The three of them walk to the bathroom together. Coke time. Or as the Mexicans call it, *perico*, parakeet, because of how it makes you chirp. Malone is studying his fellow boozers, trying to decide if this is a gay joint, when Fatboy sidles up a few minutes later and whispers, "If you want a toot, go see Brian."

The men's room door is locked when Malone pushes on it.

"Who's there?" Slim says.

"Me, dude," Malone says.

He soon finds himself squeezed into a reeking stall with Slim and the little guy with the gold. Slim dips a key into a bindle of coke, then holds the key under Malone's nostril. The shit tastes funny going down, but Malone does a second blast, and a third.

The night revs up after that. The beers keep coming, and Slim prattles on and on. As they're walking to the next bar, he tells Malone about his first wife, and his second, and his third. He's worked for a number of real assholes, too, and someone somewhere in there is to blame for everything.

Fatboy makes them wait while he vomits in the gutter.

"You dumbass," Slim yells. "Do that in the alley."

Malone starts to get sloppy. He forgets his change on the bar at the next place they go into and has to put a hand on the wall to keep from falling over when he takes a piss.

By the time they reach the strip club, he can't tell anymore whether he's thinking or talking. The neon does a number on his eyes, and the mirrors confuse him. They sit at the rail for a while, then move to a couch, where three girls dance just for them. Malone's is short and round with dyed blond hair and bush. She places his hand between her legs, and he sticks a finger inside her to see if she'll stop him. She doesn't.

"Do you have kids?" he says to her, shouting over the music. It's the wrong thing to ask, but he wants to know.

Slim thinks he's talking to him. "I've got a daughter," he says. "She's nine."

"I had a daughter too," Malone says. He sticks another finger inside the blonde and prays that the building falls in on him. "But she died, and I died, and this is all that's left of me."

10

El Príncipe gives Jerónimo the keys to a Ford Explorer with California plates, a cell phone, and a roll of bills totaling $5,000 for expenses. He also hands him a loaded 9mm Smith & Wesson. Jerónimo almost refuses the pistol, thinking of the trouble it might land him in, but so many people these days, a gun is the only thing that scares them, and he has a feeling it's going to take some scaring to get this job done quickly.

All the Prince can tell him about Luz is that she left on foot carrying a zebra-striped backpack containing his money and his gun. As for her past, besides the fact that she was once El Samurai's mistress, he doesn't know much. He thinks she grew up in Tijuana, but she never talked about what *colonia* she lived in or who she ran around with.

"If I could find her myself, why would I need you?" he says, standing in the driveway beside the Explorer as if seeing off an old friend.

Jerónimo sticks the money and the nine in the center console and starts the truck. El Príncipe waves good-bye to him as he backs down the driveway and calls out, "I'll take care of your family."

Jerónimo doesn't reply for fear of what he might say.

His first stop is Irma's sister's house to pick up his passport, which he'll need if he has to cross the border. Irma's sister is hysterical, wants to call the police, but Jerónimo tells her that would be the death of Irma and the kids.

"I'll handle this," he says. "You know I will."

He finds his passport at the bottom of Irma's jewelry box. He also takes along a necklace of hers, a locket with a tiny photo of him and the children inside.

Back in the Explorer, he drives to Tacos El Gordo, a twenty-four-hour stand frequented by Tijuana's army of taxi drivers. He's looking for Don Rafael, a retired cabbie who knows every driver in town and acts as unofficial godfather to them all, listening to their gripes, mediating their disputes, and advising them on everything from the best mechanics to whom to bribe and how much to pay in order to be left alone to work in peace. The drivers see and hear everything that goes on in the city, so there's a good chance one of them spotted Luz.

Don Rafael is sitting at one of the stand's plastic tables with a couple of other old guys. He's a gaunt man with a deeply lined face. His thick white hair is combed straight back, and his bushy white mustache has a yellowish tinge from countless cigarettes and cups of coffee.

"*Híjole,*" he says, surprised to see Jerónimo. "You're out?"

Jerónimo pulls up a chair and sits backward on it. "I'm doing a job for someone," he says.

"You look good, healthy," Don Rafael says. He reaches out to pat Jerónimo's arm. "Can I get you something to eat? To drink?"

"*Un café,*" Jerónimo says.

Don Rafael calls to the woman at the counter and raises his foam cup. "One for my friend here."

"I need your help," Jerónimo says.

"Of course," Don Rafael says. "Whatever I can do."

Jerónimo shows him the photos of Luz.

"I need to find this girl. I want you to put the word out, see if any of the drivers might have come across her. Let them know there's a thousand-dollar reward for good information."

Don Rafael pulls a pair of reading glasses from the breast pocket of his shirt and slips them on to examine the photos. "Hot stuff," he says, then peers at Jerónimo over the tops of the cheaters. "El Príncipe?"

Jerónimo shrugs, and that's enough of an answer.

Don Rafael shows the photos to the other men at the table.

"She look familiar?" he asks.

The men shake their heads, and the *taquero* brings down his cleaver on a hunk of meat. Jerónimo feels the *THWACK!* on the back of his neck. *Stay calm,* he tells himself.

Don Rafael takes out his phone and uses it to snap a picture of one of the photos. He shows it to Jerónimo for his approval.

"I'll send it to some people with a note about the reward," he says. "News like that will spread fast."

"Fast is good," Jerónimo says. The woman sets his coffee on the table, and he lifts the cup to his lips and takes a sip while the old man pokes at his phone. The smoke from the grill drifts out into the street and rises above the traffic. A couple of drivers parked at the curb lean against their cars and eat, craning their necks so as not to drip salsa on their shirts. It's a good life, driving a taxi. Jerónimo thinks he might take it up again when he and his family move to the States. Or maybe a truck.

"Okay," Don Rafael says, pressing a last key with a flourish. "Now we wait."

The old man brings out a deck of cards, and he and Jerónimo and the other men play a few hands of La Viuda. Jerónimo has trouble focusing on the game, keeps thinking of Irma and the kids. If he gets nothing from the drivers, he has another plan. He knows some people who used to work for El Samurai, and while it's dangerous to cross the lines between crews, they might have some dirt on their late boss's old girlfriend that'll help him find her.

He's about to head over to the club where these men used to hang out when Don Rafael's phone rings. The old man greets the caller and listens to what he has to say. When the caller finishes his spiel, Don Rafael presses the phone to his chest and addresses Jerónimo.

"This guy claims that the woman you're looking for got into his cab earlier today, and he ended up driving her all over town. He's afraid of getting involved though. He doesn't want to piss someone off and end up with his balls shoved down his throat."

"I don't need his name," Jerónimo says. "Just where he took her."

Don Rafael relays the message, then says, "They went to a house in Taurinas, and then afterward he dropped her off at a body shop in Libertad. The problem is, he doesn't know the addresses."

"But he could find them again."

"He thinks so."

"Then ask him to come here now and show me," Jerónimo says. "Tell him I'll give him a thousand bucks for his trouble."

He gnaws on his thumbnail while Don Rafael makes the offer. The old man presses the phone to his chest again when he's finished.

"He's asking me if he can trust you," he says.

"On my wife and children, nothing will happen to him," Jerónimo says.

Don Rafael raises the phone to his ear and tells the caller that Jerónimo's word is gold and he'll stake his reputation on it. A few second later he ends the call and sets the phone on the table.

"Well?" Jerónimo says.

"Don't get this guy killed," Don Rafael says, lighting a cigarette. "I'll look like a real asshole."

The caller shows up half an hour later, a nervous man in a black ball cap and a T-shirt that says *Hecho En Mexico.* Lalo is his name. He doesn't look Jerónimo in the eye when they shake hands. As they walk to the Explorer, Jerónimo tries to put him at ease, apologizing for making him come out so late.

"Your old lady is probably pissed," he says.

Lalo doesn't answer, just climbs into the passenger seat.

"I'll get you home safe," Jerónimo says.

"And the money?" Lalo says.

Jerónimo reaches into the center console and removes the roll of bills. He counts out $500 and passes it to the guy.

"You get the rest when we finish up," he says.

Lalo re-counts the money, then sticks the bills into the front pocket of his baggy jeans.

"Do you know the way to Taurinas?" he asks.

"I wish I could say no," Jerónimo replies.

They glide down murky streets toward the *colonia,* traffic fading away as they get closer. Jerónimo remembers back when he had his cab, many drivers would refuse fares going this way, saying it wasn't worth the risk. Not him. Not even after a couple of *pendejos* he picked up in Zona Norte got him lost over here and tried to rob him. Their knife was no match for his gun, and one of them ran off with a bullet in his leg.

He cruises up one potholed street and down another, Lalo making him stop at every corner. The guy is having a hard time retracing his route, especially with many of the streetlights shot out. "Left here," he'll say, then, "No, no, fuck, right." He's sweating even with the air conditioner blowing on him, keeps wiping his forehead with the back of his hand. Jerónimo figures he saw the Smith & Wesson sitting next to the money in the console.

There are still lots of people out at this late hour. They sit on their porches or in their yards to escape the heat of the shacks they live in. Some have even moved TVs outside. Poor people, desperate people, breathing air that smells like shit and drinking water that makes them sick. It's as bad as prison—worse, because out here they tell you you're free. Dusty boys with no future kick scuffed soccer balls, a widow in perpetual mourning sells tacos from a grill in front of her house, and gangsters congregate in the shadows with *caguamas* of Tecate, dreaming of international hit man stardom.

Lalo finally finds the place he's been searching for, an ugly concrete box on a street lined with hovels that look like broken teeth. Fugitive snippets of soap operas and salsa commercials escape through the bars covering doors and windows.

"Are you sure?" Jerónimo asks.

"This is it," Lalo replies.

He can't help but see the gun now, when Jerónimo grabs it from the console and tucks it into the waistband of his jeans. Jerónimo takes the money, too, tells Lalo to sit tight. Every dog on the street is barking as he approaches the house. A neighbor draws back a curtain, then lets it fall. The front door of the house is open behind a steel security gate, revealing a garbage-strewn front room, dark except for a single dim bulb.

Jerónimo pounds on the gate with his palm, and a voice calls from the back room: "You're early."

A few seconds later a woman appears, pretty once, but made ugly by life, spilling out of a red negligee. She opens the gate without checking who's on the other side, then flinches, startled, when she sees Jerónimo, and tries to pull the gate shut again. Jerónimo's foot stops it.

"I need to talk to you," he says.

"Not now," the woman says.

"I'll be quick."

"I'm expecting a customer."

"Don't make me be rude. Invite me in for a minute."

The woman looks him up and down angrily, then surrenders, releasing the gate and taking a step back. "What can I do?" she says. "You're a man, I'm a woman, right?"

Jerónimo walks into the house and nods toward the back room. "Is there anyone else?" he says.

"No," the woman says.

She stands before Jerónimo unashamed in her worn lingerie, defiant even. He shows her a photo of Luz, watches her face for a reaction, gets none.

"This girl was here earlier today," he says. "What is she to you?"

"Nothing," the woman says. Her bravado is belied by her shaking hands.

Jerónimo sets the photo on a table and draws the Smith & Wesson. At the same time he pulls a hundred-dollar bill from his pocket and offers it to the woman. *Plata* or *plomo*.

"Your choice," he says.

The gun frightens the whore. Jerónimo sees it in her eyes, in the way her shoulders sag.

"What a tough guy," she says.

"I've got a job to do," Jerónimo says.

"Yep, a real tough guy."

The woman takes a deep, bitter drag off her cigarette.

"She's my daughter," she says.

"Why was she here?"

"She wanted the name of a *pollero,* to go to the U.S."

"Did you know of one?"

"There's a man. Freddy. He works out of a garage in Libertad."

"And you sent her there?"

The woman licks her lower lip and fixes her gaze on the cracked and stained ceiling.

"Yes," she says.

"Was she going to L.A.?"

The woman continues to stare at the ceiling. She takes a shuddering breath and slowly releases it. It looks like she might be about to clam up, so Jerónimo points the gun at her head.

"Was she going to L.A.?" he says again.

"Maybe," the woman finally says. "My sister lives there."

"Your sister?"

"Yes."

"Give me an address or a phone number for her."

The woman fights back with an angry glare. "You'll go to hell for this, for making a mother betray her child," she says.

"You'll go to hell right now if you don't tell me what I need to know," Jerónimo says.

The woman walks to a cluttered shelf, opens a Bible lying there, and removes an envelope stashed between its pages. She hands the envelope to Jerónimo.

"This is the last letter I got from my sister, six years ago," she says.

Jerónimo tears the return address off the envelope and gives the letter back. The cheap perfume the woman has sprayed to cover the stink of the house is giving him a headache. He offers her the money again, and she slaps his hand away, one of her fingernails nicking him, drawing blood.

"You're going to kill her, aren't you?" she says.

"I'm going to find her," Jerónimo says. "What happens after that isn't up to me."

"She has a daughter there," the woman says. "She only wants to be with her. Don't you have someone you love?"

Jerónimo ignores her. What kind of question is that from a whore? He walks out the door and down the steps to the Explorer. Lalo stares at the woman watching them from the porch as the truck pulls away. Jerónimo snaps at him to mind his own business and tell him how to get to the body shop.

They pass a burning car on their way out of Taurinas. A small crowd has gathered, a sullen, silent bunch transfixed by the hunger of the flames and the smoke rising blackly into the night sky to blot out the stars.

"Jesus Christ, Jesus Christ!"

The fat man, Goyo, presses one hand to the bloody gash below his eye and raises the other for mercy. He was reluctant to call this Freddy, so Jerónimo smacked him with the nine to encourage him. He's had enough of fucking around after scaling the locked gate of the body shop in order to sneak up on the fat man, who was asleep on a cot in his office.

"Dial the number and hand me the phone," Jerónimo says.

Goyo obeys quickly this time, then uses his filthy bedsheet to stanch the bleeding from the cut, which looks like an evil red smile on his cheek.

"What the fuck are you calling me so late for?" Freddy says.

"I'm at the shop," Jerónimo says. "Goyo is about to tell me

where you live. I can come there and wake your family or you can come here."

"Who is this?"

"I have some questions about the woman who came to see you today."

"What woman?"

"Do you think I'm playing around?"

"I don't know what the fuck you're doing."

"Do you think I'm playing?"

There's a pause, then Freddy mutters, "I'm on my way."

Fifteen minutes later a Nissan truck pulls up in front of the shop and honks twice. Goyo opens the gate, and the truck drives onto the lot and parks next to the Explorer. Freddy flies out of the truck before the engine even dies, a whirlwind of exasperated energy.

"What's this about?" he says.

Jerónimo plays it cool, rising slowly from the couch where he and Lalo have been waiting and casually positioning the gun in his waistband so Freddy can see it.

"Thanks for coming so quickly," he says as he extends his hand.

Freddy reaches out to shake, confused. "So who was she?" he says. "Your wife? Your sister?"

"That's not important," Jerónimo says.

"Oh, I get it," Freddy says. "You're working for somebody."

"She came to see you about going to the U.S.," Jerónimo says.

"Did she?" Freddy says.

"Where did you send her?" Jerónimo says.

"Let me explain something to you," Freddy says. "I'm a businessman, and part of what people pay me—"

Jerónimo shoots out his hand and pinches Freddy's Adam's apple between his thumb and forefinger. He shoves him backward until he's against a wall, then runs his other hand around the guy's waist to see if he's carrying a gun. Freddy glares at him, eyes bulging, cheeks puffed. The jagged scars on his forehead stand out like lightning.

"Maybe we *should* go to your house," Jerónimo says.

"One of my men, a gringo, took her to Tecate," Freddy gasps. "A border inspector there, who also works for me, is going to pass them through in the morning."

"Call the gringo and tell him to bring the girl back," Jerónimo says.

"I don't think it's gonna be that easy," Freddy says. "She's desperate to get out of Mexico, and she has a gun. If the gringo tries anything, I think she'll use it and then find some other way across."

"Call him," Jerónimo says in the coldest voice he has.

Freddy swipes at his nose and thrusts out his chest, a rooster used to being in charge. Too fucking bad. He takes his phone from the clip on his belt and keys in a number.

"Who's this?" he says when someone answers, then, "Where the fuck is Kevin?"

A second later, he shrugs and holds out the phone. "Some crazy bitch said I had the wrong number and hung up on me."

"Luz?" Jerónimo says.

"Some other crazy bitch."

"Try again."

Freddy hits redial and starts screaming into the phone as soon as the girl picks up.

"Listen, cunt, put Kevin on now."

Jerónimo reaches out and takes the phone from him.

"What's your name?" he says.

"Angelina Jolie," the girl says.

"Let me talk to Kevin. It's an emergency."

"Talk to my fucking asshole, *puto*. And you better not call back unless you want my man to turn you out like the faggot you are."

The phone goes dead.

"If this is some kind of joke—" Jerónimo says to Freddy.

"You're the fucking joker," Freddy says. "You bust Goyo's head open, you put your fucking hands on me, and still I do everything I can to help you. In truth, I should get a piece of whatever you're getting for tracking this bitch down."

Jerónimo takes the money out of his pocket. He hands Freddy two hundred dollars and drops another hundred on the ground in front of Goyo.

"And there'll be more in it for you if I find her," he says to Freddy. "So tell me, partner, how do I catch this Luz?"

Freddy hisses and shakes his head. "Partner," he says. "You guys are hilarious."

An hour later, after paying off Lalo and dropping him back at the taco stand, Jerónimo is speeding down the toll road to Tecate. It's almost two a.m., and the chaparral, iced by the moon, glows silver and pale blue, so that the surrounding hills sparkle like the ocean frozen in mid-swell.

Jerónimo is unimpressed. All this open space makes him nervous. A city boy, a convict, he's at his most comfortable when his existence is circumscribed by four walls and a roof overhead. He dreams sometimes of his ancestors. They come to him as yipping ghosts thundering across an endless plain on their war ponies, and the vision always agitates him, because out there in the open is where your enemies can get to you, where they can sneak up and put a knife in your back or drive by and shoot you full of holes. Without cover, you're an easy target.

His reverie is interrupted by a rabbit darting across the road in front of the truck, a flash in the headlights. He instinctively mashes on the brakes, sending the Explorer into a tire-screeching skid, but it's too late. The rabbit bounces against the undercarriage two or three times as the truck passes over it, and Jerónimo glimpses the carcass in the rearview mirror as he drives away. A thing like that is a bad omen. He crosses himself, mutters a prayer, and wishes for an instant, crazy as it is, that he was back in his cell.

11

THE FENCE SEPARATING MEXICO AND THE U.S. STANDS TEN FEET high in this section between Tecate and Campo and is constructed of rusty panels of corrugated steel laid end to end and supported by steel beams sunk deep into the hard-packed earth. It's a symbol more than a barrier, however—a joke, really— because an industrious man with a sharp stick could carve out a passage beneath it in half an hour, a trench deep enough to squirm through. Then it's just a five-minute walk down one of the trails cutting through the brush to the nearest paved road, where cousin Juanito waits in his car.

Lead Agent Mike Thacker of the U.S. Border Patrol long ago accepted the absurdity of the situation, twenty years of Navy bullshit having been excellent preparation for this second career executing orders issued by idiots and futilely attempting to hold back the tireless hordes determined to cross the line in the sand he's been charged with defending. He rests his elbows on a boulder crowning a hill fifty yards from *la linea* and watches through a night-vision scope as a ghostly figure squeezes under the fence and crouches on the dirt access road to sniff for trouble.

"One," he whispers into his radio, alerting Brown and Vasquez, who are waiting in their truck at a curve in the road that puts them out of sight of the crossing point. The three of them have been staking out this spot for hours now, after an air unit spied a group of fifteen bodies who looked like they might be thinking of going for broke.

Thacker used to get a kick out of sneaking around the desert in the dark and swooping down on wetbacks like an owl pouncing on a kangaroo rat. He knew he and his fellow agents weren't making a bit of difference in the long run, that for every illegal they apprehended and shipped back to TJ, twenty more got across, but he liked wearing a uniform, and he liked carrying a gun, and, okay, he liked seeing the fear in the eyes of the wets when he pinned them down with his spotlight and ordered them to halt. He'll admit that.

He even dug it when things got hairy, when they encountered armed smugglers or took fire from snipers working with the coyotes. Nothing clears your head like rounds flying past so close that they sound like the devil snapping his fingers in your ear.

Lately, though, with all the gambling and all the trouble with Marla and Lupita—he spits a stream of tobacco juice into the sand and feels his guts pulse—the job he once enjoyed has become just another block of hours to be endured, another load he used to bear effortlessly that now threatens to bring him to his knees. Truthfully, all the fun's gone out of it.

A second ghost emerges from under the fence, then a third and fourth. Thacker whispers into his radio again—"On my 'Go'"—and adjusts the focus on the scope. When the last of the *pollos* have crossed, so many bodies are massed in front of the fence that they meld together into a glowing green blob. The coyote huddles with everyone and reminds them to keep quiet and stay together.

Thacker gives the order to move and watches through the scope as the truck whips around the bend, lights blazing, and comes to a stop in a swirl of dust. Brown and Vasquez hop out with guns drawn and sprint toward the illegals. Their shouts of *"Alto! Alto!"* and "Sit down! Sit your ass down!" carry all the way up the hill.

Most of the group comply immediately, but two bodies break away and make a run for it. They plunge into the thick chaparral and pick up a trail that circles the hill where Thacker is stationed. He stows the scope, pulls his P2000, and sidesteps down the back of the hill to intercept them. The stars and a bit of moon give him enough light, and he reaches the trail in plenty of time to conceal himself in a thicket of manzanita.

Breaking branches and the thud of footsteps herald the approach of the runners. Pistol in hand, Thacker waits. He'll be able to see them, but they won't see him. When the first wet reaches his hiding place, Thacker launches himself, leading with his shoulder, and the *pollo* flies ass over tits off the trail. The second shadow tries to stop but can't and runs right into a blow from Thacker's flashlight. It's a young girl. Thacker catches a glimpse of her before she goes down.

"Stay there," he says, showing her his gun.

He drags the first *pollo,* a kid about the same age as the girl, out of the bushes and drops him next to her, shines his light in both their faces. The girl, near tears, is rubbing a bump on her forehead. The guy stares down at the ground. They're scared, real scared, and that's good.

"Money," he says. *"Dinero."* The words come out in labored

gasps. He's sucking wind after his trip down the hill and the ambush.

When he started with Customs and Border Patrol he heard rumors of agents shaking down illegals for cash and was disgusted. It wasn't that he was above a good scam—in the Navy he made a killing selling merchandise lifted from the PX warehouse to stores near the base—but stealing from poor people didn't sit right with him.

The ground gets slippery when it rains, however. Marla lost her job but kept spending like she had one, the boys were in private school, and he had a long run of bad luck at the tables. All of a sudden he wasn't just not getting ahead, he was falling farther and farther behind every month, a fifty-year-old man about to hit the skids. And so.

The first time he forced some terrified wetback to hand over the $300 he had stashed in his shoe, he felt like shit. The second time was a little easier. Now, it barely causes a ripple in his soul. He thinks of it as an entry tax, something to teach the little fuckers how it works up here.

"Money," he says again. "I know you got some."

"No money," the guy says. "No money."

"No money?" Thacker says. "Okay."

He steps back and unzips his pants.

"You," he points at the girl. "*Chúpame*. Suck me."

What was that old bumper sticker? Ass, cash, or gas, no one rides for free? The demand for sex usually frightens the *pollos* into coughing up their money, but if it doesn't, Thacker will gladly take a blow job instead. He's come across some real pros out here, *chicas* who definitely knew what they were doing. And this one's cute. He shines his light into her face again. Cute enough.

"Wait," the guy says. "Wait." He gestures at his stomach. "She baby. Baby."

Thacker moves the flashlight beam to the girl's belly and sees that she's pregnant. The hard-on he had going disappears, but he senses these kids are about to crack, so he keeps up the pressure.

"Come on, *mamacita*," he says to the girl and reaches into his pants like he's going to pull out his cock. *"Chupa, chupa."*

"No," the guy says. "Stop."

He opens his jacket and claws at the lining, tearing a hole in it. Sticking his fingers inside, he pulls out a wad of cash and offers it to Thacker. Thacker flips through it. Five hundred dollars. He pockets the money and gestures at the trail with his pistol.

"Go on," he says. *"Ándale."*

The guy helps the girl to her feet, and they set off at a trot, disappearing into the night. If they're caught farther down the line, no big deal. Thacker's not worried about them talking. They're terrified of uniforms, and all they'll want to do is get back to Mexico as soon as possible so they can try to cross again.

He wipes the sweat off his face with his sleeve. His uniform shirt is soaked through. A breeze comes up and rattles leaves all around him, a nerve-racking sound out here. He keys his radio.

"I'm on the backside of the hill," he says. "I thought I had the two that got away, but they were too fast."

They'll get a laugh out of that, the old man and his beer belly trying to chase down a couple of kids. "You better be careful," someone'll say, one of the young punks. "You're gonna break a hip." That's okay. Let them have their fun. There's nothing wrong with playing a part as long as you know what you're really all about.

Thacker, Vasquez, and Brown do the field paperwork for the detainees, then call for a van to transport them to Campo for further processing. Ten Mexicans, two El Sals, and a Guatemalan. Not a bad haul.

Thacker leaves the station at three a.m., changes out of his uniform, and heads over to the Indian casino in Alpine. He waves at the agents manning the freeway checkpoint as he passes through. The road is almost deserted at this hour, and he drives for miles with no taillights in front of him, no headlights behind. It makes him lonely.

If he had somewhere decent to go besides the casino, he would. But all he's got is the motel he's living in, which is a dump. The bedspread depresses him, the carpet, the bars on the windows. And the animals who stay there, if they're not fucking, they're fighting, their threats and promises passing through the thin walls to dirty his dreams.

He's been crashing there for three months now, ever since Marla decided he shouldn't live in the house that his hard work paid for. It was a hell of a deal. Their marriage died years ago, but they kept it going for the boys. When Brady enlisted in the Army last year and Mike Jr. left for college, they finally agreed to live separate lives, sharing the house as roommates, the smart play financially. No sense giving money to a bunch of lawyers. Thacker moved downstairs into Brady's old room, sleeping on a twin bed surrounded by dusty basketball trophies and posters of snowboarders.

The arrangement worked out great until Marla found some texts from Lupita, a Mexican chick Thacker had been banging, a twenty-year-old gas station cashier with a fantastic ass even after two kids. Marla hadn't fucked Thacker in years, yet she still blew her top. All of a sudden she couldn't live with him anymore. All of a sudden they were going to sell the house and split the money. All of a sudden she wanted a divorce.

Thacker did *not* hit her when she laid all this on him, only maybe bumped her on his way downstairs to pack. But the cop who responded was a woman, and the shrink was a woman, and the judge was a woman, so now he's living in Motel Hell with an order of protection against him and neither of his boys even called to wish him a happy birthday last week.

The casino is empty except for a few meth heads and elderly insomniacs scattered among the slots and poker machines. A Chinese guy in sunglasses plays by himself at a $25 blackjack table. Thacker buys a *USA Today* and carries it into the coffee shop, where he sits at the counter. It's one of those fifties-style places, burgers and shakes and Buddy Holly, the staff in white aprons and paper hats. Yoli is on this morning. She pours Thacker a cup of coffee without even asking and calls out his usual breakfast to the cook: scrambled, bacon crisp, sourdough.

"Hey, handsome," she says.

"Hey, beautiful," he replies.

But she's not. She's short and fat and all worn out. Her husband is disabled, tethered to an oxygen tank, her son is in prison, and the bank is trying to take her car. Thacker never asks about her life, she offers it up freely, like she's proud of it. When nothing's any good, he guesses, why hide the bad? She probably thinks it's healthy to get it off her chest, and if he did the same, maybe he wouldn't dream of choking on fish bones and wake up gasping for air all the time.

He skims the paper until she brings his food.

"You know anything about dogs?" she asks as she sets his plate down. She has a cross tattooed on the web of skin between her thumb and forefinger. "One of the dealers here wants me to take a pup, pit bull–Lab mix."

"It'll need training," Thacker says. "It's gonna have a lot of bad traits from both sides. Could be a sweetheart or could be a real monster."

"It's for my husband," Yoli continues, not even hearing him. "He doesn't do nothing but sit in front of the TV all day. I have to talk to the landlord first. They got rules against pets. And you got to feed them too. That's expensive."

Thacker pours ketchup onto his eggs and forces himself to take a bite. "Layla" is playing on the casino's sound system. Seems to Thacker that it's always "Layla" when he notices. He looks up from his plate to see Yoli still standing in front of him.

"Charlie Hutchinson was in earlier," she says.

"He was?" Thacker says.

"Talking crazy."

"Is that right?"

She leans in close to refill his coffee. "If I owed him money, I'd pay him," she whispers. "He's a scary guy."

Hutchinson's a loan shark who works the local casinos. Thacker got drunk one night, got desperate, and borrowed $2,500 from him. He's missed a few payments, so now he's into the scumbag for something like four grand. He doesn't put much stock in the rumors that Hutchinson uses the Vagos motorcycle club to help him collect, but all the same, he'd like to get clear of him as soon as possible. That's why he jumped at this thing Murph called him with last night.

"Say no if you want, but hear me out," is how Murph began. He's CBP too, works the Tecate crossing, and he and Thacker have been tight ever since Murph and his family moved into Thacker's neighborhood five years ago. Shooting the shit at barbecues and soccer games, they discovered they had a lot in common. CBP for one, and the fact that both were gamblers, with a gambler's problems. Also, they both took money from wherever they could get it.

Murph's hustle is that for the right price he'll wave a vehicle into the U.S., no questions asked. Last night one of his Southside partners contacted him to arrange safe passage for a client. Then this partner, a Mex named Freddy, mentioned that the client, a young woman, appeared to be carrying a large amount of cash with her. Freddy had a question: What if the car carrying this girl was to be pulled over once it crossed into the States and someone took the money off her? "A thing like that could happen, couldn't it?" he asked Murph.

"Well, could it?" Murph asked Thacker when they talked.

"It could," Thacker said, already working out how. The job would be a little more complicated than jacking wets but nothing he couldn't pull off if it was truly worth his while.

"I'm guessing it will be," Murph said. "Freddy says this girl paid him twenty-five grand, and it didn't even make a dent in her pile. Whatever you get off her, we'll split sixty-forty, me and Freddy on the big end."

Thacker thought it over for all of ten seconds before saying yes.

It's 4:30 when he finishes his breakfast. The girl is crossing around ten, and he wants to be at the Tecate crossing by eight to scope things out and be ready to intercept her. That gives him some time to kill, time for a couple of hands of blackjack. Just a couple.

The Chinese guy is still at the table, a pretty good stack of chips in front of him. Thacker sits down and tosses the money he took off the *pollo* onto the felt.

"Change five hundred," the dealer calls to the pit boss, then starts counting out green chips. "How's it going?" he says to Thacker. His name is Scott. Thacker has played with him before.

"We'll soon see," he says.

He loses five hands in a row right off the bat, the dealer never busting once. The Chinaman snaps his tongue against the back of his teeth and shakes his head like it's Thacker's fault the table's gone cold. Two more losing hands, and the chink colors his chips and walks away. Fuck him.

119

It's back and forth after that, Thacker winning one here and there, then losing two. After a shuffle he presses his bet to $50 for no good goddamn reason and is dealt a pair of aces. He splits these, and another ace falls on the first one. He splits again. The pit boss strolls over to watch. Thacker's second cards are a three, a six, and a five. The dealer, showing a three, draws into a nineteen.

Thacker wants to break something but merely purses his lips and slides out his bet for the next hand. A woman is vacuuming the carpet behind him, and the noise makes him antsy.

"Can we do something about that?" he asks Scott.

The dealer talks to the pit boss, who talks to the woman, who grudgingly rolls up her cord and goes away. Doesn't make any difference. A half hour later Thacker has lost all of the wet's money and $200 of his own. Disgusted with himself, he tosses a five-buck chip to Scott, and, after a stop in the men's room, heads out to the parking lot.

The sun is about to crest the mountains to the east and is chasing the last of the stars from the rapidly pinking sky. The cool morning air smells of dust and sage. Thacker is so pissed off he doesn't notice any of it. He scuffs to his truck, bone tired, swearing for the thousandth time that he'll never again throw away money like that.

"Excuse me, sir." A skull-faced kid beckons from the open window of a filthy Toyota. "Can I talk to you for a second?"

Thacker stops but doesn't move any closer. He adjusts his windbreaker in order to have easy access to his P2000, holstered under his left arm.

"What about?" he says.

The kid steps out of his car and stands with his hands in the air like he knows Thacker's carrying. His hair is cut short, revealing a quarter-sized sore on his scalp.

"I got my baby daughter here," he says, "and we don't have nothing to eat."

Thacker looks past the kid into the Toyota. He sees a car seat on the passenger side, covered with a Winnie-the-Pooh blanket.

"I ain't never begged in my life, sir, but she needs food," the kid continues.

"Where's her mom?" Thacker asks.

"Well, sir, she's a crackhead and run off with a bunch of Mexicans. I'm trying to get some food and gas, and then we'll go on to my mom's place in Hemet."

"You on dope too?"

"Me? Oh, hell no, sir. Hell no."

He's lying. His eyes are spinning in his head like carnival rides. Thacker pulls a twenty from his wallet and steps up to pass it to him.

"Thank you, sir. God bless you," the kid says.

"Put it in your pocket before you lose it," Thacker says.

"Right, right," the kid says. As soon as his hand drops, Thacker hits him in the temple with a quick left, knocking him to the ground.

"Please, sir, please!" the kid yelps. He curls into a ball and protects his head. Thacker steps over him and reaches into the Toyota to yank the blanket off the car seat. The seat is empty.

"You used the same story on me last week, you fucking moron," Thacker says.

The kid doesn't reply, just lies there breathing hard. Thacker kicks him twice in the ribs.

"Give me back my money."

The kid digs into his pocket and brings out the bill. Thacker snatches it from his hand and tells him to get the fuck out of there. The kid scrambles to his feet and jumps into his car.

Thacker waits until he drives out of the lot and disappears down the frontage road before walking to his own truck.

The sun is up now, and a bright creep of light spreads across the asphalt. Thacker sits behind the wheel and watches a couple of stray dogs sniff around the casino's dumpsters. He thinks about going to the motel for a few hours' sleep but decides he can't bear the place this morning. He thinks about calling Lupita, but she's made it clear there'll be no more honey without more money.

So he'll crash here for a while. He unfolds a silver sunscreen and places it against the windshield. With his shades on, it's dark enough that he might be able to doze off. Reclining his seat as far as it'll go, he closes his eyes. A black tornado spins in his head, minutes and days and years, voices and faces, his whole life. It's always there waiting for him, and he always hopes it'll slow down enough for him to pinpoint exactly when everything went wrong. But it never does.

12

MALONE WAKES UP LYING IN A PUDDLE ON THE FLOOR. HIS HAIR IS wet, his face. Luz is standing over him with a dripping Subway cup.

"Time to go," she says, her shoes already on, already holding the backpack.

The sun on the ceiling is as blinding as a welder's arc. Malone sits up and takes a moment to put together where he is and what's going on. Most of it falls into place before his headache kicks in, with only a few details eluding him, mainly how he got back to the room last night. He stands with a groan, his back feeling like there's a knife stuck in it. He's too old to be sleeping on linoleum.

A few minutes in the shower help, but there's blood on the toilet paper when he blows his nose. He pulls on his shorts and shirt and checks his watch: 9:15. The border is open, and Freddy's man is on duty. A quick call to find out which traffic lane the guy's working, and they'll be on their way.

His phone, though. It's not in the pocket where he usually keeps it. He walks back into the room and checks the floor and under the bed.

"Do you see it anywhere?" he asks Luz. She's sitting in the chair by the door, frowning at him as he searches.

"This is a joke, right?" she says.

"It's probably . . ." He pats his shorts again, all the way around. His wallet is there, his keys, but no phone.

"I don't believe this," Luz says.

"No big deal," Malone assures her, recalibrating. "We can call from the office here."

Luz opens the door and steps out into the hall. Malone decides not to get too worked up about disappointing her. All he can do now is bring this thing in for a safe landing. He makes one more circuit of the room, then follows Luz to the front desk.

The crippled woman is there in her wheelchair. Luz does the talking again. The woman shakes her head when Luz asks about using the phone, says it's not possible.

"Why not?" Luz says.

"It's not allowed," the woman says.

"Why?" Luz says.

"Does she want money?" Malone asks Luz in English. He pulls a twenty from his pocket. "Money?" he says to the woman.

The woman shakes her head.

"Don't be stupid," Luz says to her.

The woman picks up the phone. "Maybe you want to talk to the police," she says.

"What's your problem?" Luz says.

Malone takes hold of Luz's arm and hurries her toward the stairs. She's fuming when they get down to the street.

"Don't touch me again," she says, shaking off Malone's hand.

"Don't freak out," he says. "We'll buy a card and call from a pay phone. It'll take five seconds."

"Unless you find some way to fuck that up too."

They cross to the tree-shadowed park and ask a man sweeping leaves off the sidewalk where the nearest store is. He points them to a place on the corner, a small, dark shop that smells of bad meat. While Luz handles the transaction, Malone stands with his elbows pressed against his sides, afraid of knocking something off a shelf. He pays for the hundred-peso card and the bottle of Corona he pulls from a cooler. The old woman at the register slips the beer into a little plastic bag. A preacher yells in Spanish from a radio on the counter.

There's a phone at the edge of the park. Luz sits on a nearby bench, tense in the shade. Malone opens the beer and takes a big swallow before searching his wallet for Freddy's number. He thought he had it on a scrap of paper, but it doesn't seem to be there. He calls information for the number of Goyo's Body Shop. Goyo answers, and Malone is able to make him understand that he needs to speak to Freddy.

"*Dígame,*" Freddy says when Malone finally reaches him.

"It's me," Malone says. "What's up with our man in Tecate?"

There's a pause, then Freddy says, "Where were you last night? I called and some crazy woman answered."

"I guess I lost my phone."

"You should be more careful."

"Excellent advice."

After another long pause, Freddy says, "Our friend is in the booth on the left."

"Got it."

"Good luck."

Malone finishes the beer and leaves the bottle on top of the phone. There's Tylenol in the Beamer, he remembers. He cleans his sunglasses on his shirt as he walks over to Luz. Strange black birds sing strange black songs in the park, and the shoeshine guys are opening their stalls.

"We're all set," he says.

The announcement doesn't cheer Luz up any, and Malone feels dumb for thinking it would. She lifts her arms to straighten her ponytail, and the glimpse Malone catches of a red scallop of bra strap gives him a thrill that's all kinds of wrong. Sneering at him like she can read his mind, Luz picks up her backpack and sets off for the car.

Traffic has died down since the early morning rush. The Explorer is parked in an empty lot overlooking the one-way road leading to the Tecate border crossing, and Jerónimo sits behind the wheel, watching the occasional car or truck pass by. He scouted this vantage point when he arrived last night and has been here since before the crossing opened, knowing that Luz and the white boy driving her will have to use the road to reach the port of entry.

He's too close to the checkpoint to stop the BMW before it gets to the border, so what he'll do is slip in behind it, follow it through the crossing, and grab Luz once they're in the U.S. If she decides to come easy, fine; if not, he'll do what it takes. Either way, El Príncipe will have his woman by noon, and Irma and the kids will be free.

The truck heats up as the sun climbs higher in the dead-white sky. Jerónimo sips from the gallon jug of water he bought last night and eats some of the bread. His eyeballs feel like they've been rolled in sand, and his blood fizzes in his veins. He hasn't slept in twenty-four hours and is slightly out of phase. It's as if the morning is being projected onto a screen and he's watching it brighten and busy there.

126

A loud bang startles him. He ducks and reaches for the Smith & Wesson. Something hits the side of the truck, and the rear window shatters. He lifts his head above the dash and sees a ragged, barefoot boy hurl a rock at the Explorer. Slipping out of the truck, he points the gun at the kid.

"What are you gonna do now, *pendejo?*" he yells.

A rock strikes him in the small of his back and another bounces off his knee. He whirls and spots two more boys and waves the gun at them, but the barrage continues, targeting both him and the truck, until he finally raises the pistol and fires a shot into the air. The urchins scatter, five or six of them, and disappear into scrub. All that's left behind are their taunts.

"Fuck you!"

"Fucking faggot!"

"Tecate Locos for life!"

Sweat rolls off Jerónimo's shaved head and stings his eyes. He rubs his back where the rock hit him and walks around the truck, checking for damage. His phone rings. Freddy again.

"The gringo called just now," Freddy says. "They're on their way to the crossing."

"Good," Jerónimo says. "And you didn't say anything to your man at the border about me, right?" He doesn't need any kind of cop up in his business.

"Of course not," Freddy says. "This is between me and you."

"Excellent," Jerónimo says. "I trust you."

But that's a lie. Freddy's a rat like all the other rats. The ones in prison and on the street, in the churches and police stations and government offices. More rats than men. It's a plague.

Jerónimo moves the truck closer to the road so he'll be ready. He keeps the engine running. Five minutes later a battered silver BMW rattles past, a white man driving. Jerónimo puts the Explorer into gear, but in the time it takes him to pull onto the asphalt, a black Honda and a big rig get between him and the Beamer. That's cool. It's better that he hangs back anyway, so he can come out of nowhere when he wants to.

Tecate being fifty miles from anyplace, there are only two lanes for passenger vehicles at the crossing, a couple more for trucks. Two lanes, two booths, two inspectors. Malone is in the left lane like he's supposed to be, but Luz still feels anxious when she sees the backup ahead, three or four cars deep.

A uniformed inspector is walking a German shepherd past the waiting vehicles, encouraging the dog to sniff tires and bumpers and door panels. All Luz can think about is the money and the gun hidden in the trunk. Her heart pounds as the dog approaches the car, but it merely circles the BMW twice, then moves on.

Malone stares straight ahead, silent behind his sunglasses. He was shaky back in town—dropping his keys while unlocking the car, fumbling with the Tylenol bottle he took from the glove compartment—but he seems to be doing better now. Which is incredible, considering what a mess he was when he returned to the room last night, reeking of tequila and a whore's perfume.

Luz hadn't slept since he left—didn't sleep all night, in fact. She lay in bed seething as he staggered into the bathroom to piss and then stood unsteadily in front of the window, hands pressed to the glass, head lowered.

"If you fuck this up for me, I'll kill you," she said to him.

"Go ahead," he replied, and it didn't sound like he was joking.

The line of cars moves forward. The BMW is next up at the booth. Luz tries to figure out the best way to sit so she doesn't look nervous. She puts her hands under her thighs, then rests them in her lap. The inspector examines the documents of the driver ahead of them and keys something into a computer.

Malone is whistling softly. He turns to Luz and says, "Ten-nine-eight-seven-six-five-four-three-two-one," as the BMW rolls up to the booth. Luz tenses the muscles in her legs to stop them from shaking. She reminds herself to breathe.

"How long have you been in Mexico?" the inspector, a big man with a gray flattop and mustache, asks.

Malone hands over his passport and Luz's expired California ID.

"Just for the night," he says. "Visiting Freddy."

The inspector nods slightly.

"Bringing anything back with you?" he says.

"Nope, nothing," Malone says.

The inspector glances at the passport and ID, then hands them back.

"Have a nice day."

"You too," Malone says.

Luz tries to tamp down her happiness, not wanting to jinx the successful crossing by celebrating too soon, but relief gets the best of her as they begin climbing the narrow, winding road leading away from the border, and she laughs and claps her hands.

"Thank God," she says.

"God?" Malone says, giving her a stupid look. "You should be thanking me."

Luz ignores him. She's already thinking ahead to her next move. She'll have Malone drop her at the Greyhound station in San Diego, where she'll catch a bus to L.A. Her aunt Carmen will be surprised when she shows up, and probably angry. Luz hasn't sent money like she promised, hasn't even called in the three years she's been with Rolando. Partly it was because she worried that Rolando would find out about Isabel, but she was also ashamed of how badly she'd screwed up her life. But what's

Carmen going to say when Luz opens the backpack and hands her a big pile of money? No?

And then she'll grab Isabel and hug her for a solid hour. She's imagined the moment many times, run through it in her head again and again. The past will be the past, and they'll begin anew as mother and daughter somewhere Rolando will never find them. They'll be happy like nobody else has ever been happy, just the two of them. She smiles thinking about it, beams at the dirty sky and the desert and the road cutting through it.

"Oh shit," Malone says, staring into the rearview mirror.

"What?" she says. "What?" But he waves her quiet.

Thacker's truck is backed onto a dirt turnout that's shielded from the road leading up from the border by a thick stand of scrub oak. He changed into his uniform, covered the truck's plates with duct tape, and now he waits, crouched behind the trees, watching the crossing through a pair of binoculars. Murph won't be able to call from his booth when he passes the BMW through, so this is the only way Thacker will know the car is headed in his direction.

A big green fly keeps trying to crawl into his ear. He can see over the fence into downtown Tecate, and the breeze brings him bits of music. Some Saturdays when the boys were young, he and Marla would take them over there for lunch at a restaurant they all liked. He remembers the time Mike Jr. played a trick on Brady, pretending to eat a jalapeño from a dish on the table but actually palming the pepper and dropping it into his napkin. Determined not to be outdone by his big brother, Brady bit into a pepper himself and ended up spitting it out and crying furious tears when he realized he'd been duped. The whole family used to laugh at that story whenever anybody brought it up, back in the days when they used to laugh.

The sun glints off a silver car leaving the inspection area. Thacker messes with the focus on the binoculars until the image sharpens. Older-model BMW, white man driving, Mexican female passenger, just like Murph said. He hurries to his truck and slides into the front seat.

Pulling to the edge of the road, he idles there and waits for the Beamer. The radio is playing country music. He snaps it off and turns on the loudspeaker he added a few years ago, clicks the mike to check the volume. He notices his shirt is missing a button over his gut. It must have popped off somewhere between the casino parking lot and here. This irks him. He hates looking like a slob. Using his thumb and forefinger, he pinches shut the gap to hide his sweaty undershirt.

The BMW clatters past, struggling up the hill. Thacker bumps onto the road behind it but keeps his distance. Where he wants to do this is in a canyon about half a mile up. Railroad property, nice and secluded. The pair in the car won't know what hit them. "Huh? What?" and he'll be gone. If the girl is carrying as much money as Murph says she is, it'll be as close as Thacker's come to winning in a long time. He'll pay off fucking Hutchinson, fucking Marla, and start making plans.

He hits the gas as the car nears the top of the hill, crawls up the Beamer's ass, and presses the switch of the mini–light bar suction-cupped to the inside of his windshield. The red and blue strobes catch the driver's attention right away, and the guy slows and drifts to the shoulder. Thacker gets on the mike and orders him to keep moving.

"Take the dirt road ahead and then proceed until I tell you to stop," he says.

The driver makes the turn, bumps down off the pavement, and continues on the road, which winds along the floor of a steep, rocky canyon the color of old bones. Thacker follows, leaning forward to peer through the billows of dust that come and go between them. When both vehicles are out of sight of the highway, he says "Halt right here" into the mike, and they ease to a stop, his truck twenty feet behind the car.

The canyon funnels the breeze into a larcenous wind that snatches up anything not rooted and drags it away. A tumbleweed glances off the truck's fender and spins in place for a second before regaining its momentum and rolling on toward Mexico. The way Thacker looks at it, this thing is already three-quarters done and going off with no problems. All that's left is to take the money. He steps out of the truck and removes his P2000 from its holster. Murph warned him the girl is carrying a gun, so he stands behind his door and shouts, "Hands where I can see them, both of you!"

The guy and girl comply immediately, thrusting their arms out their respective windows, and Thacker pulls a black balaclava over his head and charges the BMW. Moving quickly up the driver's side, he points his pistol at the guy's face.

"Yo, yo, yo," the guy says. "Wrong car, man, wrong car." He's some kind of surfer. Blond hair, suntan.

"Hand over the money," Thacker says. "The backpack."

"There's no money. We're tourists, coming from Ensenada."

Thacker fires a shot across the hood of the Beamer, low enough that Surfer Joe can see the flash and feel the heat on his cheek. Then he lines up on the guy's head again.

"That's the last round I'm gonna waste," he says.

"Please," the girl says. She's cute. Real cute.

"In the trunk," the driver says.

Jerónimo passes through the same booth the BMW did. The inspector checks his passport and waves him on, not even glancing at the broken window. When he's a safe distance away, Jerónimo takes the Smith & Wesson from under his thigh, where he had it ready in case he needed it, and places it on the passenger seat.

There are no other vehicles between him and the BMW now. The big rig was routed to the truck inspection area before they crossed, and the car, the Honda, pulled into the first gas station on the U.S. side. The BMW is making its way slowly up the hill, and Jerónimo gives it plenty of line. He'll make his move when they're farther from the border and all its cops. But not too far. He's decided he has to kill the white boy in order to keep things simple. That means stopping them before they reach a populated area, somewhere out here in no-man's-land.

A white Dodge Ram swings into the road in front of him, blocking his view of the Beamer. He finds that if he moves into the other lane a little bit, he can still see it just fine. It's noisy inside the Explorer with the broken window. The air coming in whirls around in back and makes a kind of roar. There's also a new rattle. The kids' rocks must have knocked something loose. Jerónimo takes a drink of water, steering with his knees while opening the jug. It's warm as piss.

The truck speeds up and pulls away. Jerónimo jukes into the other lane and sees that it's right on the BMW's rear bumper, and, if his eyes aren't fooling him, it's flashing police lights. Garbled words from a loudspeaker fly past, and both vehicles slow down. Jerónimo eases up on the gas, too, maintaining his distance. He needs to let what's going to happen happen so he can figure out what to do next.

The car veers off the pavement and onto a dirt road, followed by the truck. Jerónimo quickly loses both vehicles in a fog of dust. This hide-and-seek stuff doesn't add up. Cops aren't usually so cagey. He turns onto the road himself and creeps forward. It leads into a narrow canyon, one wall of which is deep in shadow, the other too bright. The BMW and the truck are already out of sight around a bend. He rolls down his window and inches along, watching and listening for any sign of them.

Another blown-out loudspeaker command and a plume of dust let him know he's close. He comes to a stop, gets out of the truck, and proceeds on foot, keeping to the shadowy side of the canyon. His gun hand is sweaty, the Smith & Wesson seemingly giving off its own heat. The BMW and the Dodge soon come into view parked about seventy-five feet ahead. Spotting a boulder that overlooks the vehicles, Jerónimo climbs the wall to take cover behind it. He presses his shoulder into the rock and cranes his neck to see what's going on down below.

A fat man in a Border Patrol uniform and ski mask is pointing a pistol at the driver of the car. The driver, the white boy, gets out and walks to the rear of the Beamer, hands on his head. When he gets there, he unlocks and opens the trunk. The fat man gestures with his gun, and the white boy reaches in and removes a backpack.

Jerónimo feels a sting on his arm, a spreading chemical burn. He pulls away from the boulder and slaps at the pain. A big red ant is smeared across his fingers, and a hundred more scurry over his shirt. They bite him on the neck, on the chest. Swatting wildly, he loses his footing in the dry, crumbly soil, falls on his ass, and rides a small landslide down the hill and out into the open. Every time he tries to stand he triggers another slide. The fat man and the driver turn toward the clatter of shifting stones and see him flailing.

"Stay down," the fat man shouts at him, then fires a shot that ricochets off the boulder with a metallic whine. Jerónimo sends two rounds downslope before rolling sideways toward a shallow wash. The fat man runs back to his truck and crouches behind it while the BMW driver, carrying the backpack, dashes to the open door of the car and dives inside.

By the time Jerónimo is on his belly in the creek bed, forearm propped on the bank, pistol ready, the BMW is pulling away. He and the fat man loose a volley of shots at it, breaking windows and popping a tire. The Beamer swerves and slows and drifts toward the brighter wall of the canyon, but then someone inside starts returning fire, and the car picks up speed and disappears in a taunting swirl of wind-whipped dust.

Malone isn't thinking about the possibility of escape when he runs back to the car, he's merely seeking cover, but then Luz yells at him to drive, and that seems like a good idea. He starts the BMW and hits the gas, and for a second it looks like they might actually get away, until the thief in the Border Patrol uniform and the Mexican who came out of nowhere open up on them. The windshield spider-webs, the car gets squirrelly, and bullets and broken glass are everywhere.

Fucking Freddy, Malone thinks, certain this is his doing. He was a fool to fall in with the guy, and now his foolishness is going to get him killed. Luz, however, isn't ready to give up. She pulls the .45 from the pack, gets on her knees facing backward in the passenger seat, and starts blasting away through the shattered rear window. The sound is deafening, and Malone cringes as ejected casings bounce off his bare arms and legs.

"Drive! Drive! Drive!" Luz says. Her shouts shock him into action, get his body working instead of his mind. He yanks on the steering wheel and stomps the accelerator. The engine screams like a dying rabbit, and the power steering is almost gone, but he manages to straighten out the car and head off down the road.

They limp around a curve, putting them out of range of the shooters. The car shudders and jerks, and it's all Malone can do to keep it on course.

135

"This thing isn't gonna take us much farther," he says.

"So we run then," Luz says. She's still kneeling on the seat, watching out the back window.

"You don't want to try to talk to them?"

"Is that what you think?" Luz says. "They're here to talk?"

The oil light on the dash flashes red, and the car loses power. The canyon walls are only thirty feet high here, and not as steep as they were near the entrance. If they can make it to the top and out into the scrub, who knows? It'll be dicey with no water, but at least they'll have a chance.

"All right," Malone says, hitting the brakes. "End of the line."

He bolts from the car and starts up the east wall of the canyon. Panic supercharges him, and he's halfway to the top before Luz even gets her door open. She climbs up after him, but, carrying the pack, has trouble making progress and keeps sliding back down.

"Wait," she calls to Malone. "Please."

The desperation in her voice hangs him up. He pauses on an outcropping and watches her struggle, the sun beating down on him like a judgment. Any minute now those motherfuckers are going to come around the bend, intent on finishing what they started.

Luz is on her knees now. "Please," she says. "You can have the money. I just want to see my daughter."

Malone considers leaving her to her fate and getting himself to safety but then imagines hearing a shot ring out behind him and knowing he might've saved her. He already has one soul on his conscience; he doesn't need another.

He sidesteps down the hill, setting off cascades of rock and sand. Reaching Luz, he takes the backpack from her and pulls her to her feet.

"Hang on to my shirt," he says, "and go as fast as you fucking can."

She grabs the hem of his T-shirt, and they climb together. Malone takes his time, planting each foot carefully. It's slow going, hot and dusty. He keeps thinking he hears the sound of an approaching vehicle, but when he turns to look, nothing. Luz does a good job of keeping up, rarely relying on him to pull her forward. When they near the top, she hustles past him to get there first, then offers him her hand.

"Come on," she says.

He pauses to catch his breath after letting her haul him up the last few feet, doubles over so the sweat dripping off his face pocks the dirt like a rare rain. But there's no time to rest. Those guys, those guns, they're still coming, so he and Luz set off at a dog trot across a rocky plain dotted with manzanita and sage and scrub oak, headed north, he hopes.

13

Trailing oily black smoke, the gut-shot BMW disappears up the canyon, and a windy silence replaces the gunfire and the howl of the dying engine. Like an animal peeking out of its den, Thacker slowly raises his head above the hood of his truck. He's pretty sure the guy who blew the holdup as he was about to put his hands on the money is still hunkered down in the shallow, brush-choked wash across the road.

"U.S. Border Patrol," he yells in that direction. "Toss your weapon and show me your hands."

"Who you trying to kid?" the guy shouts back, staying under cover.

"You're interfering with an official CBP operation," Thacker says.

"Come over here and get me then."

So the fucker's going to be like that, huh? Thacker ducks behind the truck again, even though it's murder on his knees.

He pulls off the balaclava he wore during the robbery attempt and tosses it aside. There are only a couple more rounds in his gun, so he drops the nearly empty magazine and slides in a full one.

This thing has gone to hell, and he needs to make a decision: Either muck his cards and walk away or commit to seeing it through to the end, which means catching up to the BMW and doing whatever it takes to get the money. It sure would help if he knew what the joker in the bushes was up to.

He rocks back and forth a few times to get some feeling into his feet, then stands and peers over the hood.

"Let's talk," he shouts.

"Just get in your truck and go," the guy in the bushes says.

"If anyone's going, I think it's you," Thacker says.

"You know what I think?" the guy says. "I think you're a thief. I think you were out to rob those people."

"Why would I want to do that?" Thacker says, feeling the guy out.

"Because you heard something," the guy says. "From Freddy, right?"

So he knows this Freddy character too. Thacker chuckles softly to himself. That bastard must be cutting deals left and right. A shrub clinging to the edge of the wash quivers unnaturally, and there's a flash of color against the dull tan of the landscape, the guy's shirt maybe. Thacker contemplates sending a few rounds that way, but if he misses, where will they be then? The sun is scorching his bald spot and the back of his neck. He wishes he had his hat.

"I'm not after the money," the guy in the bushes says.

"Then we don't have a problem," Thacker says. No sense in playing dumb anymore.

"I'm after the girl," the guy says.

139

"The girl? In the car?"

"Somebody wants her back in Mexico."

Thacker sucks at his teeth, trying to work up some saliva. He's wasting time here and giving the pair in the Beamer a big head start. If he wants a second shot at the money, he needs to get moving. So he takes a chance. Rising to his full height, he sets his pistol on the hood of the truck and lifts his hands.

"It's too fucking hot for this," he says. "Come on out, and let's put our heads together."

Nothing but the wind. An empty plastic jug bounces past, riding the gusts. Then a big, angry-looking Mexican suddenly climbs out of the ditch and steps to the edge of the road. Shaved head, mahogany skin, tattoos covering both arms and boiling up out of the neck of his T-shirt. Some shithead gangster. The guy holds his gun at his side, pointed at the ground, but a quick bend of the elbow . . .

"Are we gonna have a showdown or a conversation?" Thacker says.

The Mex hesitates for a second, then lays the gun in the dirt at his feet. Thacker walks around the front of the truck to stand facing him in the road.

"I've got water, if you want some," he says, jerking a thumb over his shoulder.

The Mex approaches slowly, each step birthing a dusty sprite that's instantly whirled away. He's got some Indian blood in him, and his scowl looks to have been carved out of flinty red stone. When he's halfway across the road, Thacker opens the door of the truck to get a bottle of water. The guy sprints the last few feet and barrels into him, pinning him against the Dodge with a sweaty forearm across his throat.

"So you know, I don't need a gun to kill you," he says.

Thacker gestures downward with his eyes so that the Mex notices the just-sprung switchblade aimed at his belly.

"Back at you," he says.

The Mex lets up on his windpipe and retreats a couple of steps. He's still scowling, but Thacker is sure enough he made his point that he takes a moment to shove the tails of his uniform shirt back into his pants and get himself squared away before leaning into the truck and bringing out the water. The Mex accepts the bottle with no change in expression and downs half of it in a series of deep gulps. Thacker drinks the rest, swishing the last bit and spitting.

"You know this road?" the Mex asks him.

"It ends in a set of railroad tracks about a mile on," Thacker replies.

"That's where they'll get out and run for it," the Mex says.

"Is that what you think's gonna happen?"

"If the girl figures out who sent me, it is."

"You mean Freddy?" Thacker says.

The Mex scoffs at him. "No, man, not fucking Freddy."

Thacker squeezes the empty water bottle three times, and the sound bounces around the narrow canyon. He's waiting for the Mex to put all the pieces together and come up with the obvious next move, but the guy continues to stand as still as a statue, eye-fucking him with his meanest jailhouse glare. They'll never get anywhere like this.

"You know," he says, "every second we hang here, they're getting farther away. How about we hop in the truck and chase them down? The girl's yours, the money's mine."

The Mex considers the suggestion. "And the dude, the driver?" he says. "If I take him out, are you gonna have a problem with it?"

"Should I?" Thacker says.

"Aren't you a cop?"

For one weird instant Thacker feels as hollow as a dead steer he came upon the other day, a sun-bleached hide stretched taut over a cage of bones. The wind races through his emptiness like it did through the carcass, the moan it makes coming dangerously close to thickening into a message. He shrugs and clears his throat.

"Not today," he says to the Mex.

The Mex smirks at this response and starts back across the road.

"I'm getting my gun," he says.

Thacker retrieves his P2000 off the hood of the truck, then slides behind the wheel and sticks the pistol in the door's storage well. The Mex climbs in on the passenger side and fumbles with the seat belt.

"*Vamos,*" Thacker says.

He rolls down his window and notices that his side mirror is broken. The bitch got off a lucky shot, and he worries that might not be the only one, but everything sounds fine under the hood as they head down-canyon.

They creep along at 10 mph, rocks popping under the tires. The Mex sits with his gun in his lap and fingers a fresh scrape on his elbow. The canyon swings to the east, then straightens out for a bit, the sun so high now that the ravine is full of light. Thacker puts on his shades, Oakleys, a once-upon-a-time Christmas gift from his sons, before they turned against him.

They startle a few coyotes when they round another bend, send them scrabbling up the canyon wall. The landscape begins to flatten out. As Thacker recalls, the ravine isn't much more than a sandy ditch by the time the road reaches the rail bed.

"There," the Mex says. The BMW is stopped up ahead, angled toward the eastern wall. Thacker mashes on the brakes and reaches for his gun.

"Go easy," the fat man says. "They could be holed up anywhere along here."

Jerónimo gives him a look. When did *he* become the shot caller? Jerónimo teamed with him because it seemed like two guns might be better than one for now, but if this *pendejo* thinks he's in charge, he's got another thing coming.

To prove it, Jerónimo steps out of the truck into the heat and glare and wind and walks alone toward the car, which is about fifty yards down the road. He holds the Smith & Wesson at arm's length in front of him, pointed at the vehicle.

"Wait, now, wait!" the fat man calls after him.

Jerónimo looks over his shoulder. The cop is out of the truck, fumbling with his hat and using his open door as cover. He raises the mic of the truck's PA system to his lips. A loud squeal makes Jerónimo wince, then fatso's voice is everywhere.

"You. In the silver BMW. Step out of the vehicle with your hands in the air."

The words buzz around the canyon like angry insects, but there's no response. Jerónimo resumes his approach to the car. He eases up to it and moves slowly alongside, from back to front, eyes alert for any movement. The *click, clack, click* of rocks tumbling down the canyon wall stops him cold. He crouches and scans the steep slope, his gaze tracking the barrel of his gun.

"You see something?" the fat man yells. He was halfway to the BMW when the rocks fell but now backtracks to the truck and his hiding place behind the door.

Jerónimo ignores him, intent on the craggy scarp. He half expects Luz or the white boy to lean over the edge and open fire.

After a few seconds, though, his caution begins to embarrass him, and he stands and lowers his weapon.

"All clear?" the fat man calls.

Jerónimo tosses off a wave in his direction and inspects the BMW more closely. Two tires are flat and a couple of windows are shot out. Fluid the color of blood has leaked from the engine and run in a thin stream down the road to puddle around a fist-size stone, stranding a big green beetle.

Inside the car, blue bits of broken safety glass sparkle like spilled gems. Jerónimo picks up a spent shell casing and sniffs it. The gunpowder smell reminds him of the Fourth of July when he was a kid. Piccolo Petes, Crackling Cactuses, War Drum Fountains.

The fat man rolls up in his truck and leaves the engine running when he hops out. He takes the casing from Jerónimo and bounces it in his palm. "A .45," he says. "They aren't messing around." He bends to peer inside the car. "The money?"

"They must've taken it with them," Jerónimo says.

"Well, shit," the fat man says. "Looks like we're gonna have to work a little harder then."

He lowers himself to one knee next to the driver's-side door and peers intently at the ground, sifting sand through his fingers.

"Let me see the bottom of your shoe," he says to Jerónimo.

Jerónimo lifts his foot, shows him the sole of his prison-issue sneaker. The fat man nods and stands with a grunt, then walks to the other side of the car. He kneels again, head down like he's praying, and, after a few seconds of concentration, reaches out and draws a circle in the dirt.

"Some decent prints here," he says. He stands and looks at the canyon wall from under the bill of his cap. "As far as I can tell, they went straight up."

Jerónimo tucks the Smith & Wesson into his waistband. If

they climbed, he's climbing. He walks to the wall and begins picking his way up the steep slope.

"Where you going?" the fat man says.

"After them," Jerónimo says.

"That's great, but listen for a second."

"They're getting away."

"One second, okay?"

Jerónimo looks down at the fat man, who walks over to stand at the base of the cliff.

"How's this sound," he says. "You go up and see what you can see, and I'll make sure they didn't come back down to the road farther along."

"Do what you want," Jerónimo says.

"You got a phone?"

"Why?"

The fat man pulls his phone from his pocket. "Give me the number, and I'll call if I see anything."

Jerónimo's first instinct is to tell the *cabrón* to go on and get the fuck out of here, but there's actually some sense to his plan, it being a way to be in two places at once, so he steadies himself on the wall and fumbles for the phone El Príncipe gave him.

"It's new," he calls down to the fat man. "I don't know the number."

"Call me then," the fat man says and slowly recites his digits so Jerónimo can key them in. When the dude's phone rings, he holds it up and says, "We're good to go."

Jerónimo resumes his climb as the truck drives away. It's harder than it looked like it was going to be. A rock he's using as a handhold pulls free from the wall, almost toppling him, and seemingly stable ledges crumble when he puts his weight on them so that he slips down the slope until some sturdier outcropping stops his slide. *Climb, you motherfucker,* he whispers to himself. *Climb, climb, climb.*

When he finally gets to the top, there's sand in his shoes, in his teeth, in his ears. He wipes the sweat out of his eyes with his T-shirt and blinks at the brittle dun-drab sweep laid out before him. Boulders; stubby, twisted oaks; dry grass. Buzzards circle in the bleached sky, and a snagged, shredded shirt flutters on a barbed-wire fence.

Inspired by the fat man, Jerónimo crouches to look for prints, but the ground is too hard to hold an impression. Luz and the white boy could be anywhere out here, or they could have already found an escape route and be on their way to L.A. He surveys the area once more, a shading hand across his brow, then digs in his pocket for the address he got from Luz's mother, makes sure it's still there.

His phone rings as he picks his way down the wall, descending into the canyon again.

"Nothing over this way," the fat man says.

"Nothing here either," Jerónimo says.

"I'm on my way back," the fat man says. "I'll pick you up."

Jerónimo doesn't wait for him. When he reaches bottom, he walks back up the road to the Explorer, the neck of his T-shirt pulled up over his nose and mouth to keep out the blowing dust. This dead end has taken up too much of the day. The most important thing now is to beat Luz to her aunt's house. He's not exactly sure what he'll do when he gets there, but he has money and a gun, and that's a good start.

The fat man pulls up behind him and taps the horn. "Get in," he yells out the window.

It's tough fighting the wind, and the Explorer is still a half mile away, so Jerónimo drops back and climbs into the truck.

"They booked, huh?" the fat man says.

Jerónimo shrugs. He doesn't want to give too much away to a crooked cop. But the fat man doesn't back down.

"Do you know where they're headed?" he says.

"Just drop me at my truck," Jerónimo says.

"What? I thought we had a good thing going."

"Don't be corny, man. I'm not playing."

The fat man exhales loudly and slips a finger behind the lens of his sunglasses to rub his eye. He's silent for a minute, then says out of nowhere, "You know you need my help."

Jerónimo stares out the windshield, doesn't even blink.

"Do I?" he says.

"Think about your next move, whatever it is," the fat man says. "What's going to get you farther?" He points at the tattoos on Jerónimo's neck and arms. "This shit?" he says, then taps the badge pinned to his own chest. "Or this?"

The fucker's pulling rank, saying, "You're down there, and I'm up here." He thinks everybody's afraid of what he's afraid of, that his world is the only one there is. Typical cop. Learned everything he knows off TV. Jerónimo's been running circles around fools like him forever. He draws his gun with a flourish, like a lawyer brandishing courtroom proof.

"How about this?" he says.

"Please," the fat man says. "You're smarter than that."

They pass the site of the shootout and round the bend in the canyon to pull up beside the Explorer. Jerónimo opens the door and hops out as soon as the truck stops. He's had enough talk. He walks to the Explorer and starts to get in, but then notices that the left front tire is flat. Part of him panics, the other part refuses to. He steps to the back of the vehicle and bends over to check underneath for a spare. Nothing there. The first option that comes to mind is the one he goes with. He turns to face the Dodge, gun in hand.

The fat man has seen the flat too, and anticipated Jerónimo's move. He's already out of the truck, already crouched behind the door, already has his pistol pointed at Jerónimo's head.

"Here we go again," the fat man says.

Jerónimo feels like an idiot for letting the bastard get the jump on him.

"I need your truck," he says.

"Well, I need the money that bitch is carrying," the fat man says. "So what are we gonna do?"

"I bet you've got an idea."

"Just the same one I had before," the fat man says. "I'll drive you where you need to go and put myself at your disposal. Use me. Use my uniform, my gun, my ugly white face. I can talk to bad guys for you, I can talk to cops. You need a plate run, I can do that. You need me to put the fear of God into someone, I can do that too."

Jerónimo grinds his teeth, thinking it over. He can shoot it out with the asshole, may the best man win, or he can take him up on his offer. A partner on this might not be a bad thing, at least for now. He can always get rid of him later if it doesn't work out. What's important is catching up to Luz as quickly as possible, getting her back to TJ, and freeing his family. He can't let his pride screw that up.

He lowers his gun but continues to stare into the fat man's eyes like he can see all the way through to his thoughts.

"What's your problem?" he asks him.

"What do you mean?" the fat man replies.

"Why do you need this money so bad that you're willing to rob motherfuckers in order to get it?"

"You go first," the fat man says.

"What?"

"Who are you working for?"

"Fuck that," Jerónimo says. "You got to read me my rights first."

The fat man's face hardens. He doesn't like getting the runaround, the big, bad cop.

"I suck at blackjack," he finally says. "How about that?"

Jerónimo grins, can't help himself.

"So we on or what?" the fat man says.

Jerónimo shoves his gun in his waistband. The fat man holsters his piece and steps out from behind the door of the truck.

"The girl has a kid in L.A., a daughter," Jerónimo says.

"And you think she'll try to get to her?" the fat man says.

"That's what I've been told."

"Let's hit the road then," the fat man says. "I'll have you there in three hours."

Jerónimo returns to the Explorer and gathers up the money and the jug of water and bag of *bolillos* he bought in Tecate, then walks over to the Dodge. The wind catches the door when he opens it, would bend the hinges back if he wasn't holding it.

"We'll pick up a tire on the way back," the fat man says as Jerónimo settles into the passenger seat.

"Don't worry about that," Jerónimo says. "Just get going."

They head for the mouth of the canyon. Jerónimo tries not to think about the long drive ahead, about Irma and the kids, about El Príncipe. The job is the job, and the circumstances that led him here don't matter. Get. That. Girl. He sends her a message, wherever she is, sends it on the wind, through the telephone lines, trying to break her spirit from afar: *No sense running. No sense hiding. You know I'm going to find you.*

14

LUZ CAN'T BELIEVE IT. THEY'VE BEEN RUNNING FOR MAYBE THIRTY seconds, and Malone already wants to stop.

"To see . . . to see . . . if they're following," he pants.

He drops to his stomach next to some coyote bush and motions for her to do the same. Reluctantly, she stretches out beside him in a narrow patch of winking shade. Licking her dry lips, she scans the plain for pursuers. She can see all the way back to the canyon. Boulders and chaparral bake in the heat, and a shimmering quicksilver mirage reflects the sky like a pool of standing water. Malone's breathing gradually slows. He stinks of liquor and sweat.

Five tense minutes pass. A buzz, an electric sizzle, fills the air. Cicadas. The sound tickles the back of Luz's brain, makes her wish she could scratch it somehow. She's about to get up and start running again when she sees movement at the lip of the canyon. A man appears, the tattooed one from before. He stands staring in their direction with hawkish intensity.

"Keep still," Malone says.

The man crouches to examine something on the ground, then stands again. After another glance their way, he turns and climbs back down into the canyon.

Luz raises herself onto her elbows, but Malone stops her from sitting up.

"Not yet," he whispers.

She watches the spot where the man disappeared. Her attention wanders after a few minutes, the sleepless night catching up to her. A tall clump of grass sways in the breeze with undersea gracefulness, and she drowses staring at it. Suddenly, she's back in the bedroom of Rolando's house. He wants to show her a knife he bought, joins her on the bed, and mimes stabbing someone. She snaps back to attention, angry with herself for drifting off.

"This is dumb," she says. "He's not coming back."

She scrambles to her feet and slaps the dust off her shirt.

"Come on."

Malone glares at her, irritated, but then stands himself and picks up the backpack.

They continue across the plain, jogging at first, then walking. Coming upon a trail worn into the hardpan, they follow it without discussion, like water grateful for a channel. Luz lets Malone lead because he seems to have some notion of where they're headed. She hopes she's not giving him too much credit.

The trail takes them to a set of train tracks on a raised bed. They climb to stand on the rails, which run forever in both directions. On the other side of the tracks is a dirt road. To the left, it parallels the tracks until it fades into the distance. They follow it to the right, where it turns to enter a copse of willows and cottonwoods.

It's at least twenty degrees cooler in the shady grotto formed by the overhanging branches, and the road dips quickly to cross a small but noisy creek. Luz kneels beside the stream and splashes water on her face while Malone lowers his mouth to the trickle for a drink. After one swallow, he spits and grimaces.

"Not good," he says, warning Luz away.

She notices a paw print in the mud, then another, and another. The track crosses the creek and continues up the other bank before disappearing into the thick undergrowth. She reaches for a rock, imagining some animal preparing to pounce.

Malone is lying on his back with his eyes closed like he wants to stay here all day. Luz tosses the rock so that it thumps on the ground next to his head. He sits up and stares at her.

"What's your problem?" he says.

"Let's go."

He gets up but then sits again and lowers his head between his knees.

"What's wrong?" Luz says.

He leans over and vomits into the bushes. Luz scoots away until she's backed against a tree. Her own stomach kicks when the sour smell reaches her. He's probably just sick from the heat, but what if it's something worse? It makes her angry to think that this bum, this surfer boy, has so quickly become her only hope.

Malone wipes his mouth with the back of his hand. He's pale and sweaty but still grins when he says, "Got any gum?"

"Can you go on?" Luz says.

He dismisses the question with a wave of his hand. "I knew a football player in college who puked before every game," he says. "He claimed it was his body getting rid of fear."

"Well, you must really be scared then," Luz says.

The rumble of an approaching engine drowns out the warbles of the birds and the hiss of the breeze through the leaves. Luz sits stock-still, trying to pinpoint where the sound is coming from, but Malone jumps to his feet. He snatches her up with one hand and grabs the backpack with the other, then pushes her in front of him to a fallen tree lying on the bank of the creek.

They step over the trunk together, and Malone pulls her to the ground so that they're both hidden behind it. The feeling of him lying on top of her starts her hands shaking. She can't stand being pushed, being held down. Too many bad memories.

The noise is louder now, the vehicle definitely coming closer. Luz's cheek is pressed to the dirt, but she can see under the tree to where the road crosses the stream. A Border Patrol truck roars into the grove and skids to a stop straddling the creek. The driver, a short Latino in a green uniform, steps out and stands facing their hiding place as he unzips his pants.

"Not in the water, man," another uniform calls from inside the truck.

"Fuck off," the first agent says.

He pisses long and loud, all the while staring up at a squirrel cavorting in the branches of a cottonwood, a chittering gray spasm anchored by an angry plume of tail. Luz's panic gets the best of her, and she tries to squirm out of Malone's grasp. He holds her tightly, whispering "Shhhhhh" until she settles.

The agent finishes with a grunt, then zips up and slides back into the truck. He revs the engine a couple of times before climbing out of the creek bed and turning to follow the road along the tracks. The sound of the motor fades away.

When the birds begin singing again, Malone rolls off Luz, and she stands and paces the clearing until she feels human. This takes some time. There's a part of her that can't bear to be touched by a man. It goes back to the day she left her mother's house for good.

She was thirteen, lying in bed, watching TV. Her mother

153

came in with some guy, some fat pig in a dirty shirt, a customer. Luz sighed and turned off the television, got up to go for a walk like she always did while Mamá took care of business. This time, however, Theresa stopped her, told her to sit.

"This is Ramón," she said.

"So?" Luz said.

"He wants to get to know you."

Luz understood immediately what her mother meant. A trembling started deep inside her, and to this day it's never quite gone away.

"Look," Mamá said. "How much do you give for rent here? How much for food?"

Luz couldn't speak.

"I'll tell you," Mamá continued. "Nothing and nothing." She gestured at the pig, who scratched his belly and licked his lips and looked just like a man who would pay to fuck a little girl. "This is Ramón."

Ramón stepped up to the bed and reached for Luz, put his fat, sweaty hands on her cheeks, and smiled into her face.

"Don't worry," he whispered. "I'm very gentle."

Luz tried to pull away, but he held her tighter. She lashed out like an animal desperate to escape a trap, pummeled him with fists and feet until he released her, then sprang up, pushed past her mother, and ran out the front door.

For the next couple of weeks she bounced between the homes of various friends. Another fight with Mamá, she told them, too ashamed to reveal what had really happened, and they fed her and lent her clothes like they had every other time she'd run away. But this time was different. This time she wasn't going back.

One of her friends had a cousin visiting from the U.S., an eighteen-year-old marine named Victor. Luz noticed how he looked at her, and it gave her an idea. She told the kid she was sixteen and flirted hard with him for the few days he was in town, let him tongue-kiss her and stick his hands up under her blouse. The poor *pendejo* fell for her like she knew he would and was almost in tears at the thought of leaving her behind when it was time for him to return to San Diego.

"So take me with you," she said, putting tears into her own eyes.

That night he hid her inside the toolbox in the bed of his pickup and managed to sneak her across the border. They checked into a motel afterward, where he planned to celebrate their success by fucking her for the first time. Luz jumped up off the bed as soon as he dropped his pants, though, and locked herself in the bathroom and refused to come out.

"What's the matter?" the kid asked through the door.

Luz began to cry for real then, blubbering out the truth: "I'm only thirteen."

"No way," the kid said.

"I swear," Luz replied.

Victor was upset at being played like that but eventually calmed down. He put his pants back on and was kind enough to drive her to the bus station and buy her a ticket to L.A.

"I'm gonna come looking for you in five years," he said. "See if you're still pretty."

It was a nice thought, but Luz never heard from him again.

Something stirs in the bushes, making her jump. Nothing, just a bird. She shakes off the past and refocuses on Isabel. Malone is now sitting on the log with his head in his hands. If he's not ready to move, she'll have to leave him behind.

"Are you going to vomit again?" she says.

"Nah, nah," he replies, pushing himself up and grabbing the backpack. "Let's do it to it."

★ ★ ★

Luz takes the lead now, sticking to the road, eyes and ears alert for more vehicles. Her mouth is full of dust. She spits weakly, and the wind blows the gob back onto her shirt. As she trudges along she replays the shootout in the canyon. Freddy betrayed them for sure, but she'd bet Rolando was also somehow involved. The thought sends a shudder through her and makes her walk even faster.

The road swings around the base of a hill, and the landscape changes abruptly. A fire burned through here recently, leaving in its wake gray ash, scorched boulders, and the skeletons of oaks and sagebrush and spiny yuccas. Barbed wire still clings to the charred posts of a fence defining some boundary in the midst of the desolation, and the blackened chassis of an abandoned car lies rusting in a ditch.

Luz hurries through the blight, but Malone lags behind, plodding along with his head down. Luz doesn't dare risk shouting for him to hurry, but she's not willing to slow down either. When the road curves again and she loses sight of him completely, tension builds inside her, agitation on a slow boil. She decides she'll wait for him up ahead, where the way straightens some.

An unexpected sight greets her when she reaches the spot: A hundred feet further on is an expanse of unburned ground with a couple of trees and a bit of green grass growing on it. A sunbaked trailer sits on the property, a few sheds, and, most important, an old blue pickup truck. Her frustration is suddenly washed away by a rogue wave of joy, and she thinks this must be what it's like to be saved.

★ ★ ★

Malone feels as if he might puke again. Counting his steps in order to keep his mind off it, he places one foot in front of the other and attempts to get a rhythm going. He smells smoke and then notices the burned landscape he's now walking through. It seems like a trick, some blasted vision brought on by heat and thirst.

Luz runs up the road toward him, motioning for him to stop.

"There's a trailer," she says when she gets close.

"How far?"

She points back the way she came. "There. Right there."

They creep around a bend and come upon a dilapidated aluminum Airstream sitting on a green island in a sea of black and gray. Malone goes first as they approach it and keeps a lookout for any sign of the residents. You've got meth labs out here, Nazi bikers, drug runners, coyotes—all kinds of outlaws who are serious about being left alone.

A dog the color of sand rockets out of its shady haven beneath the trailer to charge them when they turn into the driveway. Malone raises his foot, ready to fend off the animal, but the gristly old mutt stops short, plants its paws, and howls its guts out.

"Cassius!" a man's voice shouts. "Quiet!"

The dog returns to its lair, and a geezer in filthy jeans and a T-shirt advertising a liquor store appears in the doorway of the trailer. What's left of his white hair sticks straight up on his head, and a cigarette dangles from his lips.

"Howdy," Malone says, hand raised in greeting.

"Howdy," the old man says.

"Our car broke down," Malone says. "Do you have a phone we could use?"

What good a phone is going to do them, he doesn't know. It's the first thing that came to mind is all.

"Broke down?" the old man says, a suspicious squint crinkling the thin skin around his blue eyes. He waits with his hands on his hips as Malone and Luz draw nearer.

"Overheated, most likely," Malone says.

"Whereabouts?"

Malone gestures vaguely. "Ten minutes away. We just need to call someone to come get us."

"I have a cell phone," the old man says. "But you have to go up to the highway to get a signal."

"We'd appreciate it if you'd let us use it," Malone says.

"No problem."

"And if you could spare some water, too, that'd be great."

The old man points him to a hose attached to a pipe sticking up out of the ground. Malone walks over, sets down the backpack, and turns on the spigot. The water gushes so hot at first that he spits out his initial gulp, but the stream soon cools, and he guzzles until he sloshes.

"Don't be such a pig," Luz says.

She drinks daintily when he hands her the hose, like a cat lapping milk.

The old man is sitting at a rickety wooden picnic table shaded by a partially burned oak. Malone lowers himself onto the bench across from him, but Luz remains standing, radiating impatience.

"When was the fire?" Malone asks the old man.

"Couple weeks back."

"Looks like it was a close call."

The old man chortles. "Scary as hell," he says. "The flames charged over that hill there fifty feet high, roaring like a semi."

"Wow," Malone says.

"Yeah, wow," the old man says. "I fought them off with that

hose you were drinking out of, if you can believe it. Came real close to getting crispy-crittered."

A chipmunk sneaks across the grass to drink from the puddle beneath the spigot. Cassius shoots out from under the trailer to chase it off. Malone runs his fingers through his hair and tries to figure out who to call. Not Freddy, that's for sure. Maybe it'd be better to ask the geezer to drive them to the nearest town where they can catch a bus to San Diego.

"So it's only you?" he says to the old man.

The man's smile fades.

"Why?" he says. "You planning a robbery?"

"Come on," Malone says. "I was just wondering how someone out here all alone all day would occupy himself."

The old man shrugs, still wary. "I hike. Read a little."

"Oh yeah?" Malone says. "What do you like to read?"

"Westerns," the old man says. "Spy books. They've got paperbacks two for one at a store in Calexico and let you trade them in when you finish. Shakespeare."

"Shakespeare?" Malone is about to say when the old man flinches and raises his hands over his head.

Malone turns to see Luz pointing the silver-plated .45 at the guy. Hot as he was before, he's that cold now, like someone doused him with a bucket of ice water.

"We want to buy your truck," Luz says to the old man.

"And I guess I'm selling," the old man replies with acid in his tone.

Malone gets past his shock and steps in to take control. Luz has decided their next move by bringing out the pistol, but he needs to make sure the transaction goes smoothly.

"It's not like that," he says to the old man. "We'll pay you a lot more than it's worth."

"Still called stealing," the old man says.

"It can't be," Luz says. "We're *paying* you."

"Put that away," Malone says to Luz, gesturing at the gun. She lowers it but keeps it in her hand. He reaches inside the backpack, pulls out a stack of bills, and flips through it. All hundreds. He tosses the money onto the table in front of the old man.

"There's five grand there," he says.

The old man doesn't acknowledge the cash, just reaches into the pocket of his jeans and drops a red plastic keychain with one key on it onto the table.

Another thought hits Malone, and he reaches into the pack again.

"And here's"—he counts out a few loose bills—"a thousand more for your phone."

He sets the bills down next to the stack, tucks them under the abalone shell ashtray when the breeze ruffles them. The old man shakes his head and chuckles wryly.

"I suppose you want me to go in and get it for you too," he says.

"If it's not too much trouble," Malone says.

"Oh, hell no. No trouble at all," the old man says with sarcastic solicitousness. He pushes himself up from the table and turns toward the trailer.

Luz nudges Malone between the shoulder blades.

"How do you know he doesn't have a gun in there?" she whispers.

Malone beats the old man to the door but lets him enter first. The trailer is cluttered but tidy. There's an institutional, almost military orderliness in the way the canned foods are stacked on the counter of the tiny galley kitchen and the flower-print throw pillows are propped against the armrests of the sofa. Down a short hallway Malone sees a neatly made bed, and the air even smells good, like oranges.

The old man grabs a phone off a table and hands it to Malone.

"I'm sorry about this," Malone says.

The old man shrugs. "Who steals my purse steals trash," he says.

"Things aren't going well for us."

"And now they're not going too well for me either."

Malone follows the old man out of the trailer and has him sit again at the picnic table. Luz stands at the edge of the oak tree's lacy shade, looking like she's about to pop. Now that they've got the truck, all she's thinking about is going.

"It'd probably be best if you just counted that money and kept your mouth shut," Malone says to the old man. "You don't want a visit from the guys we're running from."

"Whatever you say, boss," the old man replies.

His attitude is beginning to irritate Malone. The way he's acting, like they're a couple of idiots whose antics amuse him to no end, reminds him of his dad.

He picks up the backpack and walks to the truck without another word, Luz on his heels. The door groans when he opens it, but the interior of the cab is as tidy as the trailer was. He slips the key into the ignition and twists it. The engine strains once, twice, then turns over as Luz slides in on the passenger side.

The old man is still sitting at the picnic table when Malone wheels the truck around and bounces down the driveway to the dirt road. The vehicle is a little sticky going from first to second and there's a long crack in the windshield, but it'll get them where they're going. Malone rolls down the window for some air, then rolls it back up because of the dust.

"That didn't have to go that way," he says to Luz.

"You were gonna sit there all day talking about books," Luz says. "I need to get to L.A."

"You're lucky he didn't have a heart attack."

Luz stares out the window, done talking about it.

"So where to?" Malone says. "The bus station?"

"As fast as you can," she says.

A few minutes later they turn off the dirt road onto two-lane highway 94, which runs along the border from San Diego all the way out to the Imperial Valley. The fire zone ends here, and they wind through parched grassland and scattered groves of oaks. Luz keeps opening and closing the phone, checking for signal. When she finally gets one and punches in a number, Malone can hear the ring on the other end, and the message that the number is no longer in service. Luz's face falls, and the despair revealed unnerves him.

"What?" he says.

"Nothing," she says.

"Tell me."

She sits quietly, composing herself, then says, "My aunt that was keeping my baby for me? The number I have for her doesn't work anymore."

"Is there any other way to get in touch with her?" Malone says.

"I know where she lived," Luz says. "I'll go there and see."

Annie. A single memory of her, the smell of her skin, slips through the bulwark Malone has built against the past. Even that hurts.

"Do you want me to drive you to L.A.?" he says to Luz, the words spilling out before he can stop them.

"I'll be okay," she says.

"Take a minute," he says. "Think about your daughter. Do you want me to drive you?"

He watches Luz's struggle with the offer play out on her face. After a few seconds, she says, "You can have the money."

162

"It's already mine," he says. "You gave it to me back in the canyon."

"The gun, too, then," Luz says, sliding the .45 across the seat. "It's worth a lot."

"Okay," he says. "Deal."

They ride in silence after that, the old truck's rattles and squeaks soothing in their constancy after the chaos of the last few hours. Chaparral gives way to suburbs as they skirt San Diego and turn north toward L.A., and Malone is strangely at peace. It seems to him he's not driving anymore but falling instead, tumbling helplessly, blissfully, into his fate.

15

THACKER'S TRUCK IS LOW ON GAS, AND HE NEEDS TO TAKE A LEAK. The Mex doesn't say anything when he tells him he's going to stop, but Thacker can read his irritation in the line of his clenched jaw and the momentary narrowing of his eyes. The guy hasn't spoken two words since they left the border—told him his name, Jerónimo, and that's about it—and Thacker wonders what's going through his mind. A quiet fucker can be a dangerous fucker. Or just stupid.

He pulls off the freeway in Temecula and has a choice of Shell, Standard, or Arco. Arco's cheapest, so he drives in, eases up to a pump, and steps out of the air-conditioned bubble of the cab. He decides to pay cash. Better not to leave a paper trail today.

Walking across the lot to the mini-mart, he's almost run down by a couple of girls backing up too fast in a Mustang convertible. They're talking and laughing and blasting music and don't even notice him until he shouts a warning. The driver, a ditzy blonde, looks like she's going to mouth off, but then his uniform registers and she thinks better of it.

"Sorry," she calls out, scrunching her shoulders.

Thacker approaches the Mustang and looks it over appraisingly. Where the hell's a chick her age get the money for a car like this? Someone has a sugar daddy, that's for sure.

"Nice ride," he says.

"Thanks," the blonde says. Tanned. Big tits. Her friend isn't bad either.

"Where you off to in such a hurry?" he says. Let them guess whether it's an official query or friendly conversation.

"We're late for work," the blonde says.

Thacker moves in closer, rests a hand on top of the windshield.

"Oh yeah?" he says. "Where at?"

"Over at Applebee's."

"Mmmmmm, good cheeseburgers," he says.

"Yeah, but I'm vegan, you know, so . . ."

"So, no cheeseburgers for you."

"No cheeseburgers for me."

"Plenty of dick, though, I bet," Thacker says.

The girl's big, fake smile disappears. *Yeah, you heard right, you dumb bitch,* Thacker thinks.

"Excuse me?" the girl says.

Thacker backs away from the car. "You gals be careful, okay?" he says, then lets them drive away. They'd scream bloody murder if someone called them whores, but that's what they are, and if he had that Luz's money, he'd prove it. He'd have both of them sucking him off in no time.

He enters the store and walks to the men's room, finds it occupied. Annoyed, he joins the line of customers waiting for the cashier. When it's his turn, he tells the Mex behind the counter that he'll be filling up and hands him his last eighty bucks.

Back at the pump, he washes the windshield while the tank fills. As he draws the squeegee across the glass, Jerónimo turns away, staring out the side window to avoid eye contact.

It costs $74 to top off. Thacker replaces the cap and opens his door.

"I'm gonna grab a hot dog," he says to the Mex. "You want something?"

"No," Jerónimo says.

"A Coke? Some water?" Thacker couldn't give a shit if the guy starves, but he needs him to be in good shape for whatever's coming next.

"Nothing," Jerónimo says.

Thacker walks back into the store and checks the men's room again. The door is still locked, but the women's is empty, so he uses that instead.

Before picking up his change, he pulls a Jumbo Beefy out of the warmer and covers it with chili, nacho cheese, and jalapeños. He wolfs it down standing in a sliver of shade in front of the store, gulps from a bottle of Mountain Dew between bites.

Jerónimo is sitting with his head tilted back, eyes closed, but comes back to life when Thacker opens the door.

"Siesta time?" Thacker says, fucking with the guy.

"Thinking," Jerónimo says.

Thacker gets back on the 15 and works the truck over into the far left lane, where traffic is whipping along. Past Lake Elsinore the freeway enters a range of rocky hills, and the country station he's been listening to fades to sputtering static. He presses the scan button on the radio, and a few seconds later an angry drawl fills the cab, backed by an eerie, moaning organ.

"Brothers and sisters, you know how folks are always day-dreaming about heaven, about pearly gates and streets of gold and harp-playing angels? Well, I'm here to tell you it's time they started thinking a little bit less about heaven and a little bit more about hell. Because hell is reality, people. The flames are real. The unimaginable, unending pain is real. The torment is real. 'But that's so depressing,' you say. Ha! Listen up: If you aren't scared of going to hell, there's a darn good chance you aren't going to see heaven."

Thacker grins at the fire and brimstone rant. It takes him back to the summer when he was fifteen, and Clyde Waters showed up in his hometown of Taft and took over as preacher of the Pentecostal Holiness church.

Word went out that Waters was something to see, a natural man of God with a message of grace for all, and Thacker's grandmother decided to investigate for herself. A lifelong Baptist, she'd been dragging Thacker to services since he was a toddler, determined to give him some sort of religious foundation, an effort his parents wholeheartedly supported because it got him out of the house every Sunday so they could nurse their hangovers in peace. As for Thacker, he enjoyed the post-sermon lunches at Sno-White Drive-In.

So it was that one blazing July morning, instead of driving Thacker to the tidy little First Baptist church he'd memorized every warped board of, Granny turned her Buick toward the edge of town, where Pentecostal Holiness occupied an old Quonset hut set in a dirt parking lot across the road from an oilfield full of nodding pumpjacks.

The inside of the church was hot and stuffy, and Thacker felt like Pinocchio in the belly of the whale, the way the ribbed metal ceiling arched overhead. He and his grandma slid into the last row of pews, drawing curious glances from the congregation, twenty old folks who fanned themselves with collection envelopes and folded newspapers. One of the deacons, a short, fat man bristled like a hog, made a few announcements about upcoming meetings and events and then introduced Brother Clyde Waters.

Waters was a tall, stringy, baldheaded man, as dried up as a stick of jerky from too much sun and wind. He stepped up to the pulpit in a white shirt buttoned to the throat, a stiff pair of new Levis, and shiny black cowboy boots. His sermon started slowly, with corny jokes and too much scripture, and Thacker quickly grew bored. He was half-dreaming of dove hunting when a roar startled him awake. Something had taken hold of Waters. The man's face was beet red, the tendons in his neck stood out like tree roots, and his voice had slipped into an incantatory cadence.

For the next half hour he railed against the sickness of this world, the sin that stained mankind, and the everyday demons waiting to drag you down. He was a man for whom hell was as real a place as Taft or Bakersfield or New York City, who could describe the devil crouching on his tarnished throne as clearly as if he'd seen the sight himself, who was haunted to tears by midnight visions of sinners in the lake of fire, unfortunate souls who could have been redeemed if only they'd accepted Jesus as their Lord and Savior.

Thacker hung on every word, transfixed by the preacher's furious righteousness and caught up in the passion that led the man to pound his chest with his fist and wail, "I can't wait to lay down this filthy body and go home to meet my God." And when, at the conclusion of his sermon, Waters dropped to his knees, gasping for air, out of words at last, Thacker held his breath, halfway convinced that the man was about to burst into heavenly flame and be reborn as an avenging angel.

"He was quite the performer," was all Grandma had to say afterward, but Thacker was an instant convert. Astounded that a prophet like Clyde Waters walked the same dusty, potholed streets he did, he took to following the preacher whenever their paths crossed in the tiny town, ragingly curious about the man's day-to-day existence.

One Saturday afternoon he tailed him into the diner and observed from a few stools away as he ordered a patty melt. Another time, after spotting him and his wife in the grocery store, he pushed a cart up and down the aisles behind them and discovered that Waters liked bologna and Kraft Singles, orange juice, frozen lasagna, and sourdough bread. He also watched him get his hair cut and dawdled in the post office while he bought stamps and a money order.

In little more than a month, though, Thacker lost interest in the preacher, because it turned out that Clyde Waters not only walked the same streets he did, he also lived the same stupid life. Who knew a messenger of God could be so boring? Thacker stopped following Waters and returned to his old pursuits: honing his shoplifting skills and trying to get further than dry-humping a neighbor girl he was hot for.

It had been a couple of weeks since he'd even thought of the preacher when he happened upon the man's car one evening, parked in a willow grove on the banks of a reservoir. Thacker had ridden his bicycle there to shoot tadpoles with his pellet gun. Curiosity piqued, he stashed the bike in a patch of weeds and crept up on the bird shit–spattered station wagon.

The vehicle appeared to be empty, but a moan came from inside, a giggle, a whisper. Thacker almost ran off right then, but scolded himself for being a pussy. Slowly, slowly, he raised up to peek in the window. What he saw, he saw for only an instant before the fear of being discovered sent him fleeing: Russell Hall's wife splayed out on the backseat, tits flopping, dress up around her hips, and Waters's bald head between her legs.

When Thacker tells the story now, it's as a joke, and he never tells the last part, how he rode over to the Hall house one day soon afterward when he knew Russell was at work and let Mrs. Hall know what he'd seen. She asked if there was anything she could do to keep him from telling her husband, and before he could say boo, he was fucking her himself. He knows there was all kinds of right and wrong mixed up in that, but he's never let it bother him too much. One thing *is* for certain, however: Nobody ever fooled him again.

He hits the scan button over and over until an Eagles song comes up. Either he or the Mex stinks, so he adjusts the vent to blow more air his way.

"You speak good English," he says to Jerónimo. "Where'd you learn?"

"I was born in the U.S., lived here most of my life," Jerónimo says.

"Oh yeah? Whereabouts?"

The Mex grimaces and looks away. "Not to be an asshole," he says, "but the less you know about me, the better for me, and the less I know about you, the better for you."

"Ten-four," Thacker says. "No problem."

These punks and their shove-it-up-your-ass attitudes. Then they wonder why they end up wearing stripes on the wrong side of the wall. Fucking tough guys. Fucking idiots.

When they get close to L.A., the fat man, Thacker, puts Luz's aunt's address into his phone and pulls up a map. She lives in Compton, in what used to be, in Jerónimo's day, a black neighborhood, Spooktown Crip territory. Things must have changed. Thacker hands Jerónimo the phone and has him call out the directions, and he complies without kicking. Whatever gets them there fastest.

They take the 91 west to Alameda, then head north. Thacker announces that he has to piss again.

"For real?" Jerónimo says.

Thacker chuckles to show he's joking.

"You wanted to kill me, didn't you?" he says.

Jerónimo doesn't reply, just stares down at the map, at the little blue bubble that shows their current location. If you laugh at a clown, he'll keep going, and Jerónimo doesn't want to hear any fat cop's jokes.

They're rolling through an ugly jumble of small factories, auto repair shops, and taco stands separated by trash-strewn empty lots carpeted with broken glass. The sky is the color of a bathtub ring, the sun a festering boil. A woman jogs from her car to a zipper factory with one hand clasped over her nose and mouth against the chemical haze, and psychotic pigeons strut along the deserted sidewalk, grudgingly stepping aside for a can man rattling by, his gimpy shopping cart piled high with recyclables.

Jerónimo directs Thacker to cross a set of train tracks and make a right on Alondra and a left on Burris, a narrow tree-lined street of tidy stucco residences. The place they're looking for turns out to be a Spanish-style house with arched windows and a large covered porch. There's a square of lawn out front and a concrete statue of the Virgin of Guadalupe. A hand-lettered sign is wired to a telephone pole on the curb. SLOW, it reads, CHILDREN PLAYING.

They cruise past and continue to the end of the block, Jerónimo watching the house in his mirror. The minivan in the driveway doesn't look like the police, and neither do any of the cars parked on the street. Still, he's a little worried. Luz's mother might have gotten in touch with her and told her about his visit.

Then Luz might have called the cops and said anything, trying to make trouble for him. The ringing of the phone in his pocket reels his thoughts back in.

"What's going on?" El Príncipe says. "I'm waiting."

"I'll be heading back shortly," Jerónimo says. "I'm right on her tail."

"You found her?"

"I'm close. I'll have good news for you soon."

"Perfect, because that's the only kind of news I want."

"I get it," Jerónimo says.

"You get it?"

"Yes."

"Good," El Príncipe says. "Hey, did you know your son doesn't know how to swim?"

"What?" Jerónimo says, forgetting about the house, about Luz, about everything.

"I asked him if he wanted to go in the pool, and he told me he doesn't know how to swim," El Príncipe says.

"He's young," Jerónimo says.

"If he's here long enough, maybe I'll teach him," El Príncipe says.

It's scare tactics, straight up, but Jerónimo swallows his rage, keeps his cool. "I'll call soon," he says.

"You know how I learned?" El Príncipe continues. "My father threw me in. It's a fucked-up thing to do, but it works."

"An hour, maybe two," Jerónimo says and ends the call, acting like he didn't catch the threat.

Thacker grins his stupid gringo grin.

"Who was that?" he says. "Your *jefe?* The hog with the heavy nuts?"

"Take me to the house," Jerónimo tells him. "I'm going in."

"Hold on, now."

"Man, you don't understand. I got no time to fuck around."

"I *do* understand," Thacker says. "But you can't go in there guns blazing. Let's do this right."

What he comes up with is simple enough: They'll both be Border Patrol. His uniform will get them through the door, and he'll give Jerónimo his badge to flash in case there are any questions about him. Once they're inside, Thacker will do the talking and feel the situation out.

"And don't go all loco if it looks like a dead end at first," he says. "Let me work on them."

They park across the street from the house, and Jerónimo steps out of the truck and slides the Smith & Wesson into his waistband at the small of his back. He and Thacker walk up the driveway and peek into the minivan. Kids' toys, a dream catcher hanging off the rearview mirror.

The driveway continues past the house to a detached garage out back, but passage is blocked by a five-foot chain-link gate. A German shepherd and some kind of pit bull mix rush the gate and cut loose with a grating chorus of frantic barks. Thacker taps the corner of his eye with his finger, then points to the garage. Jerónimo moves to the gate and keeps watch on the rear of the house while the fat man lumbers to the porch and knocks at the front door. The dogs, eyes rolling, teeth bared, bellow at Jerónimo, letting the whole neighborhood knows he's here.

A woman answers the door, a chubby Latina, thirty-five, forty, wearing a tank top and shorts. Thacker says something about immigration and shows her one of the photos of Luz that El Príncipe gave to Jerónimo. Jerónimo can't hear what's going on over the dogs, but Thacker soon gestures for him to join them on the porch.

"This is my partner, Agent Vasquez," Thacker says to the

woman, whose brow is knitted in confusion. He turns to Jeró-nimo. "She doesn't *habla inglés*," he says with a smirk.

Jerónimo takes the photo from Thacker and holds it out to the woman again. "We're looking for this girl," he says in Spanish. "Do you know her?"

"No, sir," the woman says. She's a terrible liar.

"Look again," Jerónimo says. "Her name is Luz."

The woman waves the picture away. "Please, sir."

"She's your niece, isn't she?"

"I don't want any trouble."

"We don't either. Tell us what we want to know, and we'll go."

"I'm afraid," she says and nods toward Thacker. "This man has a gun."

"Everything will be fine," Jerónimo reassures her. "Just a few questions."

She considers this, then opens the door wider and motions him and Thacker inside.

The living room is a cool, dark cave, the curtains shut tight, a window-mounted air conditioner working hard. Two little girls lie sprawled at opposite ends of a couch, watching cartoons on TV. They barely look up when Jerónimo, Thacker, and the woman pass through on their way to the kitchen. The family photos hanging in the hall trip Jerónimo up for a second, put him in mind of Irma and the kids, but then he glimpses a teenaged Luz in one of them, cradling an infant, and things begin to fall into place.

The kitchen is like the rest of the house, lived-in but clean where it should be. A rack of freshly washed dishes drips next to the sink, and the room smells of soap. Jerónimo pulls out a chair for the woman at a small table cut in two by a slash of sunlight and sits down across from her. Thacker stands in front of the buzzing refrigerator, arms crossed over his chest.

174

"What's your name?" Jerónimo asks the woman.

Trembling fingers hiding her lips, she replies, "Carmen Rosales."

"And you're Luz's aunt?"

She nods. "But we haven't seen or heard from her in years, not since she went back to Mexico."

"No calls from her lately? No texts?"

"Nothing. What's happened?"

Jerónimo leans forward, rests his elbows on the turquoise Formica tabletop, and stares into Carmen's eyes. He wants to frighten her just enough.

"Luz has a daughter," he says.

Carmen's hand slides from her mouth to her throat, to the gold cross hanging there.

"One of them?" Jerónimo says with a nod toward the living room, playing his hunch.

"We've been looking after her," Carmen says. "She's like one of our own."

"That's good," Jerónimo says. "That's kind of you. But we've heard something."

"What?"

"Luz is coming here to see her today."

"No. Who told you this?"

Jerónimo frowns and scratches the back of his neck. "That's confidential," he says. "You understand how these things are. What I can tell you is that Luz is in big trouble. She's made a very bad man very angry, and my partner and I have been sent here to protect her child."

Fear sharpens Carmen's features. She glances over at Thacker, then turns her gaze back to Jerónimo. "I need to call my husband," she says.

"Later," Jerónimo says. "There's no time now."

"No, I'm going to call," she says and starts to get to her feet. Jerónimo reaches out and takes one of her hands in his. He squeezes it hard as he pulls her back down into the chair.

"Listen to me," he says. "We're here to help you."

"Help me?" Carmen says, her voice tilting toward hysteria. "You're not the Border Patrol. You're not any kind of police."

"Shhhh," Jerónimo says. "Calm down." She's a good person, he can see that, but he'll hurt her if he has to.

"What's happening?" Thacker asks in English.

"Stay quiet," Jerónimo says. "Let me handle this."

16

MALONE AND LUZ ARE ON THE 91 SOMEWHERE BETWEEN CORONA and Yorba Linda, coming into Orange County, Malone's old stomping ground. He grew up in Anaheim Hills; he and Val and Annie lived in Tustin, not too far away; and his parents still live in Newport. It was here that he went to school, worked, married, was a daddy, and bumped into happiness once or twice.

He hasn't been back since he slunk off to L.A. after Val left him, intending to lose himself among strangers and burn off what remained of his life. His chest tightens as he gazes at the familiar flatness stretching to the ocean, the orderly grid of wide streets and freeways, and the pall of smog that turns the colors strange. It hits him all of a sudden that he shouldn't be here, that whatever he fled might be waiting for him like a vengeful spirit.

Luz is staring out the window, and Malone tries to think of something to say to her to stave off the foreboding that's descended upon him.

"How old's your daughter?" he asks.

"Hmmm?" Luz replies, coming back from wherever she'd drifted off to.

"How old's your kid?"

"She'll be four on Tuesday."

"And it's been how long since you last saw her?"

"Three years."

Malone can tell she's uncomfortable, but he keeps talking, can't stop himself.

"Why'd you leave her?" he asks.

Luz shoots him an angry look, then shrugs and turns away.

"I'm not judging you," he says. "I'm curious."

"I was stupid," she says.

"But now you're gonna make it right."

"I'm gonna try."

"That's good," Malone says. "I hope you do." A smear on the windshield catches his eye. He reaches up to wipe it away with his thumb but finds that the mark is on the other side of the glass. They pass a gas station where he used to fill up once in a while and the pizza place where Val worked when she was in high school. One memory leads to another.

"Who'd you take the money from?" he says to Luz, desperate for distraction.

"Nobody you want to know," she says.

"Does he have any idea what you're doing, where you're going?"

"Yeah, I left him a map," she scoffs. "What do you think?"

"I think that Border Patrol guy knew we were crossing this morning, and maybe the other guy too."

"Don't worry about it. You'll be rid of me in half an hour."

"I'm not worried about me. I'm worried about you."

"I can take care of myself."

They ride in silence until the pressure builds again inside Malone's skull. *Leave her alone,* he scolds himself even as he's saying, "What's your daughter's name?"

Luz cocks her head, angry now. "You know what," she says, "I'm gonna ask you some questions. Are you married?"

"I was," Malone says.

"What happened?"

"She left me."

"Because you cheated on her?"

"No."

"Yeah, you did. You cheated on her."

"No, I didn't."

"Why'd she leave you then?"

"Our daughter."

"Oh, a daughter. What's her name?"

"Annie."

"How old is she?"

"She'd be ten."

"What's that mean?"

"She's dead."

Shock registers briefly on Luz's face, but she keeps going.

"From what?"

"She got hit by a car."

"How?"

"She ran into the street," Malone says. "I looked away for a second to unload some groceries—"

He wants to embarrass Luz with the particulars, make her sorry she ever asked, but he falters. Even after all these years he can't bring himself to relate what happened that morning, to describe the squeal of brakes, the fleshy thump, the moment he turned to see the truck that had run Annie down still sitting on top of her. "Move!" he screams on the nights when he relives it. "Move!" But it's always too late, she's always already dead.

"Ask me something else," he says when his voice returns to him, but now that Luz has drawn blood, her indignation has dissipated. She stares silently out her window again while Malone tightens his grip on the wheel and drives on.

A Highway Patrol cruiser sneaks up on them, coming out of nowhere to speed past with its flashers winking maniacally. It begins to swerve across all four lanes of the freeway, a maneuver designed to gradually slow traffic. Malone tries to escape via an upcoming exit but ends up trapped between a panel truck and a Corvette when everything comes to a standstill. Sticking his head out the window, he watches the cruiser make a U-turn and park in the middle of the freeway facing a sea of idling vehicles. Luz clutches the door handle like she's about to make a run for it.

"Easy," Malone says, having discovered the reason for the stop: A brown leather couch lies in the fast lane. At least one vehicle has already hit it, exposing white stuffing and a broken wooden frame. Stepping out of the cruiser, the patrolman pulls on a pair of black gloves. He grabs the couch and, with a series of tugs, drags it to the shoulder.

"Thank you, officer," a woman's voice calls from somewhere nearby.

The patrolman returns to the cruiser and swings it around so that it's facing in the right direction. Traffic starts to flow again as soon as he zooms off down the eerily empty roadway, and in a matter of seconds it's as if it had never paused at all.

A couple of miles later Luz says, "If we come to a mall or something, could we stop?"

"I thought you were in a hurry," Malone says.

"I don't want Isabel to see me like this," Luz says. "I need to clean up."

"Isabel," Malone says. "That's nice."

Luz looks at him sideways for second, then says, "I'm sorry about the way I am."

"Don't worry about it," Malone says.

"I've been through a lot of shit."

"You don't have to apologize to me."

A smile flits across Luz's face. Malone reaches up and tries to rub away the spot on the windshield again.

Luz points out a sign. "There's a Target up here."

"Target it is then," Malone says.

He takes the next exit and drives down a frontage road that leads to a shopping center. Target, Best Buy, BevMo. The competition for parking spaces in the vast lot is too much for him, so he retreats to the outer edge and finds an empty spot there.

The cab of the truck heats up as soon as he shuts off the engine. Luz uses her filthy shirt to swipe at the dirt and ash streaking her face.

"Do I look okay to go inside?" she says.

"Good enough," he says.

He decides to accompany her. The store will be air-conditioned, and he needs food. He opens the backpack and pulls some money from it, a few hundreds, puts them in his pocket. He then zips up the pack and slings it over his shoulder. He and Luz walk across the parking lot together. He can feel the hot asphalt through the soles of his Converses. Once inside the store, they head for the restrooms.

Malone splashes water onto his face and uses a paper towel to wipe away the grime on his neck and arms, slides it up under his shirt to get at his chest and pits. Not much he can do about his hair. He removes a twig stuck in it and combs it into place as best he can with wet fingers.

When he leaves the bathroom he almost trips over a little boy. The kid is standing alone right outside the door and crying loudly.

"What's up, dude?" Malone asks him.

"Daddy!" the boy yells, on the verge of hysteria. "Daddy!"

Malone pushes open the bathroom door and sticks his head inside.

"Anybody missing a kid, a little boy?" he says.

A man standing at the sink says, "Not me."

Malone squats in front of the boy. "They've got a place here where they can call your dad," he says. "You want me to take you there?"

The boy puts his hand in Malone's and lets him lead him toward the customer service desk. Before they've gone too far, a short, skinny man in khakis and a denim shirt comes running up.

"What's going on?" he snaps at Malone.

"You left me," the boy wails.

"I did not," the man says.

"I found him over by the bathroom," Malone says.

The man gives Malone a look that makes Malone want to punch him in the face, a glance filled with suspicion and distrust.

"Thanks," he says as he picks up the boy and carries him off.

Malone walks back to the women's room to wait for Luz. She smiles when she emerges all scrubbed and smelling of soap. He'd forgotten how pretty she is.

"I need some clean clothes," she says. "Can you loan me some money?"

He hands her two of the hundreds he took out of the back-pack.

"I'll be in the snack bar," he says.

He orders pizza and coffee from a Chinese kid with a lisp. When it's ready, he carries his tray to one of the little plastic tables. The pizza is the first food he's eaten all day, and even though it's barely warm and has a cardboard crust, he wolfs it down and considers having more. The man and woman at the next table are staring at their phones. Beyond them, a young mother spoons frozen yogurt into her squirming toddler's mouth. Malone sips his coffee and wishes it was whiskey.

After he drops Luz off, he'll drive the pickup back to San Diego and ditch it in Old Town, take the trolley home. Then he's going to sleep for twelve hours. The past couple of days have been too fucking much. Just look at his hand. It's shaking like an old man's. He's starting to think he really should take Gail to Maui. Luz's money will be more than enough to get them going. He'll ease off the booze, give regular life another shot. He's only thirty-five. There's no reason he can't try to string together however many good days he has left into something decent. But, goddamn, look at that hand.

Luz wonders about Malone as she walks through the store. At first she thought he was sticking with her because of the money, but that can't be it because now the money is his, and he's still here. It would have been nice to have the cash to start her new life, but if she had to give it up to get Isabel back, it must have been meant to be. In fact, *everything* must have been meant to be. And that means that Malone, raggedy-ass fool that he is, is actually the person God sent to help her out today. And he's getting something out of it, too, something besides the money. He's bringing her to her baby because he can't be with his own, and this is going to make him feel better about losing Annie. At least Luz hopes it will. She'd like to think that she understands what he was feeling back there in the truck when he was talking about what happened to his daughter but knows that she doesn't. Because that kind of suffering, you do alone.

Worry is getting the best of her now that she's so close to reuniting with Isabel, and question after question pops into her head.

What if Carmen has moved?

I'll talk to the neighbors.

And if they don't know anything?

I'll go to the restaurant where Carmen's husband used to work.

And if she's dead? It's the voice of her mother asking this.

Who? Who's dead?

Isabel. What if she's dead? Like Annie.

Don't think that, don't think that, don't think, Luz tells herself.

Isabel had a cold the day Luz left for Tijuana. She was cranky and feverish, and Luz sat holding her on Carmen's couch, rocking her and kissing her again and again.

"Mamá," the little girl wailed. "Mamá," as if she knew that soon a car was going to pull up outside and Mamá would have to go. She was wearing just a diaper and a T-shirt, but still her hair was damp with sweat.

"*Cálmate,*" Luz whispered as she wiped snot from the baby's nose and pressed her lips to her burning forehead. "I won't be gone long, I promise. And when I come back, we'll have everything we need: a place of our own, furniture, good food, and every beautiful thing you deserve."

She pictured her love for Isabel as one of those charms, a heart made up of two sections that fit together like pieces of a puzzle. She'd leave half with Isabel, praying it would be enough to keep the memory of Mamá alive until she returned. The other half she'd take with her and conceal deep inside her, where its fire would warm her on the coldest nights and its glow would be a comfort to her in her darkness.

She nearly backed out when El Samurai arrived, almost sent Carmen to tell him she'd changed her mind about going with him. But it was too late. She'd led him on for too long, and to reject him then would have wounded his pride. He'd have punished her, punished Isabel, punished Carmen and her family. She wept as she handed Isabel over to Carmen and spent her last few seconds desperately trying to memorize the baby's face.

Ever since, she's struggled to live with what she did. She realized soon after leaving that it would have been better to have been poor, to have starved to death, than to be parted from Isabel, and she's grieved and yearned and drugged herself into oblivion trying to escape her shame. Her only prayer has been *Let me get back to her,* her only dream to hold her little girl again and finally, once and for all, knit together the two jagged halves of her heart. And she's so close now, so close.

It's a thrill for Luz to be able to shop on her own after never being allowed out by herself while she was with Rolando. If he didn't go with her, one of his men did, trailing her up and down the aisles of the stores and tapping his foot while she had her nails done. For her protection, he claimed, but really he was afraid that, given half a chance, she'd slip away. And now she has. She outsmarted him and made her escape, and now she's as free as all the other women here.

She flips through a rack of hoodies and chooses a sky blue one with a silver glitter design on the back. She also picks out matching sweatpants, a T-shirt, and a bra and pair of panties. Then it's off to the toy department, where, after a few minutes of deliberation, she grabs both a stuffed panda and a baby doll and takes them to the register.

She changes in a bathroom stall and drops her dirty clothes into a trashcan. Malone is where he said he'd be, at a table in the snack bar, restless fingers shredding a paper napkin.

"Better?" he says.

"Not until I see Isabel," Luz says.

"You should eat something," he says. "I'm gonna get another pizza. Want one?"

"Yeah, maybe," she says. "Cheese only."

Malone goes to the counter, and Luz closes her eyes and presses her fingertips to her eyelids. She wishes there was music or something to distract her from thinking about all the ways things could still go wrong.

The pizza smells good when Malone brings it to her. Luz eats it right up, then shows him the toys she bought for Isabel.

"Cute," he says.

He carries them to the truck for her, across the busy parking lot. The seat is hot against the back of her legs when she slides in. She rolls down her window after Malone starts the truck and tries to figure out how to turn up the air conditioner.

"Does it go any colder?" she says.

Malone doesn't answer, and she looks over to find him staring out the windshield and tapping his thumbs on the steering wheel.

"I need a drink," he says.

"A drink?"

"A *drink* drink."

"Right now?"

He nods his head.

Please, she wants to say, *let's go,* but she's been around drunks her whole life and knows how strong their weakness is.

"Where you gonna get it?" she says.

Malone shuts off the engine and points across the lot to the liquor store, the BevMo. "I'll only be a second," he says as he opens the door and steps out of the truck.

"Leave the air on," Luz says.

Malone smiles and sticks the keys in his pocket. "I love you like a sister," he says, "but I don't trust you as far as I could throw you."

He walks off toward the store. Luz tells herself to hold on, it's almost over.

Five minutes later he reappears toting two bags. One contains a twelve-pack of Bud Light, the other a fifth of cheap vodka. After starting the truck, he opens the vodka and takes three long swallows, then pops a beer and downs it in a couple of gulps.

Luz turns away, disgusted.

"Want some?" he says, offering her the vodka.

"That isn't going to help you," she says.

"What do you know about it?" he says.

He opens another beer, sets it between his legs, and starts to drive out of the parking lot.

"Hey," Luz says, grabbing for the can. "What if we get pulled over?" She rolls down her window and tosses the can out. "After you drop me off you can do whatever you want."

They get back on the freeway and cross into L.A. County. It's a tense, silent ride. Luz tells Malone to exit at Alameda, and there it is: Compton, California.

Luz remembers the first time she saw this place, back when she was thirteen years old, a scared little girl running from somewhere bad to somewhere she hoped would be better. Her fantasy of Los Angeles had been shaped by MTV and gossip magazines, so what a disappointment it was when Carmen picked her up at the bus station and brought her here. Compton was sad little factories and roaring freeways. Compton was bunker liquor stores and ghetto swap meets. It was a million miles from the beach, from Sunset Boulevard, from the Hollywood Hills.

An hour after she arrived, one of her cousins showed her the bloodstains and bullet holes from a recent drive-by, and that night she lay in bed paralyzed with fear as a helicopter circled above the neighborhood and sirens wailed in the distance. She'd come all the way from TJ for this? It felt like someone had lied to her.

There wasn't time to brood though. Her aunt expected her to pull her weight and fend for herself right off the bat, so Luz had to learn quickly where she could walk and where she couldn't, who it was okay to talk to and who to avoid. The city was a tricky maze to navigate, dodging cops on this block, gangsters on the next. You had to think ahead, you had to plan, and after a while those movie star daydreams she'd brought with her dried up and blew away without her even noticing.

The street her aunt lived on looks the same as it did when Luz left three years ago. So much has happened to her since then that she expected it, too, would have changed somehow, but, no, same houses, same cars, same trees, same sidewalks. She presses a hand to her chest as if that will stop the pounding behind her ribs. She's waited so long for this.

"Right here," she says, pointing out Carmen's place. She recognizes the minivan in the driveway, the one with the *Jesus Es Rey de Reyes* bumper sticker. She was living here when Carmen's husband, Bernardo, bought it. And there are the dogs, Lobo and Woof, and the rosebushes.

Malone pulls the truck to the curb, and Luz grabs the bags containing the doll and the stuffed bear and reaches for the door handle. On her way out she looks over her shoulder at Malone and wonders what she should say.

"Thanks for driving me," is what comes out.

"Glad I could help," he says.

"I'm sorry about what happened to your daughter," she says. "I hope you find peace someday."

He answers with a nod.

She starts up the walkway to the porch and is going over the speech she's been preparing for Carmen when Malone calls her name. She turns back to see what he wants.

He gets out of the truck with the backpack, brings it over to her.

"Take this," he says. "It'll just get me into trouble."

"You're a good man," she says.

"No, I'm not," he says.

She heads for the house again. Her legs are shaking as she steps onto the porch. She presses the doorbell and hears it chime inside. Footsteps approach at a run, and the door flies open. Carmen is standing there, a phone pressed to her ear, her face streaked with tears.

"What have you done?" she screams.

"What do you mean?" Luz says.

"Isabel."

"What about her?"

"She's gone. They've taken her."

Luz's knees buckle, and she collapses onto the porch, struck down for her sins. The last thing she sees before she fades away is the sun shining red through the smog, an angry, all-seeing eye.

17

THE DODGE IDLES ON ALAMEDA, THE ROAD BLOCKED BY A PASSING
train. Isabel screams and kicks and slams the back of her head into
Jerónimo's chest as he watches the freight crawl past. He counts
its cars in an effort to calm himself. The train seems endless. It's
another trial, Jerónimo reflects, another misery to be endured,
like cold rain or a sleepless night.

His first thought was that they'd wait for Luz at Carmen's
place and grab her when she showed up to see her daughter. But
while talking to Carmen, he began to worry. If Luz went to the
police or got help from somebody else, he and Thacker would
be sitting ducks at the house. Better to take the kid and go, and
then use the little girl to force Luz to meet them at another location.

"We have to get the child out of here," he said to Carmen.
"Right now."

"What?" Carmen said.

"For her own safety."

"No."

"We're not going to hurt her," Jerónimo said. He turned to Thacker, who was standing against the refrigerator. "Do you have something to write with?" he asked him.

Thacker passed him a pen, and Jerónimo plucked a napkin from a wrought-iron dispenser on the table. He took out the phone El Príncipe gave him, pulled up its number, and wrote it on the napkin.

"When Luz gets here, have her call me," he said. "If she does what I tell her, I'll return the child to you."

"Please," Carmen said. She looked up at Thacker and pleaded with him in English. "Please don't take the girl."

"We're taking the girl?" Thacker said.

Jerónimo made a face to warn him to shut the fuck up, then grabbed the distraught woman's shoulder.

"Listen," he said. "The man I'm working for is an animal. If he doesn't get what he wants, he'll come to this house and kill you, your husband, your children, your whole family. Be smart, and let me handle this. Make sure I get Luz, and everything will be okay."

Carmen's eyes were shut tight. She twisted her head from side to side.

"In the living room," Jerónimo said. "Which one is she?"

"No," Carmen whispered.

"I'll take them both if I have to."

Carmen opened her eyes and inhaled deeply. "Don't scare them," she said. "Let me explain it."

"Fine," Jerónimo said, "but do it now."

The woman wiped her face with a towel lying on the counter, then stood and walked into the hall without another word. Jerónimo followed and motioned for Thacker to come too. He thought of his own children, how frightened they must have been when El Príncipe's men took them from their home. And now here he was, terrorizing another family for that son of a bitch.

He made himself smile as he entered the living room. Both girls looked up when Carmen said, "Did you see who's here, Isabel? It's your uncle, your mamá's brother."

The smaller child, the one with the Dora the Explorer T-shirt and bright red shorts, said, "My real mamá?"

"That's right," Carmen said. "This is her brother. He's come to take you to McDonald's."

Isabel gave Jerónimo the once-over, skeptical.

"My real mamá lives in Mexico," she said to nobody in particular.

"So do I," Jerónimo said. "And she told me to stop here and visit you."

Looking past him at Thacker, the little girl said, "Are you a policeman?"

Carmen clapped her hands. "Hurry, hurry," she said. "It's hamburger time. Put your shoes on."

Isabel kept her eyes on Thacker as she sat up and slipped her feet into a pair of pink flip-flops.

"Can Lizzy come?" she asked Carmen.

"Yeah! Yeah! Yeah!" the other girl chanted and started to put on her flip-flops too.

"No, Lizzy," Carmen snapped. "This is special time for Isabel and her uncle."

Lizzy sank back onto the couch, a disappointed scowl twisting her face.

Isabel hesitated, sensing that something was up.

"I don't want to go," she said quietly.

"What are you afraid of?" Carmen said. "This is your uncle,

192

like Uncle Jorge and Uncle Rafael. He's come a long way to see you."

Jerónimo squatted in front of the girl. "It's okay," he said to her. "We're gonna have fun."

"I want Lizzy to come," Isabel said.

"Not this time," Jerónimo said. He picked up the girl. She stiffened and began to sniffle, tears flooding her big brown eyes, and he hurried for the door to get her out to the truck before she broke down.

"Say good-bye to everyone," he chirped as he stepped onto the porch. "Tell them you'll be back soon."

Isabel didn't say anything, just sucked in a chestful of air. Jerónimo carried her across the street and was sliding into the Dodge when she cut loose with a high-pitched wail.

Thacker climbed in and started the engine.

"This is going too far," he said. "You never said anything about snatching a kid."

Isabel tried to squirm out of Jerónimo's grasp, but he held her tightly.

"I'm tempted to drop your ass off right here," Thacker continued. "That's what you deserve for springing this on me."

"You want your money?" Jerónimo said. "Shut up and drive."

Thacker is still fuming when the train finally clacks off down the tracks. He mutters to himself and bounces his knee. Jerónimo considers shooting him in the head and taking the truck, but there's still a chance a cop might come in handy today.

"Where to, genius?" Thacker says.

"Find a McDonald's," Jerónimo says.

Isabel is finally running out of steam. She's stopped struggling, and her sobs have tapered off into pitiful whimpers. Thacker reaches over and pats her leg. "That's a good girl," he says. From a compartment in the dash he fishes out a quarter and hands it to her. "Look at that," he says. "Candy money."

"You ready for a hamburger?" Jerónimo asks her.

She nods, staring down at the coin.

"You like French fries too?" he says.

"I like Happy Meals," she says.

"'Cause of the toy, right?" he says.

She nods again.

Thacker uses his phone to locate a McDonald's over on Santa Fe. By the time they get there, Isabel has calmed down enough to ask Thacker if she can have a second quarter, for her other hand. She insists on coming to the counter with Jerónimo and ordering her own food, not trusting him to make sure she gets a *girl* Happy Meal. She reminds him so much of Ariel it hurts.

He carries the tray to the booth where Thacker is waiting for them. The fat man grabs his Big Mac and fries and digs in. Jerónimo snaps together Isabel's toy for her—a yellow plastic flower that spins like a windmill—then unwraps his own burger. He's too keyed up to eat, though, can't take his eyes off the phone sitting on the table in front of him.

"Would it piss you off too much if I asked 'What now?'" Thacker says.

"We wait for the call."

"Driving around until it comes?"

Jerónimo ignores him. He hates everything about Thacker—his sunburned bald spot, the faggoty way he purses his lips when he sucks his straw, how he pretends to be thinking when he already knows what he's going to say.

The fat piece of shit picks a shred of lettuce off his shirt and pops it into his mouth. "Why don't we get a room?" he says. "Motel 6, Holiday Inn. We can beat the heat, screw our heads on straight. And the kid's gonna need a nap at some point. I mean, who knows when *mamacita*'s gonna make it to town."

Jerónimo picks up the phone, checks it, and puts it back down. *Ring, you fucker.* Taking a room will be an acknowledgment that this thing might drag on longer than he wants it to. He keeps picturing El Príncipe back in TJ, staring at the second hand of his Rolex and getting angrier every time it sweeps around the dial.

"We'll be more comfortable with a home base," Thacker continues. "I don't know about you, but I think a whole lot better with my feet up and a beer in my hand."

There'd also be less chance for trouble if they laid low. All it would take to blow everything is a cop pulling them over and asking the wrong questions. Jerónimo twirls a fry in a puddle of ketchup. He's surely tempting fate, wandering around in a city he doesn't know anymore.

"Find someplace close," he says.

Thacker takes out his phone and starts searching.

A skinny black woman darts around the restaurant, placing small cards on the tables. Jerónimo picks one up and examines it. *I am deaf,* it says. *Can you help me with a donation?* On the other side is the alphabet in sign language, little drawings of hands clutching and pointing.

He knew a deaf kid once. Bobby Escobar. They used to sneak behind the guy and yell as loud as they could, then bust up when he didn't react. For the longest time they thought he couldn't talk either, until one day he got into a fight with another boy and began to bray obscenities like an angry donkey. Months later you could still get a laugh by imitating his strangled fury. Jerónimo can't believe that after killing six men and hurting many others it's this childish cruelty that's stuck in his memory.

The woman makes her second pass through the dining room,

retrieving the unwanted cards and collecting a few handouts. Jerónimo reaches into his pocket and pulls out a dollar.

"What are you doing?" Thacker says.

"What do you care?" Jerónimo says.

"She's not deaf. It's a scam."

"Don't be an asshole."

"Don't be a chump."

Thacker calls to the woman.

"Hey!" he says. "You can hear me, can't you?"

Confused, she shows him one of the cards.

"It's okay, it's okay," Jerónimo says to her as he shoves the dollar bill into her hand. Thacker shakes his head and goes back to his phone.

"There's a Budget Inn a couple blocks away," he says.

Isabel is humming to herself and rocking back and forth. She's only eaten a few bites of her burger, is more interested in the toy. Jerónimo pushes the tray closer to her and says, "Sit still and finish your food."

She ignores him and continues to fidget.

"Hey!" Thacker shouts at her.

She looks up at the fat man, wide-eyed.

"Eat," he says. "That's an order."

Pouting, she reaches for her burger.

The floor is sticky under Jerónimo's feet. There's a sucking sound when he lifts one sneaker, then the other. He opens and closes his phone and wonders why Thacker can't chew with his mouth closed. A kid brings in a bunch of balloons and presents them to a girl working behind the counter. She blushes and giggles as the whole crew sings "Happy Birthday." Isabel stands on her seat to watch, and Jerónimo's patience runs out. He can't sit here any longer. He packs what's left of the girl's meal back into the box and says, "Let's go."

★   ★   ★

The motel is an anonymous stucco heap wedged in beside an off-ramp from the 91. Nothing good has ever happened here, no happy reunions or thrilling trysts, nothing nice. It's all husbands who've been kicked out, family members in town for funerals, and high-functioning dopers on weekend benders. Thacker pulls into the parking lot and backs into a space well away from the office.

"You check in," he says. "I'll watch the kid."

"Why me?" Jerónimo says.

"Number one, I don't have any money," Thacker says.

"I want to go home," Isabel whines.

"Shhhhh," Jerónimo says to her. "Carmen's coming to pick you up in a few minutes."

"Number two," Thacker says, "you fit in here better than I do."

Jerónimo can't tell if the fat man is trying to be funny when he says shit like this, or if he thinks he's getting away with something. Maybe soon he'll beat the answer out of him.

The Indian manning the office is asleep in his chair. Jerónimo slaps the counter to wake him. He writes the first numbers that come into his head where it asks for the truck's license plate on the registration card and leaves the deposit in cash.

"The swimming pool is closed," the Indian says.

"That's okay," Jerónimo says.

"Spa too. Broken pipe."

"Whatever."

Isabel is in the throes of another tantrum when Jerónimo returns to the truck. He watches it through the windshield like a movie with no sound, the girl red-faced and thrashing, her mouth stretched wide in a silent howl, Thacker sitting glumly behind the wheel, jaw set, knuckles white. The kid's fury spills out when Jerónimo opens the passenger-side door and slams into his chest like a two-handed shove.

"Hey, hey, hey," he says. "What's the problem?"

"I want—" Isabel sobs, "I want—" but is unable to get the rest out.

Thacker, meanwhile, slides out of his door and makes his escape.

"Give me the key," he says. "I raised two sons already, and that was enough daddying for a lifetime."

Malone pulls the beer from under the seat and opens a can as he watches Luz walk to the house. He's in no hurry to get back on the road. It's after three already, and traffic is going to be terrible all the way back to San Diego. The smart thing would be to go to a movie or find a bar and wait it out.

Luz is on the porch now. A woman opens the door, and she and Luz talk briefly. All of a sudden Luz goes down. Malone is out of the truck and halfway across the lawn before he thinks about what he's doing. The shotgun in the hands of the Mexican guy who steps out onto the porch brings him back to his senses, the shotgun that's pointed at his head.

"Stop!" the guy says in thickly accented English.

Malone jerks to a halt and raises his arms.

"I'm a friend of Luz's," he says. "It was me who drove her here."

"Go," the guy says. "Now."

"I just want to check on her," Malone says. "I saw her fall. Is she okay?"

The guy consults with the woman, who's now standing beside him on the porch. After a short discussion, he walks out onto the lawn, the gun still trained on Malone.

"Lift you shirt," he says.

Malone pulls his T-shirt up to his chest.

"Turn," the guy says.

Malone faces the street and shivers as the shotgun brushes his spine. The Mexican's breathing is loud in his ear as the guy pats the pockets of his shorts. Malone watches the pale ghost of a plane descend toward LAX.

"Okay," the guy says. "Come."

He trails behind Malone as they walk to the porch. Luz is lying on her back with her eyes closed. The woman is crouched beside her. She reaches out to nudge Luz as if trying to wake someone who's fallen asleep.

"Hey," she says. "Hey."

Malone goes down on one knee next to her.

"What happened?" he asks.

"I don't know," the woman says. "She fainted."

Malone can see that Luz is breathing, her chest expanding and contracting regularly. He lays a hand on her upper arm and gently squeezes it.

"Luz," he says. "Can you hear me?"

Her eyes flutter, then open. She inhales sharply upon seeing everyone staring down at her, and a sudden spasm of fear curls her into a ball. In the next instant, however, she seems to remember where she is and relaxes a bit.

"You passed out or something," Malone says. "Are you okay?"

Her reply is a desolate moan.

"They took Isabel," she says.

Malone looks to the woman for confirmation. She nods curtly, her expression grim.

"Fuck," Malone blurts, raising a hand to his forehead. He's at a loss about what to do next. "What's your name?" he says to the woman. "You're her aunt, right?" Turning to the man, he says, "Can I take her inside?"

The man and woman exchange looks, and the woman stands and opens the door wider.

"Only for a minute," she says. "We have children."

"Can you walk?" Malone asks Luz.

He can't make out whatever it is she murmurs, so he slips one arm under her knees and one under her shoulders and lifts her from the porch.

Inside the house he lays her on a couch in the living room. She's shaking all over. The man closes the door and stands in front of it, shotgun pointed at the floor. The woman watches Malone and Luz warily.

"I'm Kevin," Malone says, trying to put her at ease.

She ignores his outstretched hand. "I'm Carmen. This my husband, Bernardo."

Bernardo, a short, burly man wearing paint-stained coveralls and work boots, doesn't acknowledge Malone's nod in his direction.

A little girl sneaks into the living room and stands against the wall. She's hoping not to be noticed, but Malone points her out to Carmen, who says, "Back to your room."

"Where's Isabel?" the girl asks.

"To your room! *Ahora!*" Bernardo shouts.

Frustrated, the girl stomps off down the hallway. A second later a door slams hard enough to rattle the photos hanging on the wall.

"There's two more that'll be home from school soon," Carmen says to Malone. "You and her have to go now."

Luz sits up, startling them all. Tears glisten on her face, but there's a coldness in her eyes that spooks Malone.

"Who took my baby?" she says to Carmen.

"It was two of them," Carmen says. "The one who did the talking looked like a *narco*. The other was a white man in a uniform. At first they said you were in trouble and that they were here to protect Isabel, but then they admitted they'd been sent by someone. To get you."

"How long ago?"

"An hour, a little more. I tried to stop them, but they said if I didn't give them Isabel, they'd kill us all."

Bernardo shifts uneasily and looks out the peephole in the door. Malone feels the tension too, like all hell could break loose at any second.

"You have to call them, and then they'll bring Isabel back," Carmen says. She hands Luz a napkin. "Here's the number."

Luz gets up from the couch. "Where's your phone?" she says to Carmen.

"You're not calling from here," Carmen says. "Go somewhere else and deal with this."

"Fine," Luz says. Her eyes scan the couch and the floor. "Where are my bags?"

"On the porch," Carmen says.

Luz heads for the door. Carmen follows her.

"What the hell is wrong with you, dragging us into your shit?" Carmen says. "And Isabel. Your own daughter."

"I'm sorry," Luz says.

Bernardo unlocks the door and opens it to let her out. Sunlight floods the darkened room, and Malone loses sight of her until she steps forward and is silhouetted on the threshold.

"Did you really think you could come back and be her mom again?" Carmen says, one hand raised to shield her eyes from the glare. "You abandoned her, remember? Ran away and left her here all alone. What the hell do you even know about being a mom?"

Malone cringes. Val said something similar to him shortly after Annie was killed. He was in the backyard, drunk by the pool, which was where and how he spent his time in those days. More than a month had passed since the funeral, but it was still hard to walk, to breathe, to blink. He hadn't been back to work, hadn't even called his dad to discuss it, and was starting to think he never would.

Val came out to the pool deck carrying a drink of her own. She stood over him, her anger stronger than her sorrow that night, a newly kindled fire blazing inside a cold furnace. A drop of condensation fell from her tumbler and hit Malone square in the chest, but he didn't move, didn't speak, just kept watching a cloud overhead that was about to swallow the moon.

. "Tell me something," she said. "What made you think you'd be any kind of father?"

Even if he had an answer, she didn't want to hear it.

"I trusted you," she continued. "Annie trusted you. You were her daddy. You were supposed to protect her. You were supposed to keep her safe. But you didn't, and nobody's going to understand that. Oh, they'll say this, and they'll say that, but you're always going to be the man who let his baby get run over."

She was right, and he knew it, and that was the moment when he gave up. Gave up, stopped paddling, and sank like a stone. And soon, sooner than you'd think, he found himself among the bottom-feeders—the creeps and cutthroats, the scuttlers and the slime. Settling in with his bottle and his grief, he waited to drown, and it would have been so much easier if he had.

He walks to the door, needs some air, and almost bumps into Luz on the porch. She's holding out the backpack to Carmen.

"Take this," she says. "There's money in it."

"Money?" Carmen says. "Whose money? Are you *trying* to get us killed?"

Luz sets the pack on the welcome mat, next to the bags containing the doll and the stuffed bear.

"It's for Isabel," she says.

Carmen kicks the backpack, knocking it over.

"We don't want your money," she says.

Luz turns to Malone. "Can I use the old man's phone?" she says.

"It's in the truck."

She steps off the porch without another word and walks away across the lawn.

"Isabel will always have a home with us," Carmen calls after her, "but I don't ever want to see you again."

Malone picks up the backpack and follows Luz. When she gets to the truck, she yanks open the passenger-side door and climbs in. Malone sets the pack on the seat between them.

"You might need this," he says, sliding behind the wheel.

"Please get me away from here," Luz says.

They drive past a group of kids tossing a baseball. It's late afternoon, and the shadows of the trees have begun to creep toward the houses on the east side of the street. Luz stares straight ahead. Her face is blank, but her mind is working a mile a minute. When they come to a stop sign, Malone asks which way.

"Just park somewhere," Luz says.

He takes a left and continues until he hits a strip mall containing a Laundromat, a beauty salon, a check-cashing place, and a liquor store. He swings into the parking lot and finds a spot in the shade. They're looking into the window of the Laundromat, where a tall black man folds a pair of pants in front of a dryer, and a little Mexican boy pushes a little Mexican girl in a laundry cart.

"I should have known," Luz says, her voice flat, dead.

"Known what?" Malone says.

"He told me he could find me anywhere."

"Who are we talking about? Your boyfriend? Your husband?"

"The devil," Luz says. "The fucking devil."

"I'm trying to help you," Malone says.

"You can't help me," Luz says. "It was my husband who sent those men. He's a gangster, a *narco*. You know what that is?"

"A *narco*? Sure."

"You don't know anything. He . . . he beat me. He raped me. He threatened to kill me if I ever left him. But I wanted to be with Isabel." Luz breaks off here, takes a deep breath and turns away. "I stole some money from him and ran off. The maid tried to stop me, and one of my husband's bodyguards, and I killed them both."

"Jesus," Malone says.

"That's what I'm paying for now," Luz says. "That's why they have my baby."

Malone tugs on the collar of his shirt. His clothes feel like they're suffocating him.

"What'll happen to you when you go back?" he says.

Luz smirks at him like he's dense. "What do you think?"

He's not going to give her false hope, doesn't want to insult her that way. He can see in her eyes that she knows what she knows.

"Will you do me one favor?" she continues. "Will you stay with me until I find out where they want to meet and then drive me there?"

"I'll stay with you as long as you need me," Malone says.

She reaches over and lays a hand on his thigh.

"You can have the money back," she says. "And if you want, I'll . . ."

Her voice trails off, and the unspoken offer fills Malone with sadness. Putting his hand over hers to keep it from sliding any higher, he says, "Don't."

Luz pulls away, her embarrassment coming out as anger.

"Sorry," she snaps.

"There's nothing to be sorry about," Malone says. "It's just that you don't have to do that to keep me around."

Luz can't look at him while she processes this, stares out her window instead. Eventually she gets herself together and takes the napkin that Carmen gave her from the pocket of her hoodie.

"So can I use the phone?" she says.

Malone passes it to her, and she punches in the number written on the napkin. He gropes under the seat for the vodka, opens it, and has a swig. Inside the Laundromat, mama is mad at the kids playing with the cart. She lifts the girl out and sets her on the ground and swats at the boy, who laughs and runs away. Malone closes his eyes. He can't watch anymore. He's done with this world, has been for years. He closes his eyes and listens to the beeping of the phone as Luz calls up her doom.

18

THE SQUAWKING OF THE KID'S CARTOONS IS GIVING THACKER A headache, but what's he going to do? If he tells her to shut off the TV and take a nap, she'll start screaming again, and this is the quietest she's been since they grabbed her. She's happy as can be now, sitting cross-legged on the other bed, eating cold French fries and watching a bunch of monkeys or mice or whatever they are kick the shit out of each other.

Jerónimo, on the other hand, is wound tight as a speed freak at the tail end of a three-day run. He's hunched over the room's little table and looks like he's about to get on his knees and beg the phone sitting in front of him to ring. There's more than money driving him, that's for sure. He's got some sort of personal stake in seeing that this girl Luz gets to where she's wanted, and this worries Thacker, because when it gets personal is when people get stupid, and stupid people do stupid things, like kidnapping children.

He should have said *Fuck it* right then, should have slipped away. But that cash, man, it's so close now he can smell it, and if the Mex will listen to him, they can still snatch this out of the fire without burning their fingers. Everything will work out fine: Jerónimo will get Luz, he'll get the money, the kid will be returned to her aunt, and they'll all go their separate ways with a friendly wave and a hearty "Fuck you."

That's *if* he listens. Right now it looks like he's sitting over there coming up with a whole bunch of bad ideas, Plan B's and doomsday scenarios. Step one is to get him talking instead of thinking.

"So the phone rings," Thacker says, adjusting his pillow against the headboard of the bed he's lying on.

"What?" Jerónimo says.

"The phone rings, and it's—" he glances at Isabel and lowers his voice—"you know. What are you gonna say?"

Jerónimo hisses derisively and mumbles, "I'm not playing games with you."

"It can't hurt to figure out in advance how you're going to respond," Thacker says. "Things have already gotten a little out of hand, after all."

The Mex puffs up and crosses his arms over his chest. It pisses him off to have a gringo point out his mistakes. Too bad.

"Ring, ring," Thacker says.

"I'm gonna tell her to get her ass over here," Jerónimo says. "What do you think I'm gonna say?"

"With the money?" Thacker says.

"Yeah, yeah, with the money."

"But don't let her come up to the room."

"I won't."

"In fact, don't even mention the motel. Only tell her the corner."

Jerónimo gets up and steps over to the window, pulls the curtains aside. The room is on the second floor, off an open-air walkway. A no-name gas station and mini-mart skulk at the edge of an empty lot across the street.

"I'll meet her down there," Jerónimo says, pointing at the station. "I'll tell her to come alone and wait out in the open."

"That's good," Thacker says. "We can watch from up here to see if she tries to sneak in any backup."

"Right," Jerónimo says. He closes the curtains and returns to the table. "So relax."

"I *am* relaxed," Thacker says. "I just want to get it straight. So she does what you tell her and shows up when she's supposed to. Then what?"

"I go down and talk to her, and when I'm sure everything's cool, I signal you, and you put the little one in the truck and come pick us up."

"She might go nuts when she sees her daughter."

"I'll handle that."

"She might try to grab the kid and make a run for it or causes a commotion."

Jerónimo pulls his nine from his waistband. "Not with this between her legs," he says. "This'll keep her quiet while we drop the kid off and drive back to the border."

Isabel is watching them now, instead of the TV. She can't make out what they're saying, but she's old enough to know what a gun is, or at least to know that it's something to be afraid of. Thacker is about to tell Jerónimo to put the damn thing away when the phone on the table flashes and plays a song. Jerónimo snatches it up.

The conversation is a quick one and entirely in Spanish, but Thacker gets the gist. Luz asks Jerónimo who he is, and he tells her it's none of her business, just be at the gas station in an hour, her and the money. She wants to know how the kid is doing, and Jerónimo says, "Fine, as long as you follow orders." Then she says something like "Prove it," because after a lot of *no*'s, Jerónimo gets up from the table and walks over to Isabel.

"Say hello," he tells her, and holds out the phone.

"Hello?" Isabel warbles, close to tears. After listening to Luz for a few seconds, she says in English, "I want to go home."

Jerónimo pulls the phone away, makes a quiet threat, and ends the call.

"She get the message?" Thacker says.

"She got it," Jerónimo says.

"Good. Good deal."

Thacker settles back onto the bed and stares up at the stucco ceiling, acting like everything is cool even though it's not. Worry coils around his backbone like a jungle vine. He's always known he's not what you'd call a good man and admitted it to himself readily enough, but this, the kind of bad he's knee-deep in now, is way more serious than fucking with wetbacks and stealing pussy from whores. This shit is hard-core.

The air conditioner is roaring, but he can still feel the heat from outside pressing against the windows, the walls, the roof. Jerónimo peeks out between the curtains like Luz might already be waiting across the street, then turns to Isabel, who's lying on the bed, crying softly, her face buried in a pillow.

"What's the matter, *mija?*" he asks her.

"I want my aunt," comes the muffled response.

"You'll be back there soon," he says. "Right in time for dinner."

The room is closing in on Thacker. He gets up from the bed and grabs a Styrofoam cup off the table. When he goes to step outside, however, Jerónimo stops him with a hand on his arm.

"What's up?" the Mex says.

Thacker shows him his tin of Skoal. "Having a dip," he says. "Want one?"

Jerónimo takes his hand off him but says, "Leave the door open."

Out on the walkway, Thacker steps to the rail and tucks a bit of tobacco between his cheek and gum. A car exits the gas station across the street and speeds off, leaving behind a cloud of black smoke that hangs in the air for some time afterward. A man comes out of the market with a broom and a long-handled dustpan and begins sweeping up. Jerónimo's right; they'll have a clear view from here when Luz arrives—the parking lot, the surrounding streets. That's one thing in their favor.

But Thacker is still uneasy. The kid changes everything. With her around the possibility for disaster is huge. She gets hurt or, God forbid, killed, and the shit storm that will rain down on them will be fatal, as in Special Circumstances, as in Death or Life-Plus-One. He spits into the cup and scratches a new mole he discovered on his neck last week. *What the hell did you get into?* he asks himself.

Luz closes the phone and sets it on the dashboard. One hour, the man said. Don't be early, don't be late. He won't be the one to kill her, Luz is pretty sure of that. He'll take her back to Tijuana and let Rolando have his fun. She's also pretty sure he's not going to listen to any pleas for mercy. Rolando wouldn't have trusted this job to someone who could be swayed.

Perhaps a small request. Five minutes with Isabel. If she's going to believe that this guy will release the little girl when she turns herself over to him, she might as well also believe that he'll grant her five minutes to hold her and tell her how much she loves her. It's something to look forward to at least, something to keep her going.

The resignation she feels now is a relief after the agony that overwhelmed her when she learned they'd taken Isabel from Carmen. At first, she was so ashamed of putting her daughter in danger that all she wanted to do was die. But then it hit her that she was the only person who could save the girl, and that gave her the strength to finish this. Her escape attempt was a failure, but at least she'll have a chance to clean up the mess she made before she pays for crossing Rolando.

Malone is trying to pretend he's not watching her out of the corner of his eye. He looks sadder than she does. The man had a shotgun pulled on him and still hasn't cut and run. God sure picked a crazy one.

"He wants me to come to Central and Walnut in an hour," Luz says. "A gas station there."

"Do you know where that is?" Malone asks her.

"Right off the freeway, I think," she says.

"All right," he says and takes a swallow of vodka.

His face ripples like the surface of a pond disturbed. He's not done yet, Luz can tell. He's got more to say. He caps the bottle and slides it under the seat, straightens his shirt and brushes back his hair.

"I know the cops are out of the question," he begins.

"Stop," Luz says.

"It's just, there has to be—"

He needs to leave it alone. Now.

"I stole from him and killed his people," Luz says. "I made him look stupid. He's not American, okay, he's Mexican, and for a woman to do that, he's not gonna quit until he gets back at me."

"What about someone above him?" Malone says. "He has a

boss, and that's the guy you need to talk to. You go to him with the money and make your case, tell him how this asshole treated you and why you did what you did."

"They've got my baby," Luz says. "I'm going to do whatever they want."

Malone strokes the stubble on his chin and turns away from her.

"I wish I was smarter," he says. "Smart enough to come up with something else."

Luz wishes she was smarter too. She starts going over things she might have done differently when it came to planning her escape, and in seconds her mind is revving toward panic. She concentrates on her surroundings—a woman unloading a washing machine in the Laundromat, a stray dog trotting past, the little girl who tries to pet it and the old man who warns her not to, the way the reflection of the parking lot in the window of the liquor store pulses every time the door opens and closes—but it doesn't help.

She tries to think of somewhere quiet nearby where they might wait out the hour left to her. The answer is like a kick in the stomach when it comes, and she rouses Malone and tells him there's one more place she'd like to see before he drops her off.

They get onto Greenleaf and go west. The sun is low enough now that it's shining right into their eyes. Even with her visor down, Luz has to squint through her lashes to see the road ahead. They drive past the entrance to the cemetery the first time and end up circling the block to get back to the gate.

SACRED GROUND, 15 MPH a sign orders. Malone cruises slowly past the graves while Luz tries to find the spot she's looking for. She remembers a tree and a fountain. It's been almost four years, though, and a whole lot of life since she was last here. The best she can do is get them what she thinks is close.

"Do you want me to wait in here?" Malone asks when she opens her door.

"It's okay," she says. "You can come if you want."

He gets out of the truck, too, and follows her up a hill toward a sickly pine with downcast needles. The ground is covered with more weeds than grass, but at least they keep the place mowed. The markers in this section are all identical granite rectangles that lie flat on the ground, row after row of them. There's enough room on each for the name and dates and maybe a brief tribute or a small etching of a cross or a lily.

Luz moves from stone to stone, searching for Alejandro's. She passes a baby's marker decorated with a drawing of Minnie Mouse—*Camilla Washington, May 19, 2006–January 5, 2007*. A wilted bouquet sits on Daniel Martinez's grave, and someone has left a New Testament for Donita Hughes, *Beloved Mother, Sister, and Friend*. Luz is jealous of them all. Nobody will remember her when she's gone, and there'll be no grave to visit.

She comes to the end of one row and moves on to the next. Malone trudges along behind her, head down. He's thinking about his little girl, Luz knows. After being with him less than a day, she already recognizes the face he gets when the memories come blacking. Three ravens circle overhead, their ugly croaks like curses. Luz almost trips, glaring up them, and then there it is, right at her feet.

Alejandro Delgado Gonzalez, May 19, 1991–October 5, 2009. His nickname's on it too: Smiley. Luz is sad to see it again, but the sadness is different now, after so much time, mellower but truer. For a month after he died she came here every couple of days, her and baby Isabel. She'd bring a boom box to play her and Alejandro's favorite CDs—Morrissey, Selena, RBD—and sit on the grass beside the stone and weep until her eyes burned and her chest ached. Her grief was real back then, but she realizes she was crying mostly for herself, for her loss. The tears that sting her eyes today are for a sweet, big-eared boy with a silver tooth and the softest lips in the world.

Malone is standing beside her. "Who is it?" he asks.

"Isabel's daddy," she replies.

"So young."

"Something was wrong with his heart."

It's true. One day he just fell down dead. He was the first and last boy Luz ever loved, the embodiment of so many words that have lost their meaning for her since then: good, kind, honest. He lived on the same street as Carmen and her family, but Luz barely noticed him during her first hectic years in L.A. Thinking about it later, she wondered if that's how it was when it was real. You didn't crash into each other and hang on for dear life the first time you met. Instead, you came together slowly, a long succession of revelations and reassessments gradually closing the gap.

How clearly she remembers some of the things that made her love him. There was the time she watched him comfort his little sister after she'd fallen off her bicycle, rocking and tickling her until she laughed away her tears. There was his voice when he tried to sing a song he knew Luz liked, even though they were still months away from holding hands.

And she'll never forget the morning they were walking to school with all the other kids and the two of them fell behind because they were talking so much and the sun hit his green eyes exactly right and whatever had been smoldering between them for so long finally burst into bright, billowing flame.

They were inseparable after that. If Luz wasn't at his house, he was at hers. Carmen was as crazy about him as Luz was, and

Alejandro's parents treated Luz like a daughter. None of them were happy when Luz got pregnant, but her and Alejandro's love was like a steamroller, flattening any opposition. In the end, both families swallowed their disappointment and did what they could to help. Isabel was born with Alejandro's eyes and Luz's mouth. The nose they couldn't figure out.

Three months later Alejandro went to play basketball with some friends and didn't come home. He collapsed on the court and was gone before he hit the ground. The doctor told Luz he didn't feel any pain, but how could he know that?

And so she was alone again. An eighteen-year-old illegal with a new baby. The daughter of a whore with her back against the wall. She's glad Alejandro can't see what a mess she made of everything.

She crouches to brush a leaf from the stone and lets her fingers trace the letters carved there. Malone shifts from one foot to the other, uncomfortable.

"I'm gonna wait over there," he says, pointing to the fountain.

Luz says a prayer for Alejandro and another for Isabel. *Keep her safe a little longer.* Something is wrong. She's always believed in a God who listens to the pleas of the wretched, but today she feels like she's talking to herself, like the words are going nowhere. He's turned away from her, she realizes, even Him.

She walks to the fountain. It's not working, hasn't in a long time. Four angels stand back-to-back blowing trumpets. The pool surrounding them doesn't have any water in it, only dead leaves, a Burger King cup, and a condom wrapper. Malone is staring at the freeway in the distance, where ten lanes of cars and trucks crawl along under a noxious pall. To the west a few wispy clouds are starting to color as the sun drops lower.

"I better get going," Luz says.

"Whenever you're ready," Malone says.

"I'm ready."

On the way back to the truck, Malone suddenly reaches out and wraps an arm around Luz. Her first instinct is to pull away, but she stops herself, and then, just like that, folds into Malone so that he's supporting her as they walk. She says sorry, and he says it's okay, and it feels so good to be propped up for a second, to not have to bear everything by herself.

19

THIS LAST HOUR WILL BE THE WORST. EVEN THOUGH JERÓNIMO
trusts that Luz is going to show up, he still can't relax. He's been
to the window three times in the last five minutes to check the
gas station. Thacker is lying on one of the beds again, pretending to be asleep, and Isabel has settled, gone back to watching
TV. Jerónimo picks up a pen from the table and scribbles on a
Budget Inn scratchpad. He draws a star and a crescent moon, a
spaceship, and a dwindled Earth.

The cell phone ringing almost does him in. He sees that it's
El Príncipe and steps out of the room to take the call.

"You got my wife?" El Príncipe says.

"She's on her way here," Jerónimo says.

"So the answer is no."

"She's coming," Jerónimo says. "I have something she wants."

"What's that?"

"Her daughter."

"Daughter?" El Príncipe says. "She doesn't have a daughter."

"Yeah, she does," Jerónimo says. "About four years old. She's been living with her aunt up here."

El Príncipe's silence pleases Jerónimo. It feels good to catch him off guard. But the bastard recovers quickly. "I knew it," he says. "I always sensed it."

"Luz was coming to see her," Jerónimo says. "I got to the aunt's house first and took the girl, so now she has to come to me."

"What balls," El Príncipe says. "That's thinking like a man."

"Once I have her, I'll take the kid back to the aunt and bring Luz to you."

"The sneaky fucking bitch," El Príncipe says, then goes silent again.

A woman emerges from a room on the first floor and walks to the ice machine. Jerónimo pulls back so she won't see him if she happens to look up. Thacker was right about things getting sloppy. It's time to tighten up and make a clean getaway.

"I have an idea," El Príncipe says.

"What?" Jerónimo says.

"Bring me the daughter as well."

The words jolt Jerónimo like a raw electric shock. He holds the phone away from his mouth, afraid some noise coming from him will give him away. A few seconds pass before he feels calm enough to resume the conversation.

"Is that smart?" he says. "Involving a child?"

"I don't know about smart, but it's what I want," El Príncipe says. "So do it."

"But, *jefe,* the kid has no part in this."

"Are you—" El Príncipe begins, but Jerónimo keeps talking.

"You'll have Luz, and she's the one you're pissed at," he says. "Taking the little girl will only lead to trouble."

"Hey, hey, hey," El Príncipe says, raising his voice to cut Jerónimo off. "Where were you yesterday?"

"Where was I?" Jerónimo says.

"Where were you before I had my guys come get you?"

"I was in La Mesa," Jerónimo says.

"That's right!" El Príncipe shouts. "In fucking prison. And where was I? In a fucking mansion. So you tell me, you piece of shit, who's smarter, you or me?"

"All I'm saying is that you should have mercy on an innocent child," Jerónimo says.

"And your family, do they deserve mercy too?" El Príncipe says.

Jerónimo closes his eyes and grits his teeth. It's all over. The son of a bitch has won. "Of course," he says.

"So here's your choice: Save the whore's kid, or save your own."

"I understand."

"Make sure you do, because the next time you defy me, I'll beat your son to death in front of his mother. I'll break every bone in his body. And then I'll think of something to do to your daughter."

"You'll have the woman and the girl by midnight."

Jerónimo ends the call and drops into a squat, his back pressed against the rough stucco wall. He glances at his watch. Still forty-five minutes to go until Luz is supposed to arrive. He reaches into his pocket for the necklace he took from Irma's jewelry box. Opening it, he stares down at the faces of his children. Then he makes a fist and punches himself in the head once, twice, three times. He doesn't feel a thing. That's good. That means he's almost there. Not his own man for the next few hours, but another man's monster instead.

★   ★   ★

Thacker opens one eye when the Mex pokes his head into the room and asks him to come outside. He gets up off the bed and tucks in his shirt, wonders what the hell has gone wrong now. Stepping onto the walkway, he pulls the door shut so the kid can't hear them.

"Things have changed," Jerónimo announces. "The little girl's coming too."

"What?" Thacker says. "To the border?"

"You heard me."

"You're batshit."

"It's not my decision," Jerónimo says. "It's what the guy I'm working for wants."

"Well, he's batshit then," Thacker says.

Jerónimo shrugs. "He's the girl's father, and he wants to raise her over there."

"Her father, huh?"

"It's against the law what Luz did, bringing her up here and giving her to her aunt. It's kidnapping."

"Yeah?"

"My man's got papers and everything to prove it."

Thacker can tell the guy is lying but rolls with it because there's nothing to stop this *ese* from cutting his throat and taking his truck if he thinks he's turned against him. Hell, the way things have spun now, he might end up killing him anyway, to get rid of a witness.

"You know what?" Thacker says. "Fuck it. I'm just the driver."

"That's right," Jerónimo says.

"I'll take you and whoever back, get my money, and go."

"That's all you got to do."

"That's all I'm *gonna* do."

"Then we got no problems," Jerónimo says.

Thacker follows him back into the room, silently weighing his options. If he sticks to the original script, transporting Jerónimo, Luz, and the kid to the border, there's a good chance he'll wind up dead by the side of some dirt road. These people are fucking animals, he realizes, fucking apes, and he was nuts to think he could trust them. So what if he bugs out then, first chance he gets, and leaves Jerónimo stranded here? That'd be fine except he'd be giving up the money, and he really, really wants that money.

The Mex walks into the bathroom and closes the door. A few seconds later the shower goes on. The little girl is asleep now, curled around a pillow at the foot of the bed, one arm thrown over her eyes. Thacker looks at her, then toward the bathroom. A new scheme begins to come together in his head. He's not clear on the details yet, but if it's going to work at all, he has to get moving.

He takes his gun belt off the chair and buckles it around his waist, checks his pockets for wallet and keys, pulls on his hat. Next, he needs to put Jerónimo out of commission in order to give himself a decent head start.

He goes to the bathroom door, shouts "Sorry" as he's pushing it open.

"What the fuck?" Jerónimo yells from the other side of the opaque shower curtain.

"I gotta piss something fierce," Thacker says.

"Hurry your ass up."

"I will, I will."

Thacker stands in front of the toilet and scans the bathroom. Jerónimo's clothes are in a heap on the floor, his gun and phone on top. Swiftly and silently Thacker gathers everything up and carries it out, closing the door behind him. Just then, Isabel, on the bed, sighs and wiggles into a more comfortable position, the very image of the goddamn lamb in the lion's den. Thacker's scalp is tingling as he picks her up, lays her over his shoulder, and hurries to the front door.

The sky is on fire when he slips out of the room and jogs for the stairs. His foot hits funny coming off the last step, and he staggers right, then left, before recovering his balance. Dashing across the parking lot, he points his remote at the truck and presses the unlock button with his thumb. He's breathing hard by the time he clambers behind the wheel, all the fat in his belly pushing up against his lungs.

Isabel opens her eyes as he's strapping her into the passenger seat, but then her head lolls to the side, and she's asleep again. His boys used to sack out like that. A war wouldn't have roused them. He sticks his key in the ignition and glances up at the room. No sign of the Mex. So far, so good. Sometimes one smart move can make up for ten bad ones. And with this new plan, he might even still come out ahead today.

When the fat man finishes pissing and leaves him alone again, Jerónimo shuts off the hot water and lets the cold pound his back and shoulders. El Príncipe's phone call started his pulse throbbing in his temples, and he jumped into the shower desperate for another sensation besides rage and helplessness. The frigid drenching helps some, but he's still close to snapping when he cuts off the stream, draws aside the shower curtain, and steps out of the tub.

Something's wrong. His clothes are missing, the money in the pocket, the gun, the phone. Yanking open the bathroom door, he sticks his head into the other room. Thacker is gone, and so is the little girl. If they get away, it's a death sentence for Irma and the kids.

Jerónimo is almost to the front door before he remembers that he's naked and goes back for a towel. He bursts onto the walkway and leans over the rail. The spot where the truck was parked is empty. He hurries down the stairs and walks the entire lot, then goes to the corner to check the streets. There's no sign of the Dodge, but a passing car honks, and the teens inside hoot and shout insults at him, a tattooed loco wrapped in a towel, dripping wet, barefoot, ridiculous.

Back in the room, a quick survey of what he has left doesn't make him feel any better about his situation. What good are a cheap watch, a pair of socks, and some sneakers? Luz will be here in half an hour. He's going to have to call for help. The only people he knows around here who'll be able to get him what he needs are his old Inglewood homeboys, the *vatos* he ran with as a kid. It's been eight years since he last spoke to any of them, but he's got nowhere else to turn.

He sits on the bed and picks up the room phone. The first number that comes into his head is Ruben's, who they used to call Looney. He was in on the robbery Jerónimo went down for in 2000 but didn't get nabbed, and Jerónimo, being a righteous homie, didn't roll over on him. It takes a few calls to track him down. Jerónimo talks to the dude's mom, his brother, and his old lady before getting through to Looney himself.

"Apache?" Looney says. "I heard you was dead down in Mexico."

"Not me, *ese,* I'm still kicking," Jerónimo says. "I've been working for someone in TJ, and I'm up here in Compton doing a thing for him."

"Oh yeah?" Looney says. Jerónimo hears the wariness in his voice. "And you got close to the old 'hood and decided to call me?"

"Truthfully, man, I need you to do me a solid," Jerónimo says.

Looney pauses. There's a TV playing wherever he is, and a couple of kids jabbering in the background. Jerónimo runs his finger over the bedspread, tracing the arc of a stitch, and waits for the man to compose a response.

"I'm not really down with too much dirt no more," Looney says. "I'm an electrician, you know, union and shit."

"If it wasn't serious, *ese,* I wouldn't be bothering you, believe that," Jerónimo says.

"Yeah, but still . . ."

"Yeah, but still I did two years for jacking that motherfucker with you, took 'em like a man. You could have been in there with me real easy."

A siren spirals past outside the motel, and Jerónimo puts his hand over the phone so Looney won't hear it and get any more spooked than he already is. The dude sighs and clears his throat.

"This is fucked up, holmes," he says.

"Life's fucked up," Jerónimo says.

"What do you need?"

"A car and a *cuete*—any kind."

"Is that all?" Looney scoffs.

"And some clothes. Pants, a shirt. I'll send you money to cover it when I get back to TJ, to more than cover it."

"Check's in the mail, huh?"

"How soon can you get here?"

"How soon do you need me to get there?"

"How about now. How about right this minute."

Looney chuckles. "Come on, man," he says. "Compton? Fucking Friday, fucking rush hour?"

"I know, I know," Jerónimo says.

"Gonna be at least an hour or two."

"Quick as you can. I appreciate it."

"Yeah, yeah," Looney says.

Jerónimo gives him the address of the motel and hangs up. He has twenty minutes to figure out what to do about Luz, how to approach her when she arrives at the gas station and get her back to the room. He checks the bathroom again, to make sure the gun is really gone, then looks around for something else to use as a come-along.

The pen he was drawing with earlier could work as a shank with some sharpening on a patch of concrete, or what about a piece of the bed frame, brandish it like a club. The trick will be running up on her fast enough that all she gets is a glimpse of whatever he's carrying before he grabs her and hustles her across the street. She won't be paying much attention anyway, worked up as she'll be about her kid.

Malone pulls over in front of the gas station where he's supposed to drop Luz. In the end there isn't much to say. Good-bye. Good luck. He wonders if he should add something else, an acknowledgment of her courage in accepting her fate, but what good is that going to do? And maybe the commonplace phrases they exchange are a source of comfort to her, a well-marked path through hostile terrain where any deeper sentiment would only complicate matters.

He offers to wait nearby in case she needs him for anything, but she's adamant that he leave right now, worried about upsetting the men holding Isabel. He reaches for her hand at the exact moment she pulls it away to grab the backpack, and then she slides out of the truck and slams the door. It's not as easy as he'd like it to be to drive away and leave her standing on the sidewalk. He follows a sign for the freeway, takes a corner, and she's gone.

There's drinking to be done, but he doesn't want to do it here. He'll drive up to Palos Verdes, find a cliff overlooking the ocean, a patch of sand to pass out on. The phone rings as he's approaching the ramp to the 91. Day is making its last stand against night, and the battle lights up the sky.

"Hello," he says.

"Who's this?" the man on the other end says.

"Who do you want?"

"Are you the guy that was with Luz?"

Malone drives past the on-ramp and swerves into the parking lot of a storage facility tucked beneath the freeway.

"Could be," he says.

"Put her on."

"I just dropped her off."

"At the gas station?"

"That's where you said, right?"

"Go back and get her. Quick."

"What do you mean?" Malone doesn't know what's going on, but he's already turning the truck around.

"The Mexicans were gonna kill the kid, so I took her," the man on the phone says. "And now all I want is the money Luz is carrying. If she hands it over, she can have the girl."

"Where are you now?" Malone says. He makes a dangerous left and crosses three lanes of traffic to an angry chorus of horns.

"I'll call later with that. If she's not at the station, go to the motel across the street. Room 215. The Mex is unarmed, but you'll have to fight him."

Malone drops the phone onto the seat and concentrates on driving. He swings onto Central, tires squealing, and sees that Luz is still on the sidewalk. As he speeds toward her, a shirtless *vato* with a towel wrapped around his waist comes jogging out of the parking lot of the motel. Malone palms the truck's horn, and both Luz and the *vato* turn to look, the *vato* pausing in the middle of the street. This moment of hesitation is enough to allow

226

Malone to steer the truck between them. He screeches to a stop, the vodka bottle rolling out from under the seat.

"Get in back!" he yells out the window at Luz.

"No," she protests. "I told you—"

"He doesn't have Isabel!"

The *vato* in the towel, a big, brawny dude with tattoos twining over his chest and arms, moves to the front of the truck and points a gun at Malone through the windshield. Malone ducks behind the wheel and shouts again to Luz.

"Come on!"

She slings the backpack into the bed of the truck, then clambers over the side herself. The *vato* drops his gun and runs toward her. He grabs one of her feet, but she kicks it loose and scrambles away from him.

Malone presses the gas pedal to the floor. The *vato* runs alongside the pickup, trying to climb in. He loses his grip as the vehicle gains speed, trips, and sprawls onto the asphalt. Malone rounds the corner and leaves him behind.

"No way!" Malone yells. "No fucking way!" He lets out a whoop and bounces on the seat. The streetlights all flicker to life at once and stretch on and on, as far as he can see, a bright, safe passage to somewhere.

20

Luz is stuck in midair, doesn't know whether to fly or fall. She climbed into the truck in a panic when she saw the half-naked man charging her, not even sure what Malone was yelling, only hearing Isabel's name. She needs Malone to explain what's going on so she can be sure she did the right thing by leaving.

She keeps her head down as he whips around one corner, then a second, slinging her from one side of the bed to the other. He finally comes to a stop on a deserted street lined with dark warehouses hunkered behind chain link and concertina wire.

"All clear," he calls out.

She grabs the backpack and steps over the tailgate onto the bumper, then down to the ground. A light goes on in the cab when she opens the door, but she doesn't get in. She wants to hear the story first.

"I got a call as I was driving away," Malone says. "The man on the phone—I think it was the cop—said that he had Isabel, that he'd taken her from the other guy, and that I should go back and pick you up."

"The cop has Isabel?" Luz asks.

"So he said."

"Where, then? Where is she?"

"We didn't have time to get into it. He's supposed to call back later. But listen: He also said you can have her if you give him the money."

"The money."

"He claims that's all he wants."

Luz would like to rejoice at this news, but she's still skeptical. Anybody can say anything, and nothing's real until it happens. She's not sure she can stand being disappointed again.

"Why would he do that?" she says. "Why would he take Isabel?"

Malone looks uncomfortable. "That's the part I didn't want to tell you," he says.

"Why?" Luz demands. "What happened?"

Malone grimaces and bends forward in his seat, stalling.

"What?" Luz says. "Tell me."

"He said he took her because the Mexicans were going to kill her," Malone finally says in a rush.

Luz reels at the words. Rolando. The bastard. The fucking bastard.

"But she's safe now," Malone continues. "She's safe, and you're going to get her back."

"Are you sure?" Luz says.

"I'm sure."

He's not, though, Luz realizes. He's just being nice. He doesn't know any more than she does about what's going on.

A car with one working headlight turns onto the street, and Malone tenses up.

"We should go," he says.

Luz has a bad feeling too. She climbs into the truck and closes the door. The rusted-out Bonneville draws nearer, and she reaches into the backpack for the .45. The car slows to a crawl as it passes, and two hard black faces size them up. Malone twists the key. The truck's engine strains mightily but fails to start.

The Bonneville continues to the next intersection, swings around, and cruises back toward them. Luz watches it approach like a marauding shark in her side mirror while Malone keeps cranking the ignition and pumping the gas pedal. When the truck finally comes to life, he jams it into gear and quickly pulls away from the Bonneville, blowing stop signs and screaming around corners until Luz tells him it's okay, they're not following.

When they get back onto a wide, well-lit street, Luz makes him go over the phone call again word for word as he remembers it.

"Did he say when he'd call?" she asks.

"Nope, just that he would," Malone replies.

"Why can't I call him?"

Malone slides the phone across the seat. "The number's blocked. He's being real careful."

Luz picks up the phone to check for herself.

"Let's go somewhere," Malone says. They pass a Denny's. "What about there? You want a milkshake? I want a milkshake."

Luz won't be able to eat anything but says okay, sure, because sitting in the restaurant will be safer than parking on the street someplace where trouble might find them again.

The sun is down but heat is still rising off the asphalt of the parking lot. Luz hugs the backpack to her chest as they walk to the entrance. She's not letting it out of her sight until she hands it over in exchange for Isabel. Stepping into the icy brightness of the restaurant is like crossing over into another dimension. She shivers at the sudden chill and squints against the fluorescents.

The woman who seats them bustles and chirps like a little bird, and the server who comes to take their order is smiling at a secret joke—a mean one, to judge by the tilt of his lips. Malone gets a chocolate shake, and Luz orders a Coke. Malone asks if she wants to share fries, and it's easier to say yes than no.

"Not the wavy-cut ones," Malone says to the server. "The regular kind."

Their booth is against a window that looks out onto the parking lot. Luz can see her face in the glass and extends a finger to touch the circles under the reflection's eyes. She'll be glad when she's not pretty anymore.

"Once you have Isabel, you need to go someplace nobody knows you," Malone says. "Don't tell your aunt, don't tell your friends, don't tell anybody. I've got a feeling these guys are going to keep looking for you for a while."

"Don't worry," Luz says. "We're going somewhere I haven't even thought of yet."

"You can have the truck, but I'd advise dumping it as soon as you can."

"That's okay."

"What's okay?"

"I don't know how to drive."

"Huh."

"It's no big thing," Luz says. "We'll take the bus."

Malone raises his hand to silence her. "No, now, see, keep even that to yourself," he says. "I don't want to know anything."

The server brings their drinks, still with that smirk on his face. Luz peels the wrapper off her straw and has a sip of her Coke.

The phone is on the table. She picks it up to make sure there's a signal.

A man and woman are arguing over a parking space outside, their voices coming muffled through the window.

"I was waiting for that."

"You passed it by."

"I did not. I was waiting."

"I didn't see you."

"So open your fucking eyes."

"Open *your* eyes, bitch."

Luz resists the urge to duck. It's as bad up here as it is in Tijuana, people turning on each other over the smallest things.

"Are you from L.A.?" she says to Malone.

"Orange County," he says. "Anaheim Hills."

"That's like all rich over there, isn't it?"

Malone shrugs as he spoons whipped cream into his mouth. "They'd say middle class."

"I don't trust rich people," Luz says.

"I don't trust anybody," Malone says.

"Me neither," Luz says.

"Not even you," Malone says with a smile.

Luz smiles too. "Right," she says. "Not even *you*."

For a second she feels like a normal person sitting in a restaurant, joking with a friend. For an instant it seems like another way the world could be. But then Malone goes dark, sucker punched by the past again, and her arm brushes the backpack lying on the seat beside her, the one containing stolen money and a gun, and she realizes there's no hope of normal ever. Even the server knows it. He returns with Malone's fries, still wearing his strange, scornful grin, and the reason comes to Luz like a curtain whisked away: He sees right through them.

★　　　★　　　★

Thacker gets on the 91 and keeps driving until his blood pressure drops and he's breathing normally. Somewhere around Anaheim he starts feeling like he's far enough from Jerónimo that the Mex isn't going to catch up to them. The kid is awake now and a little fussy, so when he sees the giant stucco castle up ahead, King John's Fun Zone, it seems like the perfect place to make the exchange with her mom.

He takes the next exit and works his way back on surface streets. The castle is painted white but dyed an ethereal blue by the floodlights shining up at it. Thacker has to wait to get into the busy parking lot. That's fine. He wanted a place where they'd be part of a crowd. Isabel is wide-eyed as he pulls into an empty slot.

"Are we going here?" she says.

"I don't know," he says. "Do you want to?"

She nods happily, understanding that he's joking with her.

"Okay, then," he says. "But you have to promise to be good."

"I promise."

She tries to free herself from the seatbelt, but he tells her to hold on, there's something he needs to do.

Reaching behind the seat, he brings up Jerónimo's belongings. He gets out, walks around to the back of the truck, and sets the stuff in the bed. A quick search of the guy's pants turns up a roll of twenties and hundreds. He pockets the money, then unlocks the toolbox mounted to the cab and lifts out the duffel bag he keeps his civilian clothes in. He takes off his gun belt and uniform shirt and puts on a clean T-shirt, a shoulder holster, and a windbreaker to cover it.

After stowing the Mex's gun and clothes in the box, he moves around to help Isabel out of the truck. She won't let him carry her, says she wants to walk. He says okay as long as she holds his hand. She grabs his index finger and sets off across the lot, dragging him behind her.

The castle is the centerpiece of a complex containing a mini-golf course, a go-kart track, and an immense arcade. Twenty-five years ago it might have been something, but now the artificial turf is worn and wrinkled, the video games are out of date, and the stucco needs patching and paint. Still, it draws sullen teenagers with nowhere else to go and younger children whose parents are lured by bargain birthday packages.

Thacker pauses as soon as they enter. The screams of a hundred kids zip around the cavernous space like ricocheting bullets, and he needs a second to get his bearings. Isabel isn't having it. She yanks him into the midst of the unruliness and makes a beeline for the first flashing lights she sees.

"I want to do this," she says, pointing to a game played as best Thacker can tell by jumping up and down on an illuminated platform in time to tinny music. Two oriental boys with spiked hair are bouncing on it now, and a long line of other kids wait for turns.

"Let's golf first," Thacker says. "We'll come back to this later."

He pays for the putters with the Mex's money.

The course is outside, away from the worst of the noise. There's still the muted rattle of go-kart engines and the rumble of the freeway on the other side of a ten-foot sound wall, but at least here Thacker can string two thoughts together. He and Isabel stand at the first hole, waiting for the family in front of them to finish up. Isabel keeps swinging her club at a trashcan, and Thacker keeps telling her to stop.

"When am I going home?" she says.

"Soon," he says.

"Is this for my birthday?"

"How'd you guess?"

When the family moves on, he lets Isabel chase her ball around the Astroturf while he uses Jerónimo's phone to call Luz.

"Hello?" she says.

"Hey there, sexy," he says. He's remembering how she looked when he pulled them over at the border. Thin, with long, black hair and a cute mole on her lip. A hot *mamacita*. Just his type. "You're still alive."

"That's right," she replies.

"What's up with Jerónimo?"

"The guy at the gas station? We got away from him."

"You sure about that?"

"He was laying in the street, all messed up."

"And my money?"

"It's right here."

Thacker smiles. Hard to believe, but it's all working out. "So come get your kid," he says.

"Tell me where."

Isabel hits her ball too hard, and it ends up lost in the bushes. She turns to Thacker for help. He tosses her his ball to play with.

"It's this place called King John's off the 91," he says into the phone. "Big white castle. You can't miss it."

"I know where it is," Luz says.

"We'll be playing mini-golf. Look for the Border Patrol cap."

"We'll be there soon."

"We?" Thacker says. "No way, baby doll. I only want to see you and the money."

"That's what I meant. Me."

"I'm serious. If I even suspect you're fucking around, the deal is off, and your little girl pays the price."

"I'll be alone. Don't worry."

"Oh, I won't. I'm not the worrying type."

Thacker ends the call and watches Isabel kick the ball into the cup, then stand there waiting for something to happen.

"That's it, kiddo," he says to her. "How many strokes?"

He wouldn't mind being a grandpa someday, if he ever manages to get back into his sons' good graces. They're full of Sunday school superiority right now, but life will kick them in the ass soon enough, and then they can all sit down in the dirt and talk like men.

A big pink unicorn guards the second hole. Isabel swings away. A security guard approaches, a tall skinny Mexican with a shaved head and baggy uniform. *What the fuck is this about?* Thacker wonders.

"How's it going?" the guard says.

"Oh, you know," Thacker says. "Trying to stay cool in this heat."

"You Border Patrol?"

"How'd you guess?"

"Your hat," the guard says, touching the bill of his own cap. "I'm thinking about applying."

"Is that so."

"I'm finishing my B.S. in criminal justice at Argosy next semester, and my professor says I shouldn't have any problem getting hired once I got that."

"He's steering you right. We're always looking for qualified people."

"Where you stationed? San Ysidro?"

"Campo," Thacker says, then wishes he hadn't.

"I might go to Arizona," the guard says. He's doing his damnedest to grow a mustache, but getting only fuzz. "My girlfriend's family is there and everything, and it's cheaper to live, too."

"Sounds like a plan," Thacker says. Isabel is trying to climb onto the unicorn's back. "Get down," he calls to her.

"I want to play Dance Dance now," she says.

"Looks like we're going inside," he says to the guard. "Good luck to you."

"You never know, maybe we'll see each other on patrol or something someday," the guard says.

"You never know," Thacker says. Isabel is already skipping toward the arcade, and he heads off in pursuit. He's pretty sure the guy is just some idiot who's genuinely excited about joining the patrol, but all the same, he's nervous. He doesn't need him hanging around when Luz gets here.

Jerónimo lies on one of the beds in the motel room. He's holding a damp washcloth to the scrape he got on his knee when he fell in the street and staring at a cop show on the television. He's not paying much attention, but he can tell that the TV cops are smarter than real ones, like they always are in movies.

He closes his eyes and tries to relax. His foot keeps bouncing, shaking the whole bed. He can't stop thinking about the fact that every minute he wastes in this room is one more minute his family is in danger.

Looking on the bright side, nothing is broken, nothing is bleeding too much. He can still run, still scrap if it comes to that, and the pain in his knee will make him meaner and smarter. It wouldn't matter if he was missing an arm, though, he'd keep chasing Luz. The trigger's been pulled, the bomb's been dropped.

There's a knock at the door. Jerónimo wraps a towel around his waist and limps over to open it. Looney and some kid, a little *vato* of fifteen or sixteen, are standing there.

"*Híjole*," Looney says and pretends to hide his eyes. "What kind of party you having?"

"Hey, *ese*," Jerónimo says. "Come on in."

Looney steps inside and motions for the boy to follow.

"You look good," Jerónimo says.

"No I don't," Looney says. "I'm fat as a motherfucker." He gestures at Jerónimo's knee. "What happened?"

"Nothing," Jerónimo says. "I tripped on the stairs." He closes the door and locks it. "I don't have any beer or anything. You want some water?"

"Nah, we're fine," Looney says. The kid stands there fidgeting, not knowing where to look. Looney puts his hand on his shoulder and says, "This is my oldest, Ruben Junior. He's my ride home. Junior, this here's El Apache."

"Hey, Junior, good to meet you," Jerónimo says.

"Good to meet you too," the kid replies in a soft voice, uncomfortable with the formality of the exchange.

Looney holds out a plastic grocery store bag and says, "Put these on. You're making me nervous."

"Thanks again, holmes," Jerónimo says. He takes the bag and walks to the bathroom.

"It's some of my old stuff," Looney says. "I didn't know what size you were, but there's a belt."

The Lakers T-shirt fits okay, but the pants, a pair of gray Dickies, are too short in the legs and too big in the waist. Jerónimo slides the belt through the loops and cinches it tight. He'll need to make a new hole.

"You got a *filero?*" he says to Looney when he steps back into the room. Looney fishes in his pocket, pulls out a folding knife, and tosses it to him. Jerónimo uses the tip of the blade to bore through the leather of the belt. A few seconds later he's all set.

"How do I look?" he says to the kid.

"Better," the kid says with a shy grin.

Looney picks up the length of curtain rod that Jerónimo bent and then blacked with oil from a stain in the parking lot. It was supposed to fool Luz into thinking he had a gun when he went down to meet her.

"What's this?" Looney says. "Some *Escape from Alcatraz* shit?" He points it at his son, changes his voice. "Put your hands up, motherfucker."

Jerónimo shrugs while the two of them laugh. "It ain't been my day," he says.

Looney sets the curtain rod on the dresser and reaches into his back pocket for something wrapped in a small brown paper bag. He hands it to Jerónimo, who looks inside and sees a pistol.

"Ain't nothing but a .25, but it's clean," Looney says. "Got six rounds in it, too."

"It'll do fine," Jerónimo says.

"Better than that fakie anyway," Looney says.

"And you ought to know, right?" Jerónimo says. He's talking about one night when they were kids and Looney tried to hold up a liquor store with a comb held like a gun. The Korean who owned the place leaped over the counter swinging a collapsible baton and came close to catching him. Jerónimo doesn't tell the story outright, not knowing how much Looney has revealed to his son about his past, but he sees that Looney is uneasy nonetheless.

"You're thinking of that dude Clown, I think," Looney says.

"Riiiight," Jerónimo says like he's all of a sudden remembering. "*That* dumbshit." He shoves the gun, still in the bag, into his pocket.

"Let me show you this car and get out of here," Looney says. "My old lady's like, 'You better get your ass back in time for dinner.'"

The three of them leave the room and walk downstairs to the parking lot. Looney is talking about a job he's on, wiring a new shopping center, all the overtime he's pulling, time-and-a-half, double-time. He doesn't shut up, doesn't give Jerónimo the chance to bring up any more old mischief. The car he's brought is a beat-to-shit Honda Civic with mismatched headlights, a bungee cord holding the hood shut, and a temporary spare on the right rear hub.

"Don't get pulled over," Looney says, dangling a key. "I don't have the registration. And the brakes are shot too."

"That's cool, that's cool," Jerónimo says. "Could you also slide me, like, twenty bucks?"

Looney makes a face, then takes out his wallet and passes him two tens. It's funny, him bragging one minute about all the money he's making and the next giving his old friend that kind of look when he asks for a loan.

Nonetheless, Jerónimo clasps the big man's hand and pulls him close, so they're standing chest to chest.

"You came through for me, holmes, and I mean it, I'll take care of you as soon as this job is done," he says.

Looney grips him tighter and pulls him closer. Jerónimo feels something poking his stomach and looks down to see a gun, held low, so the kid won't notice.

"I don't want nothing from you," Looney whispers in his ear. "We're even now, and you're gonna forget all about me. *Comprendes?*"

Jerónimo's not angry at him. The guy has a family, a house, a life, and Jerónimo knows what it's like to lose that.

"Comprendo," he whispers back.

The gun disappears, and Looney slaps him on the back as they separate. "Say good-bye to El Apache," he says to the kid. "He was a real loco back in the day."

Father and son walk to a tricked-out Supra and crawl inside, the kid behind the wheel. Looney sticks his arm out the window as they pull away and flashes Jerónimo a peace sign.

All of a sudden it's night. Two kids roll by on skateboards, one of them tossing a cigarette that sparks when it hits the street. Jeró-nimo takes the bag out of his pocket and opens it to look at the gun again, then gets into the Honda. The seat's broken, won't move forward, but the engine turns over, and the radio works.

There's still a line for the dance game Isabel wants to play, so Thacker eases her on to something else, a race car that rocks back and forth when she steers it. The arcade echoes with gun-fire and explosions, barked orders, and the recurring groans of the wounded. Across the way two Mexican kids dressed in black aim bright pink pistols at shambling zombies whose heads erupt into mushroom clouds of blood and brain when hit.

Thacker watches the entrance for Luz. He'll call her over as soon as she comes in and take the money off her right here. He's counting on her not trying anything funny, hopes he's scared her enough. *Wait ten minutes,* he'll tell her. *I mean it. I have eyes on this place.*

"Excuse me again."

The security guard. Snuck up out of nowhere.

"Is there a problem?" Thacker says, his irritation showing.

"No problem," the guard says. "It's just, I'm thinking of tak-ing the test for the Border Patrol."

"Right. You told me that before."

"Well, I was wondering, like, if I could get your card."

"What for?"

"I figure it'd be cool if I could say I knew someone when I went down there."

Thacker still can't figure out if the kid is stupid or up to some-thing, but all of a sudden it feels like everyone's looking at him. Paranoia makes him reconsider his plan. This place was a bad idea. There's got to be somewhere better to meet Luz.

"You know what," he says as he lifts Isabel from the race car, "I'm all out of cards."

"I'm not done!" Isabel yells.

"That's okay," the guard says. "Just give me your name, and I'll write it down." He reaches into his shirt pocket for a notepad and pen.

"Johnson," Thacker says. "Don Johnson."

"I want to finish!" Isabel yells.

"I gotta go," Thacker says to the guard and carries the kid toward the entrance.

"Thanks a lot, Agent Johnson," the guard calls after him.

Isabel is in the midst of another meltdown by the time they get out to the parking lot.

"Where's Aunt Carmen?" she screams. "Where's Aunt Carmen?"

"I'm taking you to her," Thacker says, and belts her into the truck.

21

Luz spots the castle from the freeway, and it looks exactly like she remembers it from when she and Alejandro used to go there on double dates with his brother and his brother's girl-friend. She tells Malone to get off at the next exit and directs him to the entrance to the parking lot.

"Don't go in," she says. "Let me out here."

"I'm sure it's fine if I drop you off," Malone says.

"He said to come alone."

Malone eases to the curb, keeps the engine running. Luz reaches into the backpack and pulls out the silver-plated .45.

"Take this," she says.

"Maybe you should keep it," Malone says. "Just in case."

"I don't want it," Luz says. "It's bad luck, and there isn't going to be any 'just in case' this time."

Malone takes the gun from her. He turns it so that it catches the neon of the sign overhead and flashes red, yellow, and blue.

"Fancy," he says.

"He had it made special," Luz says. "You can get a lot of money for it."

Malone points to the engraving on the ivory grip, a skeleton wearing a hooded robe. "What's this?" he asks.

"Santa Muerte," Luz replies. "She's like a saint for *narcos*. They pray to her."

"Saint Death?"

"Like I told you," Luz says as she opens the door and steps outside. "Bad luck."

"Don't forget this," Malone says, grabbing the phone off the seat and handing it to her.

"Thanks," Luz says.

"Don't worry," Malone says. "Everything's going to be fine." The flashing lights of the sign claw at his face, and his smile is a little white lie.

Luz can't think of anything to end with this time. She closes the door and steps away from the truck, waits to make sure Malone drives off. When he turns the corner, she starts walking across the parking lot.

It's a confusing bustle of vehicles and people. Minivans disgorge swarms of children who carom off one another as they race to see who can get to the castle first, and teenagers slouch in their cars flamboyantly smoking cigarettes and courting through open windows.

A loud kissing sound from the shadows spins Luz around. Two boys perched on the tailgate of a Toyota pickup eye her, one of them tugging at the crotch of his baggy jeans. The little *pendejos* are lucky she gave the gun to Malone. With a disdainful toss of her head, she continues on her way, the boys' laughter quickly drowned out by the sputtering of go-karts circling the track.

*　　*　　*

Luz is rocked by a flood of familiar sights and sounds when she enters the castle. The dusty suits of armor flanking the door, the swaying shoulders of the boys hunched over games in the arcade, the radio blaring Today's Hottest Hits. She passes the bench where she and Alejandro used to sit, his lips tickling her ear and making her laugh, and the snack bar, where the same pale, bug-eyed woman still doles out popcorn and nachos.

Walking out to the golf course, she keeps her eyes open for a man in a Border Patrol hat and a pretty little girl. They're nowhere in sight, so she leaves the castle behind and sets off down a narrow path that winds among the holes. The course has a number of hills and gullies, and the candy-colored lights play tricks. A child with something familiar in her face attracts her attention, but as she moves closer, a woman calls to the girl, who skips off to join her family.

Luz makes two quick circuits of the course, from the grinning purple dragon to the haunted house, from the freeway to the jungle waterfall, and doesn't see Isabel or the border patrolman anywhere. Worried that she misunderstood the instructions, she returns to the castle and scours the arcade, then pushes through the heavy glass doors that lead out to the go-karts, where the stink of gasoline and burning rubber poison the hot air and cranky little cars rattle around an oval track beneath fiery, moth-swarmed floodlights.

There's no sign of the pair out there, either, and Luz starts to feel a little frantic. As she turns to reenter the castle, eyes darting wildly, the backpack clutched to her chest, a teenaged attendant in grease-stained coveralls regards her with suspicion.

"Can I help you?" he says.

"I'm looking for my daughter."

"Is she lost?"

Luz ignores the kid and pulls open the door to the arcade, ready to search the whole complex again. Only then does she notice that the phone, in the pocket of her hoodie, is vibrating, has been for who knows how long, the ringer having somehow been turned off.

"Hello?" she says. "Hello?"

"Hola, guapa," the border patrolman croons.

"Where are you?" Luz says. "Where's Isabel?"

"Are you at the golf course?"

"Yes."

"Alone?"

"Yes. Like you wanted."

The border patrolman chuckles. "You know what I love?" he says. "A hot chick that follows orders."

"Tell me how to get this money to you," Luz says.

"Me and Isabel are checking into a room at the Best Western on Lincoln and Euclid. Think you can find it?"

"I'll take a taxi. What room?"

"Tell you what: stay in the parking lot when you get here, and I'll be watching for you."

"I'll be there soon," Luz says.

"Goody," the border patrolman says. "I can't wait."

Back on the streets.

Jerónimo thought he'd be on his way to TJ by now, mission accomplished, but here he is cruising through Compton again, trying to remember the way to Carmen's house. He's going back to see if he can squeeze more information out of the woman. His hope is that she knows more than she let on before. Maybe Luz told her where she was headed next. Maybe she left a number. He'll get rough this time, hold her daughter's hand over the stove if that's what it takes.

He sees the sign, CHILDREN PLAYING, and recognizes the van. By the time he pulls over to the curb, the dogs are at the gate, waiting for him to show himself. So no sneaking around back. He'll have to sweet talk his way through the front door and bring the hammer down once Carmen lets him inside.

He steps out of the Honda, and the dogs go nuts. At first glance it looks like nobody's home, but he can see a glow behind the drawn curtains. *My wife, my kids*—he rehearses his plea as he moves up the walkway to the dark porch. The white flowers clinging to a trellis there give off a sweet smell.

Knocking on the door, he stares at the tiny circle of light shining through the peephole. The light disappears for a second, returns, goes dark again. He hears whispers inside. A bare bulb comes on overhead, and the door flies open. He sees a man first, some guy in work clothes, then a shotgun pointed at his head.

"Wait," he squawks. "Hold on."

He starts to reach for his pistol, but something smarter wins out, and he finds himself backing off the porch, hands in the air.

"Don't shoot!"

The man keeps coming. Jerónimo sprints for the Honda and dives behind it just as the guy pulls the trigger. Jerónimo hears the *BOOM* of the gun and the pop of breaking glass. Red-hot pellets burrow into his face and neck. He drops to the street.

The shot echoes through the neighborhood. Jerónimo presses his belly to the pavement and peers under the car, trying to track the gunman. The curb blocks his view, so he gets up and looks over the hood. The guy is standing on the lawn, staring at the smoke curling out of the barrel of the gun like he can't believe it actually went off. Jerónimo opens the car door and scrambles inside.

The windows on the passenger side are gone. Pebbles of shattered glass glint on the seat. Jerónimo gets the car running and hits the gas. The Honda slowly picks up speed, and the wind whistling through the broken windows sounds like a distant siren. The man on the lawn points the gun but doesn't fire again. He must have used up all his guts the first time.

When he's sure nobody's following him, Jerónimo checks the damage to his face. The rearview mirror reveals a bloody constellation on the left side. The worst wound is below his eye, where a pellet gouged a deep gash as it rode the curve of the cheekbone. Adrenaline dulls the pain for now, but he knows he'll be hurting soon.

He pulls into the parking lot of a Rite Aid and wipes away the blood with a dirty rag from the floor of the car. He keeps the rag pressed to his face when he walks into the store. The security guard up front is playing a game on his phone, doesn't give him a second look. Jerónimo wanders the aisles in a daze, tasting metal and feeling the buzz of the fluorescent lights inside his eyeballs.

When he finds the bandages back by the pharmacy counter, the array of choices confounds him. He grabs a box of Band-Aids and a bottle of peroxide. A skinny black girl approaches as he's searching for tweezers. At first he thinks she works here, is coming over to ask if he needs help, but she's not wearing a nametag or a smock, and her eyes are crazy bright.

"Hey," she says with a nervous glance at the pharmacy counter. "You got any pills you want to sell?"

"Huh?" Jerónimo grunts.

"Oxy or Vicodin," she says, one hand scratching at her throat, nails bitten ragged. "Anything like that?"

Begging dope in a drugstore. Fucking junkies always creating their own bad luck. Got to stay as far from that kind of stupidity as possible.

"Get the fuck away from me," Jerónimo says.

"Come on, don't be like that," the girl drawls.

"I said move along."

Jerónimo knocks a pair of tweezers off the display while snatching one for himself. The girl doesn't follow when he heads up front. The cashier is black, too, her hair piled in thick orange curls on top of her head. Jerónimo pays her with the money Looney gave him, gets back three bucks in change. The cashier acts like she doesn't see the bloody rag.

He hurries out of the store. The passenger side of the Honda is freckled with tiny holes from the shotgun pellets. Looks like somebody went to town on it with an ice pick. Jerónimo collapses in the driver's seat and lowers his forehead to the steering wheel. His face is on fire now, and he can't think straight around the rhythmic pulsing. Best to go back to the motel, get his shit together, then figure out what to do next.

"Do you have any kings available?" Thacker asks the desk clerk at the Best Western. The clerk is a Mexican kid who must be new on the job, the way he pauses before each step of the check-in process, as if reviewing it in his head.

"A king?" the kid says.

"Yeah, it's just me," Thacker says. "I have my granddaughter with me now, but her mom's coming for her shortly."

Thacker doesn't intend to be in the room for more than an hour, but he wants it to seem as if he's staying all night, like any other guest. A little too cautious, maybe, but he's doing everything he can to get out of town without making any ripples.

"Let me check," the kid says.

Isabel is asleep in the truck, parked in front of the office. She passed out as soon as they left the arcade. Thacker can see the top of her head through the window. He picks up a brochure somebody left on the counter. The Hollywood Wax Museum. The figures in the photos look more like department store mannequins decked out in wigs and mustaches than the movie stars they're supposed to be. Pretty pitiful.

The clerk lets Thacker pay the room deposit in cash and then hands over a keycard. He points out the room on a map and where Thacker should park. Thacker drives down to the shorter leg of the L-shaped complex and finds a spot, but as he's opening his door, a family spills out of a room on the first floor and begins to load into a van parked next to the truck, blocking his way.

"Sorry," the redheaded, sunburned daddy calls to him. Thacker gives him a wave and a smile, whispering "Fuck you" through gritted teeth.

The Disney parks are only a couple of miles away, Knott's a couple more, so the motel is full of rowdy kids and harried adults. That's why Thacker chose it, thinking that he and Isabel would blend right in. When the last child has climbed into the van and daddy pulls away and heads for the entrance, Thacker gets out of the Dodge. Walking around to the passenger side, he takes the seatbelt off Isabel and carries her up to their second-floor room.

He opens the door and lays her on the bed. She doesn't stir when he lifts her head to slide a pillow under it. After checking the bathroom and closet for bogeymen, he grabs a cup to spit in and steps outside to wait for Luz.

The walkway overlooks the motel's swimming pool. Lit from below, it's a quivering rectangle of the palest blue. A dozen children splash in the water, sending up reflections that wriggle across Thacker's face as he places a bit of dip in his mouth and leans forward to rest his elbows on the railing. He can see the whole parking lot from here, all the way back to the office and the IHOP across the road. The catbird seat. The kids' shouts resound into nonsense as they bounce around the motel.

"Marco!" "Polo!" Back and forth they go.

Three teenage girls leave the pool together, and the gate in the fence that surrounds the deck slams shut behind them. Thacker watches them scuff across the parking lot in their flip-flops and feels his breathing change. They're carrying towels but don't use them to cover themselves as they bounce up the stairs in their bikinis.

Thacker stands up straight when they pass by him on the walkway, sucks in his gut, and says, "Ladies." This makes them giggle, the funny old fat man. Anger flashes like lightning behind Thacker's eyes. *You don't know how lucky you are this isn't some dark road,* he thinks. Marla called him a pervert when she found out about Lupita, and he wanted so badly to say to her, "Shit, baby, you think *that's* sick?" She'd drop dead if she could see the stuff that comes into his mind sometimes.

He leans over the rail again, spits into his cup. The sky lights up with fireworks bursting silently over Angel Stadium or Disneyland, bright skittering blooms that fade into spiders of smoke. A taxi pulls into the driveway and a young woman carrying a backpack gets out and eyes the motel. Her. Thacker waves his arms.

"Hey!" he shouts. "Hey! Up here!"

Luz wants to run to the stairs but makes herself walk, her excitement building with each step. All these people standing outside their rooms, all the kids in the pool. Surely the guy wouldn't choose a place like this to double-cross her.

Two little girls with wet hair and dripping bathing suits press their faces to the bars of the fence circling the pool to watch the fireworks Luz glimpsed as she was getting out of the taxi.

"Look," one of the girls says to Luz, pointing.

Luz glances over her shoulder. "Pretty," she says.

The border patrolman watches her climb the stairs with a lecherous smile on his face. She zips up her jacket as she approaches him, an automatic reaction.

"Damn, mama," he says. "You are *fine.*"

The nasty old *cabrón,* with his clown nose and yellow teeth, his big belly hanging over his belt. And now he's holding his arms out like he wants to hug her.

"Come here and give me some sugar," he says.

"That's okay."

"Actually, it's not. I'm not letting you into the room without patting you down first."

Luz holds her breath as the border patrolman runs his hands over her. He ignores the phone but tenses when he finds the money in her jacket pocket, a stack of bills she took from the backpack right before the taxi dropped her off, some cash to get her and Isabel wherever they're going.

Waving the money in her face, he says, "Is this some of mine?"

She shrugs for an answer. They'll get along without it.

"You're a sneaky one, aren't you?" he says.

Fuck him.

He points to the backpack. "Is that the rest of it?"

She swings the pack around behind her, where he can't get to it. "Not until I have Isabel," she says.

A car alarm goes off below, and the kids in the pool imitate its whoop.

"I guess it's time," the border patrolman says. He opens the door to the room, and Luz feels like she's expanding beyond her body, like flesh doesn't mean much anymore. She squeezes past the fat man and sees Isabel asleep on the bed. She's such a tiny thing, but still where all the light in the room goes. Luz is drawn to her, too, pulled to the edge of the mattress, where she sinks to her knees.

She reaches out a tentative hand to touch her and wonders if she's worthy, having abandoned her, having forgotten her even—so terrible to admit—for weeks at a time when she was on dope. Gently brushing back a curl of jet black hair from the girl's lips, she decides that if she came all this way and did all she did only to see her for this instant, it was worth it.

The border patrolman is saying something. Words, words, words. Luz hands him the backpack without taking her eyes off her daughter. *I will never leave you again,* she promises. *Your life will always mean more to me than my own.* The child looks so peaceful that she hates to wake her back into all this, but they have to keep moving. She stands and bends to pick her up.

"Hold on a minute," the voice behind her says.

Luz pauses, arms outstretched, wondering *What now?* but already knowing.

"Turn around."

The fat man is standing too close. Close enough to touch her. Close enough that she can feel his breath on her face.

"She's a good girl," he says. "She behaved herself real well today."

"I'm glad," Luz says.

"When that fucker said he was going to kill her, that was it for me. He blew it. I snatched her right out from under his nose and decided to give her back to you."

"Thank you," Luz says. She turns back to Isabel. Maybe if she moves quickly enough.

The border patrolman grabs her arm. "I saved her life," he says, forcing her to face him again.

"And I said thank you," Luz says.

"Yeah, but you stole from me too," he says. "You didn't think I'd find that money, did you?"

He's trying to bully her, to scare her. Five years ago it might have worked, but since then she's been with men whose viciousness makes this pig look like a schoolyard punk.

"It wasn't for me, it was for Isabel," she says.

"Stealing's stealing," he says as he unzips her hoodie. Luz raises a hand to stop him, but he slaps it away, then reaches inside her jacket and squeezes one of her breasts.

"You think I'm a man you can mess with," he says. "But I'm not."

"I know that."

"Do you?"

"I'm sorry."

"Are you?"

Luz doesn't reply. She's not going to play his games. He's all worked up, trembling, sweaty, and what he wants now is for her to crumble, to acquiesce, as if she actually did something to deserve what he's going to do to her. He'll die waiting for that.

"Get in the bathroom and show me how sorry," he says.

"Go to hell," Luz spits.

She empties herself out so she doesn't feel any pain when he grabs her hair, any fear when he draws his gun and jabs it into her cheek. It's just a body that he hauls into the bathroom, just a shell that he forces to the floor.

"Let me see those titties," he says.

Luz takes off her hoodie, her T-shirt, her bra. The border patrolman sticks the pistol into a holster under his arm, drops his pants to his knees, and sits on the lid of the toilet.

"Get up here and suck on it a little bit first," he says.

He leans back so that his belly lifts out of the way and his hard-on pops into view. His keys slide out of his pocket and clatter on the tile. Luz crawls toward him, but the old tricks aren't working tonight; she's not as far away as she should be. She's going to remember the smell, the taste, the feel of his hands on the back of her head as he fucks her mouth.

She moves up between his legs, takes his cock in her hand, and that's when she sees it, a mother-of-pearl switchblade dangling unnoticed from his pants pocket, about to slip the rest of the way out and drop to the floor. Without pausing to think, she grabs it, presses the button to open it, and lays the blade across the top of his scrotum.

"What the hell!" the fat man yelps, raising a reflexive fist.

"Touch me, and I'll cut them off," Luz says.

The man lowers his hand and glares down at her. His face is bright red, and his breath comes in frightened puffs.

"You like to push girls around?" Luz says, making a little sawing motion with the knife. "You like to hurt them?"

"Please," he says.

"Please," Luz repeats, in scornful imitation. "Please."

In one swift motion, she stands and snatches the man's gun from its holster, then backs away, pointing it at his face. He's not so tough now, an old *gordo* slumped on a toilet.

"Try to fuck me now," she says.

"Get the hell out of here before you do something stupid," he says.

"The only stupid thing I'm going to do is blow your head off," she says.

And if Isabel weren't here, she'd do it. She'd pull the trigger and put this dog down. Instead, she picks up her hoodie with her free hand and shrugs it on. Then she sticks the knife in her pocket and grabs her bra and T-shirt.

"What's wrong with you?" she says as she steps into the other room. "You had the money."

The man shrugs and looks down at the floor.

"Don't fucking move," Luz says.

She closes the door and goes quickly to the bed. Picking up Isabel, she manages to lay the girl over her shoulder without waking her. The backpack is on the table. She shoves the pistol and her clothes into it, zips it, and slings it over her other shoulder.

She slips out the front door and shuts it quietly. Hitching Isabel higher, she hurries for the stairs. Down she goes and across the parking lot. When she glances back at the room, the door is still closed.

She turns out of the lot and walks toward the bright lights of a strip mall on the next block. It's not so much a decision as a destination, somewhere to run to. Better to be around other people if the fat man comes looking for them. Isabel wakes up before they get there and rears back her head to see who's carrying her.

"Who are you?" she asks, so matter-of-factly that it makes Luz smile.

"I'm a friend," Luz says. "A friend of Aunt Carmen."

"Where's the policeman?"

"He had to go."

"Where's Aunt Carmen?"

"You'll see her soon."

The little girl stares into Luz's face, deciding if this is acceptable. After a long pause she says, "It's my birthday Tuesday."

"I know," Luz says. "That's why I'm here."

"For my party?"

"Of course. I wouldn't miss it."

Isabel lays her head back down and doesn't say anything more. When they get to the strip mall, Luz ducks into a busy 7-Eleven and moves to the rear of the store where they can't be seen through the front window. She watches the door as she calls for a cab.

"Where do you want to go?" the dispatcher asks.

Isabel is humming to herself and tugging at the string that tightens the hood of Luz's jacket.

"The bus station," Luz says. "Greyhound."

Isabel leans back to look quizzically into her face again.

"Why are you crying?" she says.

"They're happy tears," Luz says, pulling the girl close to kiss her on the cheek. "Haven't you ever heard of happy tears?"

22

Malone is on his way to Palos Verdes when the past drops over him like a hood. His dad, his wife, his dead baby daughter step forward out of the darkness to deliver their lines, the litany of failure louder than ever tonight. He turns on the radio to try to drown it out, yells the words to the songs, but the testimony cuts right through. Other voices, other faces are what he needs, the distraction of strangers.

He takes the next exit and pulls into the parking lot of the first bar he comes to, a dumpy stucco box called Breezy's Hideaway. A Budweiser sign gutters in the window, and a big man with a scraggly white beard is standing out front, sucking on a cigarette.

Inside, the bar is brightly lit and decorated with a muddle of beer advertisements and sports banners. A couple of flat screens are tuned to ESPN, but the sound is dialed down in favor of the heavily reverbed racket blasting from a karaoke machine manned by a skinny bald guy wearing a tuxedo T-shirt. The frowsy blonde on the mike, a renegade mommy in high heels and too much makeup, screeches out the chorus to "Livin' On a Prayer," playing to a group of similarly decked-out women seated at one of the tables.

Malone sinks into the last open chair at the bar and orders a double vodka from a gal with a pixie tattooed on the inside of her forearm. She brings him his drink and takes his money without looking at him. Staring down at his clasped hands, he thinks of Luz. She's probably with her daughter by now, and that's good, that's at least one story that might end well. He swigs half the vodka in a gulp, but something is wrong. It sticks in his throat and comes up so that he tastes it again, caustic and sour, his best friend finally betraying him.

An old man gets up to sing "I Walk the Line." This agitates the guy sitting next to Malone. He bumps Malone's elbow, mutters an apology, then blurts, "Fucking Johnny Cash."

Malone turns to look into his face, and, Christ, it's a mirror.

"You know about Johnny Cash?" the guy asks him.

"What do you mean?" Malone replies.

"He wore black for the Indians, for the vets, for the prisoners, for every fucked-up fucker, and now look." The guy gestures at the old man singing as if pointing out something obvious.

Malone nods sympathetically without trying to figure out what his neighbor is getting at. Another drunk with a beef, he figures, another boozer trying to put words to his pain.

"You are a *cocksucker!*" the guy says to the old man, building to a shout on the last word.

This draws a warning finger from the bartender. "Strike two," she says.

The guy hunches his shoulders in apology like a chagrined little boy.

Malone sips his drink. It goes down easier this time. He's

waiting for the alcohol to kick in, for the honey to start to flow. He should be feeling better by now, a little at least. This shit should be on the verge of bearable.

"What kind of music you into?" the Johnny Cash fan asks him.

"I don't know," Malone says. "Rock, old punk."

"Old punk?" the guy exclaims with delight. "Old punk. Okay." He extends his hand, palm up, and begins reciting band names, touching his fingers to his thumb. "The Sex Pistols, the Buzzcocks, the Ramones, Bad Brains, Suicidal, Black Flag, Rancid. I played in punk bands, man, toured and everything. San Francisco, Sacramento, Phoenix."

"That's cool," Malone says.

"What are you drinking?" the guy says, happy to have found a friend. "Let me buy you one."

Malone starts to answer, but his stomach bucks and his mouth fills with saliva. The bar swells and shrinks as the music dissolves into an incoherent roar. He launches himself out of his chair and hurries past the pool table, past the video golf game to the bathroom, where he slams his way into a stall and vomits. He's been vomiting a lot lately. Sometimes he hopes it's cancer.

His head is spinning when he finishes, but he manages to get himself together enough to make it back out to the pickup. Once there he rinses his mouth with one of the beers and watches cars pull into the drive-through of the Taco Bell across the street. The echoey, amplified voice of the girl taking orders sounds late-night and lonely.

He thinks of Luz again, realizes he's half in love with her. An alternate life unspools, the one they might have had together. Christmas and birthdays. Her little girl calling him Daddy. The three of them a happy family. More bullshit, another pathetic fantasy, like starting over with Gail in Hawaii. The truth is, nothing's ever going to change, nothing's ever going to get better.

He reaches into the glove compartment and brings out the silver-plated Colt. Santa Muerte grins at him from the grip, her smile as inviting as it is horrible. He sticks the muzzle of the gun into his mouth and starts to pull the trigger. But then a thought comes to him, one last loose end he can tie up, something that might give Luz some breathing room. He takes the pistol out of his mouth and lays it in his lap. It's not over yet. Not quite.

Jerónimo's blood is a funny color under the fluorescent light of the motel bathroom. Almost purple, almost black. He grits his teeth and watches his shirtless self in the mirror as he uses the tweezers to dig another shotgun pellet out of his cheek. He drops the tiny chunk of lead into the toilet, where it spirals like a comet, dragging a pale pink tail down to join the other pellets at the bottom of the bowl.

While he works, he struggles to come up with his next move, feeling like he's reached a dead end. Returning to Carmen's is out of the question. She's his only hope for more information about Luz, but her neighborhood is probably crawling with cops right now. And meanwhile, El Príncipe waits back in TJ, growing increasingly impatient. It won't be long before he makes good on some of his threats. Jerónimo turns the situation over and over in his mind, searching for some new angle, but nothing reveals itself.

The ringing of the room phone is like a gun going off. Jerónimo jumps, startled, then grabs a towel and hurries to answer.

"Hello?" he says into the receiver.

"Don't talk, just listen," Thacker says. "I fucked up. I took the kid and tried to do my own thing. It was stupid, and I apologize. The bitch pulled a fast one on me, though, and got away with the kid and the money. So now I'm ready to make a new deal. You want to hear it?"

"Go on," Jerónimo says.

"I managed to pick up her trail after she took off," Thacker says. "I saw her get into a cab and tailed the cab, and I'm looking at her right now."

"Where?" Jerónimo says.

"That's the big question, right?" Thacker says.

Jerónimo wipes the blood and sweat off his face with the towel. He can't stand having to kowtow to Thacker but understands that working with the pig is the only way he's going to find Luz quickly, so he chokes back his disgust and says, "Whatever you want, you can have."

"I want the same thing I always wanted," Thacker says. "I want the money."

"If I get my hands on it, it's yours," Jerónimo says. He sits on the bed and rocks back and forth. His head is pounding, his face aches.

"All right then," Thacker says. "Can you get a car?"

"I already have one."

"Excellent. So this is how it's going to go: Luz is at the Greyhound bus station in Anaheim. You're going to go there and do what you have to do. You'll be on your own, because I'm done with that part of it. All I care is that when you're finished, you drive two blocks to the corner of Anaheim and Midway, drop the money there, and drive away. Got that?"

"Anaheim and Midway."

"Dump the backpack in the bushes and drive away."

"Got it."

"As soon as you do that, our partnership is over."

"Okay."

"But know this: I'll be watching you the whole time, and if

you try and fuck me over, I'll call every cop I can find between here and San Diego and tell them you abducted a little girl. I'll give them the make and model of your vehicle, the plate number, and they'll run you off the road before you've gone twenty miles."

Jerónimo stands and reaches for his shirt. He can get a map at the gas station across the street.

"I'm on my way," he says.

"The next bus for anywhere leaves in half an hour," Thacker says. "So hurry your ass up."

"I'll be there."

"And one more thing."

"What?"

"Someone's been calling that phone of yours. Someone from Mexico."

Jerónimo freezes. "Did you answer?"

"Hell no," Thacker says. "I threw the fucking thing away."

Stay calm, Jerónimo tells himself. He'll deal with getting in touch with El Príncipe after he picks up Luz and her kid.

"I'll be at the station in fifteen minutes," he says.

"Get me my money," Thacker says.

Jerónimo hangs up and collects his keys and the gun. He's just about ready to leave when a knock at the door derails him. He wipes his face again with the towel, then approaches the door cautiously and bends to look through the peephole.

He's shocked to see the shaggy-ass *pendejo* who drove Luz across the border and then came out of nowhere to help her tonight. The dude must be crazy to show up here. Jerónimo backs away from the door and points the gun at it.

"Yeah?" he calls out.

"We need to talk," the guy says.

"About what?"

"You know about what."

"No I don't."

"How about where Luz is, and your partner, and what they're up to."

What *they're* up to? Jerónimo has been trying to ignore the doubts he's been having about Thacker, and now this dude comes along talking about what *they're* up to, and a whole new kind of paranoia grips him.

"Why would you want to talk to *me* about that?" he says.

"They cut me out, and it pissed me off," the guy says. "I figured you might be willing to pay for good information."

Jerónimo smiles. Another rat. They're everywhere. He bends to the peephole again. The guy hasn't moved.

"So, go on," he says. "Tell me what you know."

"Seriously, man," the guy says. "Don't play me for a fool."

Two minutes is all it will take to hear the rat out and determine whether he's full of shit. If he is, Jerónimo will kill him and leave for the bus station; if he's not, a change of plans might be in order.

Jerónimo unlocks the door and opens it a crack, showing the muzzle of his gun.

"Hands up," he says.

The rat hesitates for a second, then complies.

"Lift your shirt and turn around."

Two Chinese men dressed in business suits step out of the next room and onto the walkway. Jerónimo can't see them, but he hears their yammering. The door to their room slams shut, and they come into view as they pass between him and the rat. Jerónimo closes his door almost all the way, reopening it when the *chinos* clomp down the stairs.

"Okay, now," he says to the rat. "Show me."

The rat pulls up his shirt to reveal his belly, then starts to turn. Halfway around he pulls a gun from the small of his back and slams his shoulder into the door with all of his weight behind it. The move catches Jerónimo by surprise, and the inside edge of the door strikes the bridge of his nose, triggering a red wave of pain that scrambles his vision and softens his bones.

Carried backward by the momentum of the rat's charge, he trips and falls across the bed. The rat follows him down, landing on top of him. They're lying face-to-face, and Jerónimo feels the rat's gun pressing against him, trapped between their bodies. The rat attempts to pull it loose, but Jerónimo hugs him with one arm and uses the .25 in his free hand to hammer the side of the guy's head again and again until he lets go of his pistol and turns his attention to stopping the blows. The weight shift gives Jerónimo enough leverage to buck him off, roll to the edge of the mattress, and drop to the floor.

Dizzy, nauseous, he scoots backward. The rat rises from the bed, panting, blood streaming from a gash on his head, and claws his pistol out of the tangle of sheets. He points it at Jerónimo, but Jerónimo is quicker. He raises the .25 and fires twice.

A ringing silence follows the shots. The rat's knees buckle, but he doesn't go down. Stunned, he examines the holes in his chest, touching them inquisitively. Jerónimo springs at him and knocks him onto the bed. Twisting the gun out of his hand, Jerónimo takes hold of his hair, yanks his head back, and jams the .25 under his chin. He's got to work fast. Once the man's brain catches up to what's happened to his body, it'll be all over.

"Where's Luz?" he asks.

The rat takes a deep, wheezing breath. Bloody saliva bubbles at the corner of his mouth.

"Gone to the police," he says.

"You're lying," Jerónimo says. "She's at the bus station. I just got a call from my partner, and I'm on my way there now."

The rat manages a smirk. "You'd trust a cop?" he says.

"Why not? I should trust you instead?"

"Go to the station, then. See what happens."

"What do you mean?"

The rat coughs and struggles to refill his lungs. Jerónimo shakes him.

"What do you mean?" he says again.

"They're setting you up," the rat whispers. His eyes are glazing over. He's on his way out.

Jerónimo stands and takes a second to think things through. The rat must be telling stories. If Luz or Thacker really went to the cops, wouldn't the cops have come for him by now, surrounded the place? Then again, maybe they felt there were too many innocent people around for that. Maybe they've decided to lock down the bus station instead, call him to come get Luz, then grab him when he shows up there. He can't risk that, not with Irma and the kids still in El Príncipe's hands. They're doomed if he goes down.

So that leaves one other option, a last-chance, all-or-nothing play: He has to return to Tijuana and kill El Príncipe before El Príncipe kills his family. He makes his decision in an instant, and once he does, he's at peace, as if he knew from the start that it would come to this. He's always resented El Príncipe's hold on him, hated the way the man kept his fingers around his throat, allowing him just enough air to survive, but he could live with it, accepting that it was his own mistakes that had put him at the Prince's mercy. When the bastard went after his family, though, that was crossing the line, and for that he's going to die.

Time to go. Somebody's called about the gunshots by now, and the police must be on their way. Jerónimo shoves the .25

into his front pocket, then picks up the rat's pistol and drops the magazine. Two rounds left. He might as well take it along. Sliding a hand underneath the guy, he gets hold of his wallet. The two hundred dollars he finds inside it means he won't have to jack someone for gas money to get him to the border.

The rat is lying motionless on the bed, staring at the ceiling but not seeing it, when Jerónimo walks out the door. Jerónimo feels lucky. If the guy had been just a little quicker on the trigger, Jerónimo knows it would be his ghost haunting this room forever, not the rat's. And that's got to mean something. Got to.

Malone wakes in the room in Tijuana, the one out by the dog track, gets up, and goes into the bathroom to splash water on his face. No. That was this morning. No. Yesterday. He tries to lift his head but can't, turns it to one side instead. Daylight already? No. The wall is white, the curtains beige. The night coming through, the night is. He walks into the kitchen late because she never remembers to set the alarm. The baby is in the high chair. Her eyes are blue, her hair is blond. She feeds Dadada a mushy slice of banana, pushes it into his mouth with. No. The pain is terrible, like two blazing coals stuck up behind his ribs, his ruined lungs the bellows. He turns his face back to the ceiling, and tears spill out of the corners of his eyes and tickle their way down to his ears. The bastard who shot him leaves. Where to? That's important. Where to? Luz sits in a. No. Luz stands. Luz trudges beside him through the snow. It never snows at the beach, but look, a fog of white flakes that sting where they touch you, that settle like ash on the water. Luz says she's scared. He takes her hand. It's the end of the world, she says. But it's not that, not the world. No. He can move the thumb and ring finger on his left hand, a few others on the right. That's all. Maybe

267

his toes. The strange taste in his mouth is blood, the stuff he keeps coughing up. No. Make a list. Yes. Takes your mind off it. Tenpenny, twelve-penny, sixteen-penny, twenty, scaffold, common, finishing, roofing, shingle. The bartender at the dog track shows him a trick, makes an olive disappear. The dogs shiver in the snow. Poor things, Luz says. How to explain how it always is? The thud in his head, the amplified beat of his laboring heart, slowly slows. Yes. A passing car's headlights sweep across the icy expanse of the ceiling, get trapped in the crystals embedded there and wink like glimpsed stars. Annie again. She sits on the kitchen floor, banging a pot with a wooden spoon. Mommy has a headache, he tells her, then squats with his own saucepan and shows her how to make some real noise. In fifteen minutes they'll leave for the store. In an hour he'll be unloading the groceries. In an hour and ten seconds. Fuck it. The sooner this is over, the better. A sleep you don't wake from, a dark that keeps its promise. Everything in him is cold now but the bullets. He trembles. His eyes want to close. He lets them. Yes. Yellowtail, dorado, bonito, sculpin, halibut, sand bass. Pablo Honey's on the pier. He bought a box of a hundred pocketknives from Home Shopping Network. "Take one," he says. "Take a couple." Malone gestures at the falling snow, wants to show him. A groan. A clotted gurgle. Okay now. Yes. Come black, come silence, come peace. Dawn. Dusk. Both minds are fading now, the one that loved him and the one that didn't. Yes. He steps out of the motel in Tijuana, into the sun. There's a store down the hill that sells beer and candy. The snow piles higher, drifting into his mouth, his nose, his eyes, and the last lie he tells himself is yes. Yes, yes, yes.

Sitting in his truck across the street from the station, Thacker watches a bus leave. The Mex still hasn't shown, so he calls the motel again. The clerk sounds funny when Thacker asks for the room, and then someone else gets on, not the Mex, and says, "Who's calling?" Thacker hangs up.

Something has gone wrong. Thacker isn't sure what, but he knows he needs to get out of here. He starts the truck and pulls away from the curb, wondering if the cops nabbed the Mex, wondering if the Mex will roll over on him. Another bus leaves the station as he drives off. Looks like the bitch is going to get away after all.

He heads for the freeway and merges onto the 5 going south. The $3,500 he found in Jerónimo's pants is small change compared to what he was hoping for and nowhere near enough compensation for what he's been through today, chauffeuring that crazy *vato* around the ghetto and nearly getting his balls chopped off. He had the money in his hands, that's what sickens him most, a bag full of cash and he blew it, let some stupid whore get the drop on him.

The important thing now is that he keep his cool. He can talk his way out of any mess if he doesn't get stuck chasing his own tail. He'll return to San Diego, lay low until Monday, then go into work like nothing happened. His missing gun? It was stolen out of his truck. He'll break a window to back up the story.

He passes a big rig hauling a load of lemons. The ocean is glowing as if lit from below, but he can't find the moon in the sky. He puts the fan on, aims all the vents at his face, and it's still not enough air. For a minute he thinks he's having a heart attack and worries that he'll pass out and crash the truck. And maybe that'd be better, quicker, than what's coming.

He's gotten away with playing dirty his whole life, with stealing from people, with hurting and humiliating them, and one day it's going to catch up to him. He's a gambler, he understands the odds. Luck runs out. Today scared him, so he'll walk the straight and narrow for a while, play by the rules, but six months from now, a year, he'll get cocky again. He'll make some *señorita* get down on her knees in the sand, and she'll have a knife, and she'll stick it in his belly. He'll bleed to death out there in the desert, alone, his last breath pluming in the cold night air, then disappearing. And nobody will give a shit.

The premonition rattles him. He shakes it out of his head and grips the wheel tighter, doing his best to reduce the world to the short stretch of road in the headlights and to make everything else mean nothing.

23

Jerónimo gets into San Ysidro at midnight and parks the Civic in a dirt lot next to a twenty-four-hour currency exchange housed in a double-wide trailer. The old man who takes his money is reading a wrestling magazine with the flashlight he uses to direct drivers to empty spaces.

"*Vaya con dios,*" he says as he hands Jerónimo the ticket.

It's as bright as day at the crossing. Powerful spotlights hold back the shadows and would-be runners, and armed men in uniform stand guard at razor-wire fences. This late there's not much foot traffic: a few drunk college kids returning to the U.S., some swing-shift workers going home to TJ. Jerónimo walks past the souvenir shops, the McDonald's, and up and over the pedestrian bridge that crosses in front of the massive border station, which looks like a shiny new office building straddling *la línea*. There's no passport control or customs inspection when he enters Mexico, only a heavy turnstile to push through.

271

He feels stronger now that he knows what needs to be done. Too many choices have always confused him, and kill or be killed is as simple as it gets. He thought of calling El Príncipe and feeding him enough lies to keep him calm until he arrived at the house but then decided surprise would give him more of an advantage. As long as he's not already too late.

The driver of the cab he hails is just a kid. Peeking in the rearview mirror at Jerónimo's battered face, he says, "Please, *señor,* I'm a family man."

"So am I," Jerónimo says. "Drive now, and I'll give you directions on the way."

He slouches in the backseat as they cruise dark streets toward the hilltop neighborhood where El Príncipe lives in his mansion overlooking the ocean with his swimming pool and his garage full of expensive cars. Somewhere in the midst of all that, Irma and the children are waiting for Jerónimo to take them home. He doesn't have a plan, doesn't need one. He'll start with two guns and six bullets and go from there.

He tells the driver to slow down as they approach El Príncipe's spread. Peering through the gate, he sees lights on in the house and yard. A large spot also shines on the gate and driveway, creating a bright puddle on the otherwise murky street. There's no sign of a guard, but Jerónimo is sure there's one on duty, and since the wall surrounding the compound is rigged with motion detectors, the first thing he'll have to do is come up with a way to get past him.

When the cab reaches the crest of the hill, he orders the driver to take a right on a cross-street and pull over. He pays the kid, then gets out and watches the car until it disappears. A five-hundred-foot radio tower juts up in front of him like the skeleton of some ancient snake god nailed to the night sky. He can see the whole world from here. The flickering sprawl of TJ to the south and east, San Diego blazing to the north, and, to the west, the dark, brooding slick of the Pacific, a watery ponderousness lurking at the edge of everything.

He punches himself in the nose. The pain makes him gasp, and blood begins to drip from his left nostril. He claws at the buckshot wounds on his face to get them bleeding again too. Taking the .25 from his pocket, he runs along the road for fifty yards or so in the direction the cab went, then returns to the tower at a trot. He's breathing hard now, sweating. He continues jogging to the corner, turns onto El Príncipe's street, and heads for the house, keeping to the shadows.

When he reaches the gate, he collapses against it, then steps back and rattles the iron bars with one hand while pointing his gun up the hill to where he just came from. Ozzy is sitting in the front seat of an Escalade that's parked in the driveway facing the gate. His eyes widen at Jerónimo's sudden, gory appearance, and he's quick on the draw, pulling and aiming a Glock through the windshield of the truck.

"It's me. El Apache," Jerónimo whispers like he's afraid of being overheard by pursuers. "Let me in."

Ozzy opens the door of the Escalade, and a *corrido* booms briefly until he shuts off the radio. "What's going on?" he says.

"I was bringing the boss's woman back, but some fuckers who used to work for El Samurai pulled me over and took her and the car," Jerónimo says.

"Where?" Ozzy says, getting out of the truck.

"Up the road, by the tower," Jerónimo says. "Let me in, *hombre*. They were right behind me."

Ozzy hits a button on the gate's control box. The gate slides open, and Jerónimo slips inside as soon as the opening is wide enough. When Ozzy pushes past him to peer in the direction of the radio tower, Jerónimo leaps onto the man's back, slamming a knee into his kidney and wrapping an arm around his throat.

Ozzy drops his gun and brings both hands up to try to ease the pressure on his windpipe. Jerónimo yanks him backward and drags him to the ground. The man lands on top of him, but not hard enough to break the chokehold. Grunting fiercely, Ozzy attempts to sit up, to roll over, to grind Jerónimo into the pavement beneath him. Without oxygen he quickly loses strength and is reduced to slapping the asphalt with his palm in a gesture of submission or frustration. Jerónimo tightens his arm and wraps his legs around the man's thighs to keep him still.

He continues to squeeze Ozzy's throat long after his struggles cease, listening all the while for any sound from the house to indicate that an alarm has been raised. All he hears is faint music and a couple of dogs grousing in the distance.

Slipping out from under the dead man, he rifles through his pockets and comes up with a ring of keys, a wallet stuffed with pesos, and a six-inch lock blade. He takes the Glock too. Ozzy's face is frozen in a horrible grimace, his tongue, protruding between his teeth, nearly bitten through. Jerónimo avoids looking at it as he drags the man's body into the bushes.

Two other vehicles are parked in the driveway, a pickup and a little Audi Spyder. Jerónimo uses the knife to slash their tires. When he reaches the house, he crouches in a flowerbed with his back to the wall and scans the compound for movement. Nothing except bugs circling a light on the porch. The detached garage with its second-story apartment is quiet too.

He creeps along the wall. The blinds are lowered on all the windows, so the only glimpses he gets inside are flashes of empty rooms seen through the narrow gaps between the slats. The music he heard at the gate is playing throughout the house, Led

Zeppelin turned up so loud that the windowpanes rattle with each bass note.

At the back of the house is a pool with a waterfall spilling into it. An inflatable raft sits becalmed in the shallow end, and another lies atop one of the deck chairs lined up under the thatched awning that covers a wet bar and a large gas grill. The music is being piped out here too. Robert Plant's wails rise up toward a trio of palm trees nodding overhead.

Jerónimo freezes when he spies a mound of towels lying on the patio and remembers El Príncipe's comment about swimming lessons. With one eye on the big glass slider that opens onto the pool from the house, he moves cautiously toward the towels and prods them with his foot until he's satisfied there's not a small body hidden beneath them.

On the other side of the slider is the kitchen, which is dark except for the bright rectangle of an entrance to a hallway and the soft blue glow imparted to the stainless steel appliances by the lights around the pool. The slider is locked, so Jerónimo moves on to another door farther along the back wall.

A window in this one reveals the laundry room—washer, dryer, bottled water dispenser. It's locked, too, but Jerónimo reaches into his pocket for Ozzy's keys and tries them one by one. Number four is it. No alarm sounds when he opens the door and steps inside. A gust from the air conditioner blows cold across his sweaty body, raising gooseflesh and making him shiver, and "Whole Lotta Love" pounds in his head. He crosses the room and twists the knob on another door.

The kitchen. It's spotless except for a couple of pizza boxes on the counter and an empty two-liter Coke bottle in the sink. Kid food, Jerónimo convinces himself, proof they've been taking care of Junior and Ariel. He quicksteps to the hallway, the pool shining through the slider like an image from a movie. Peeking around the door frame, he determines that the hall is empty and starts down it, Ozzy's Glock out in front.

He ignores the closed doors he passes, wants to clear the main part of the house first. The hallway ends in a two-story foyer that flows into the expansive living room. Jerónimo recognizes it from his previous visits. He creeps toward the living room but stops short when he spies Esteban, El Príncipe's other body-guard, sitting in a recliner and watching soccer on a flat screen.

He retreats to the hall, stows the Glock in his waistband, and takes out Ozzy's knife. He'll do this with the *filero* in order to avoid gunshots that'll alert everybody else in the house. He creeps up low and slow on Esteban until the bodyguard senses him coming and turns his way. Then it's a mad dash.

He brings the knife down hard, but Esteban is already rolling out of the chair, so the blade merely nicks his upper arm. Jerónimo keeps going, scrambling up and over the recliner and launching himself at the man, who's drawing a gun from a shoul-der holster. Jerónimo lands on top of him and begins stabbing wildly at his midsection, twisting every thrust.

Esteban pushes him off, and Jerónimo trips and falls, taking a lamp with him. He's back on his feet in an instant, charging again. Esteban has his gun out but doesn't have the strength to lift it. Blood is spreading across his T-shirt from wounds in his chest and stomach.

"Príncipe!" he yells as Jerónimo lays into him with the knife. "Príncipe!"

Again Jerónimo finds himself on the floor. Esteban grabs his own forearm and brings his gun up that way, trying to blink things into focus. Jerónimo pulls the Glock and fires five times, at least two of the rounds striking the bodyguard in the head. He drops like a hanged man cut down from the gallows, but Jeró-nimo doesn't see it. He's already looking for cover.

El Príncipe steps into the room. "Good-bye, you son of a bitch," he shouts as he squeezes the trigger of his Beretta.

Jerónimo dives behind a pool table and makes himself as small as possible. Bullets thwack into the wall behind him. He rests the Glock on the edge of the table and fires blindly, trusting that El Príncipe's survival instincts will take over and back him off.

Sure enough, when he pops up, the Prince is nowhere to be seen through the haze of gun smoke. Jerónimo makes for an open door beside the fireplace. El Príncipe reemerges and looses another barrage. Dropping and rolling, Jerónimo finds himself in a tiny bathroom, where he crouches next to the toilet until the shooting stops.

"Have you gone crazy?" El Príncipe yells.

"I've come for my family," Jerónimo replies.

"Like this?"

"Give them to me, and I'll let you live."

Jerónimo stands and wedges himself next to the doorjamb, ignoring the light switch digging into his back. The movement draws another shot from El Príncipe, the bullet shattering a mirror over the sink.

"What about our deal?" the Prince says.

"I did the best I could," Jerónimo says.

"So where's Luz then?"

"I don't know. She got away."

"And you couldn't just come here and tell me that? You had to break into my house and kill my men and threaten to kill me? I thought we were *compadres, hombre.* We always did right by each other before."

Jerónimo hesitates, wondering if there might have been another way to handle this, a way without blood, but then he remembers everything he knows about El Príncipe, every betrayal and atrocity, and tightens his grip on his gun.

"My family," he says.

"I'll give them to you after you give me your gun," El Príncipe says.

"As easy as that?" Jerónimo scoffs.

"As easy as that."

Jerónimo cranes his neck to look through the doorway. He can't see El Príncipe, but his voice sounds like it's coming from the hall. He draws the .25 with his left hand, keeps the Glock in his right.

"Where are they?" he says.

"Throw down your gun," El Príncipe says.

"It's a simple question: Where's my family?"

"You've got two more seconds."

"Are they here?"

"You already know, don't you?" El Príncipe says. He moves out of the hall and into the foyer, stupid pride making him fearless. "You already know they're dead."

Jerónimo steps into the living room to meet him. They stand face-to-face twenty-five feet apart, blasting away at each other. A round nicks Jerónimo's ribcage, tearing his shirt. El Príncipe is hit in the shoulder but keeps shooting until he empties the Beretta. He then hurls the pistol at Jerónimo and runs across the foyer to the stairs leading to the second floor.

Both of Jerónimo's guns are empty too. He searches the floor near Esteban's body for the knife, but then feels the weight of the rat's fancy .45 in his back pocket and pulls that instead.

El Príncipe is halfway up the staircase when Jerónimo reaches the bottom. Jerónimo fires one of the two rounds in the gun and hits the Prince in the back of his left leg, the bullet destroying the kneecap as it exits. El Príncipe goes down with an agonized scream and rolls onto his back to watch Jerónimo climb the stairs toward him.

"I won't beg," he says. "Not a dog like you."

Jerónimo stands over him and lets him look down the barrel of the .45. He knows that even the toughest men shit themselves when they see the end coming, and he wants this bastard to die terrified.

El Príncipe doesn't crack though. He grins up at Jerónimo and says, "I liked your family, I really did. Especially your boy."

Jerónimo plants his foot on the man's shattered knee and grinds.

"What a tight little ass he had!" El Príncipe roars.

Jerónimo can't hold off any longer. He sends his last round into the center of the man's forehead, then steps up to kick the smirk off the corpse's face.

He's exhausted by the time he reaches the second floor and collapses on the top step. His legs are shaking, and grief is like a stone in his chest. He's got one more job to do. If Irma and the kids are still here, he has to find their bodies and bury them.

He's steeling himself for the search when a sound cuts through the music and the ringing in his ears: a child's cry, short, sharp, and abruptly muffled, coming from somewhere behind him. He struggles to his feet and wobbles down the second-floor hallway. A bedroom, a bedroom, a bathroom, and then a locked door.

"Mijo," he tries to shout, *"mija,"* but the words come out garbled, soaked in bloody phlegm.

Bracing himself, he kicks the door again and again until it gives way and swings open on another bedroom. Light flooding in from the hall reveals Ariel and Junior crouched behind the bed and Irma charging toward him, a lamp raised over her head.

"It's me!" he says, ducking and throwing up an arm.

Irma pulls up short and squints like she can't believe her eyes. Jerónimo moves toward her, but she drops the lamp and turns away. The kids are crying and need her attention. He watches, grateful and ashamed, as she gathers them in her arms and whispers comforts to them that he can't make out. He doesn't deserve her, doesn't deserve them, but now isn't the time to add everything up. He tries to put a gentle tone in his voice, but it's difficult, shouting over the music.

"We've got to move," he says.

Forgetting what a bloody mess he is, he reaches for Junior, who screams and clings to his mother.

"Leave him to me," Irma says.

He turns to Ariel. "Do you know who I am?" he asks her.

She nods, her body wracked with suppressed sobs.

"We're going to run now, so I need to carry you, okay?"

She nods again.

He picks her up and lays her over his shoulder. "Close your eyes," he says.

He leads the way down the stairs, through the foyer and kitchen and around the pool. A stiff breeze is blowing, and ominous shadows lurch in every corner of the compound. As he and Irma are jogging across the yard something big gets blown over and lands with a metallic clang. Jerónimo jumps at the sound but keeps going.

"This one," he says when they reach the driveway, gesturing to the Escalade. Irma climbs into the passenger seat with Junior, and Jerónimo hands Ariel over to her. Now that they've made it this far, he's thinking about the mess inside the house.

"Give me five minutes," he says to Irma.

"What choice do I have?" she says.

He kisses his fingers and presses them to her cheek.

The side door of the garage is unlocked. Jerónimo turns on the light, revealing a couple more cars and all the tools needed to maintain them, including a mechanic's bay with a hydraulic lift. A bright red five-gallon gas can catches his eye. He picks it up and shakes it. Almost full. A paved walkway leads to the house.

Entering through the kitchen again, he works from front to back, sloshing gasoline all over the first floor. He opens every closed door and dowses every room. In El Príncipe's office he soaks the desk, the computer, the couch; in the living room, Esteban's body. He then detours upstairs to sprinkle the Prince's corpse as well. Music is still playing. Pink Floyd now. *The Wall.*

By the time Jerónimo finishes in the kitchen, the can is empty. He rolls it down the hall and goes to the sink, where he washes the blood off his face and hands. Stepping into the backyard, he grabs a barbecue lighter from under the grill on the patio. The smell of gas funneling out of the house when he squats in front of the slider makes him dizzy. He holds his breath and sparks the lighter.

The gas ignites immediately, a carpet of shimmering flame unrolling across the kitchen floor and down the hallway. Jerónimo closes the door and runs. He doesn't look back until he gets to the Escalade. Fire is visible through the upstairs windows, and smoke curls out of every gap and vent. A pane of glass shatters from the heat, releasing long fingers of flame that claw at the side of the house.

Jerónimo slides into the driver's seat and starts the truck. The kids are quiet now, mesmerized by the swelling conflagration.

"Where are you taking us?" Irma asks, flames dancing in her eyes.

"South," is all Jerónimo can think to say.

Everybody's quiet during the ride downhill into the mad heart of the city. Reflections of traffic lights and blinking signs roll up the hood and over the windshield as Jerónimo navigates the bustling late-night streets, and young badasses lounging on corners glance furtively at the Escalade, trading guesses on who might be inside. Jerónimo ditches the vehicle a couple of blocks from the bus terminal and walks the rest of the way with Irma and the kids.

"We shouldn't be seen together," he tells Irma, pressing money into her hand at the entrance to the station. "Get tickets for the next bus out of here for you and the kids, and I'll do the same for myself."

She understands the danger they're in and doesn't waste time arguing. Jerónimo waits until she's in line at the ticket counter, then walks to a stall down the street to buy a clean T-shirt. He changes in an alley, and when he returns to the terminal, Irma signals him from across the crowded, noisy waiting room, holding up two fingers and pointing at the departure board. A first-class bus leaves for Durango at two a.m. He purchases a ticket and stands where he can keep an eye on the doors to the station and his family at the same time.

The next hour drags by, the crowd expanding and contracting with each arrival and departure. It's late, and everyone's tired. The long rows of plastic chairs are filled with yawning passengers who scowl at a group of children playing tag around the vending machines. Jerónimo tenses when a trio of soldiers passes through, cold eyes scanning the throng, and again when Irma goes to the snack bar with the kids to get candy and juice. Every loiterer is an assassin, every sudden sound imminent doom. Junior stares at him over the back of his chair, and he risks a wave and a smile. The boy turns away and sinks into his seat without responding.

When it's time to leave, Jerónimo hangs back until Irma and the kids have joined the line of people waiting to board, then slips in at the end of the queue. On the bus he sits three rows behind them, resting a hand briefly on Ariel's head as he passes in the aisle. With a hiss and a jolt, the bus begins to move. Swaying like a boat on a rough sea, it lumbers out of the parking lot and muscles into traffic. There are a couple more scares on the way out of town: a police van with yowling sirens and flashing lights, a suspicious car blocking an intersection. But the cops keep going, and a passerby helps the driver push his junker to the curb.

Jerónimo relaxes a bit when they merge onto the highway. Soon they're clear of Tijuana and roaring down an empty road through the desert. For once he's happy to be out in the open. He stands in the aisle to check on Irma. She's already asleep, exhausted by her ordeal. The kids too. It's a good sign, a small step toward normalcy.

The ancient wrinkled woman sitting next to him breaks off mid-snore and lifts her head from the window. She turns to look at him, as if surprised to see him there, then dozes off again. His own eyelids grow heavy. The heat, the gentle rocking of the bus. The Apaches, his ancestors, appear, ghost warriors hunched over their horses, thundering across the endless prairie. Jerónimo forces himself awake. No dreams tonight; he's on watch. He and Irma and the kids will hit Durango with nothing, but he's not worried. He'll work hard, keep his nose clean, and woe to anyone who dares to get between his family and happiness. They'll find out just how brutal love can be.

Epilogue

LUZ SPENT TOO MUCH ON THE TREE BECAUSE IT'S THEIR FIRST Christmas together and she wants to make it special. She's not going to stress about it. She's been careful with money, and there's still plenty stashed in various hiding places around the apartment. Plus, Mr. Cardoza has promised her another shift at the market beginning next week. The way she sees it, it's things like this, the holidays, that Isabel is going to remember, and if she gives the girl enough good times, maybe the bad stuff that came before will fade away.

She's decorating alone because Isabel lost interest after a few minutes and begged to go play on the patio. The neighbor's cat hangs out there and lets Isabel fuss over him like a baby doll. She'll spend hours rocking the fat tabby, singing him songs and tickling him under the chin to make him purr. Luz cocks an ear to her happy chatter as she hangs another ornament. All of the decorations are either silver or pink, Isabel's choice.

The little girl has adjusted nicely to her new life. In the beginning she'd cry for Carmen and her cousins once in a while, but she hardly ever mentions them now. The story Luz tells her is that she left her to work in Mexico and came back as soon as she had enough money to get the two of them a place to live. Isabel accepts this as the truth, and even urges Luz to repeat the fable and elaborate on certain aspects, like how lonely she was for Isabel and how she sobbed into her pillow every night, thinking about her. The kid gets a kick out of being a character in her own bedtime tale.

The tickets Luz bought that night after the cab dropped them off at the Greyhound station were for Stockton, a city Alejandro used to talk about, somewhere his parents had lived before they moved to Compton. Luz and Isabel ended up getting off the bus early here in Fresno, though, to escape a woman who was asking too many questions about where they were headed and why. Luz decided this was as good a place as any to disappear, and, after a few weeks in a motel, found a one-bedroom unit in a nice complex on the edge of downtown. The whole apartment is smaller than the master suite of El Príncipe's house, but there's a pool and a security fence, and she and Isabel can walk to a shopping center and a shady park.

They kept to themselves for a couple of months after they moved in, settling down and getting to know each other. The real world wasn't going to go away, however, and Luz understood that they had to learn to live in it. She started at the supermarket as a bagger, but is now a checker trainee. Isabel goes to a preschool down the street and is crazy about her day care lady, Mrs. Sanchez. On Luz's days off, they sit by the pool or go to the park or see movies at the mall. Isabel loves McDonald's French fries, cherry Popsicles, and playing on the swings. It's the life Luz pictured them having with Alejandro, only they're living it alone. When men ask her out, she tells them she's married to a soldier serving in Afghanistan. When she has nightmares about shooting Maria and El Toro, she listens to Isabel's breathing in the quiet room they share and reminds herself that it was them or her.

The tree has shed needles all over the carpet. Luz wheels the vacuum cleaner out of the closet, plugs it in, and pushes it around the living room while going over produce codes in preparation for her checker's test tomorrow: Iceberg lettuce, 119. Tomatoes, 238. Navel oranges, 210.

"Mommy!" Isabel calls.

"What?" Luz shouts back.

Getting no response and thinking the girl didn't hear her, she shuts off the vacuum.

"What?" she says again, cocking an ear toward the patio.

No answer. Fear stirs in Luz's chest like a long-hibernating beast slowly rousing.

"Isabel?"

She steps into the kitchen. The slider that leads to the patio is wide open, and Luz can see that both of the deck chairs where Isabel usually sits with the cat are empty. That's crazy. There's nowhere else she could have gone. The patio is tucked under the balcony of the second-floor unit above theirs. Floor-to-ceiling walls on both sides provide privacy from the neighbors' patios, and a sturdy six-foot wooden fence serves as a back wall.

Besides the chairs, there are a few potted plants on the slab and some of Isabel's toys—a plastic rocking horse; a kid-size kitchen setup with a stove, refrigerator, and sink; a half-flat beach ball. Heart pounding, Luz drags one of the chairs to the fence and climbs onto it to check the alley on the other side. She worried about the alley before taking the place, but everyone assured her it was used mainly by garbage trucks. "There isn't even any graffiti," they said. This afternoon it's deserted, and the garage doors that open onto it are all closed.

The worst kinds of thoughts fill Luz's head. Could Rolando have found her here? She gets down off the chair and runs through the kitchen and living room and out the front door. It's a cold, gray day, the sun hidden behind a curtain of thick clouds. Luz's breath smokes as she jogs down the walkway to the street, calling Isabel's name. Her hands are freezing. Two white men, one old, one young, are painting a dresser on the sidewalk. She's seen them around the neighborhood before.

"Did you notice a little girl?" she shouts at them. "Four years old? Black hair? Wearing a red coat?"

"A little girl?" the old man says.

Luz doesn't have time to repeat herself. She steps into the street and yells in both directions. "Isabel! Isabel!" Her cries go nowhere, muffled by the gloom or snagged in the bare black branches of winter trees. The only movement is a mail truck a block away, the carrier opening the rear door to refill his pouch. Luz wraps her arms around herself and runs stiff-legged back to the apartment.

"We ain't seen nobody," the old man says as she passes by.

Her phone. Where is it? She bends over the coffee table and tosses aside coloring books and boxes of Christmas ornaments. Whatever trouble it brings, she has to call the police. "My daughter is missing." The thought of saying those words makes her throat swell. Coming up empty-handed, she heads into the kitchen. Her purse is on the counter. She grabs it and paws frantically through the mess inside. There's the phone. There. She flips it open.

"Boo!"

The room tilts and rights itself at the sound of Isabel's voice. Luz turns to find the girl pointing up at her from under the table.

287

"Ha-ha, I scared you," Isabel says.

Luz's legs give way, and she sinks to the floor.

"What are you doing?" she says to Isabel.

The girl's grin disappears when she hears the anger in Luz's tone.

"I was hiding," she says. "For like a joke."

"No, *mija,* no," Luz says sternly, her blood finally flowing again. "No hiding. It's not funny."

Isabel isn't sure how to react, it's so rare that Luz scolds her. Seeing tears well up in the girl's eyes, Luz reaches out and pulls her onto her lap.

"Mommy worries if she can't find you," she says. She rocks her back and forth. "You're my sun and moon. You're my stars and sky and my birds and trees."

"You're my kitty and my cat," Isabel says, brightening as she recognizes one of their games.

"You're my puppy and my monkey," Luz says.

"You're my flower and my water," Isabel says. "You're my mommy and daddy and sister and brother."

Luz hugs her tightly, still shaken by the chasm that opened at her feet when she thought she was gone. *This is love,* she tells herself, *this is life.* She kisses the girl's cheek and presses her nose into her hair. You can have everything else in the world, all of it. She's found her treasure, a lamp to light her way, and it's enough.

Acknowledgments

Many thanks to my agent, Henry Dunow; my editor, Asya Muchnick; and everybody at Little, Brown/Mulholland Books. Also, thanks to the John Simon Guggenheim Foundation for financial support during the writing of this book.

About the Author

Richard Lange is the author of the story collection *Dead Boys*, which received the Rosenthal Family Foundation Award from the American Academy of Arts and Letters, and the novel *This Wicked World*. He is the recipient of a Guggenheim Fellowship, and his fiction has appeared in the *Iowa Review*, the *Atlantic Monthly*'s Fiction for Kindle series, and *Best American Mystery Stories 2004* and *2011*. He lives in Los Angeles.